LOVE ON OCEAN DRIVE

Love on...
Book Two

Aubrey Parr

This novel is purely a work of fiction. Any characters, names, or events are the product of the author's imagination. Any resemblance to real persons, places, or events is purely coincidental.

French Kiss: written by Adam Brooks
Copyright 20th Century Fox

Dedication:

This book is dedicated to…

Mom – For being there every step of the way.

and

Kate – For inspiring such a great character.

PROLOGUE

"The plane will be there by 8:00am. See you then!"
Nicole added.

"See you tomorrow, Nic." Hanging up the phone,
Kate saw Ethan walk by her office. Why did she always
seem to look up just as he walked by?

Kate had been going through a dry spell for the past
few months. Maybe she should just walk right up to
Ethan and invite him over for a night of no-strings-
attached sex. Kate laughed to herself, knowing she'd
never have the nerve. Chicago was crawling with
attractive men. So what was so special about Ethan? He
was handsome, smart, and successful. He appeared to
have his life together. All the things that, on the surface,
seemed perfect. There was just one small problem: he
didn't see her as anything more than a work friend.

Kate needed this weekend to get away from work and
from Ethan. Who knew, maybe she'd meet someone to
help take her mind off him

CHAPTER ONE

You would think that Kate Olesen would be used to flying in a personal jet by now. It still felt like a dream every time she walked into the luxurious cabin. Her best friend Nicole had been married to Derek Stone, a retired MMA fighter turned vacation property developer, for almost a year now. Due to his extensive travel commitments, Derek had a private jet. A jet he was only too happy to send to pick up his wife's best friend. Kate had spent the better part of the year visiting the couple once a month in a multitude of different resorts. Usually the Stones were in Mexico, but not this time. This time, she didn't need her passport.

Kate had just landed in Miami and was in a cab on her way to the Stones' hotel. The driver seemed to be in an awful hurry, weaving in and out of traffic while they crossed the causeway to Miami Beach. It was making her sick. Even with the window down, the humidity took over, making the inside of the car feel like a million degrees. The driver was humming to salsa music that was playing far too loudly.

"Is it a far drive?" she yelled up to the cab driver, trying to sound pleasant.

"Oh, maybe another fifteen minutes. I can speed up if you like."

Speed up? Kate thought. "No rush, just curious," she answered back, hoping that he didn't dare increase the already nauseating pace. She might lose her breakfast if he did.

Kate wondered how bitchy she would feel if she was still subjected to flying coach on a commercial flight. She smiled at her embarrassing conceit. Kate didn't like it when she was crabby, and she knew full well why she was. Ethan again.

She and Ethan had worked in the same law office for the past few years, and he had immediately caught her attention. No matter how much she tried to ignore it, she had a thing for him, like a school girl with a crush. She didn't like feeling that way. She knew he liked her. Unfortunately, it just wasn't in the way she hoped. Somehow, Kate had pulled off the "acting casual" thing far too well with him; Ethan seemed to see her as just one of the guys.

Usually that was okay with her, though some days were harder than others. Being a divorce attorney had made her a little jaded about relationships and marriage. It wasn't anything she was interested in at the moment, anyway. Her career was going great; she was on track to be a partner before she was forty. That was what was important right now. She was married to her job and, so far, it was a great husband.

She leaned her head back on the seat and tried not to breathe in the sickly stale stench of the cab. Maybe that was her problem. Maybe she'd be fine once she could get out of this little sweat box. There were a lot of maybes going through her mind at the moment. So, she tried to concentrate on the fact that soon she would be in Miami Beach with her best friend, and all would be right with the world. Although Kate had traveled far more lately than she ever had before, it still felt like she needed this weekend away.

By the time Kate opened her eyes, they were in the South Beach area on Ocean Drive. She checked out the hotels, each with outdoor restaurant seating in front. She could see endless couples and groups of friends, drinking and having lunch. It was a gorgeous day, the sun shining bright. It already had her feeling better.

Nicole had told her that the hotel was a block inland. She and Derek had stayed at a hotel on Ocean Drive during one of his investigative visits and had barely slept, what with the music playing till all hours of the morning. Derek knew his clients would not want that for their guests. The location he found was perfect: in the middle of South Beach, one block's walk from the excitement, but far enough away to provide a quiet night's sleep. Collins Avenue had far more stores than bars, and its hotels had smaller bars with coffee shops, rather than a party atmosphere.

The cab driver pulled up to the Ocean Azul Hotel, and Kate immediately relaxed. She grabbed her overnight bag (she had become an expert packer), stepped out onto the sidewalk, and looked up at the hotel.

It had a beachy chic look- stark white interrupted by scattered blocks of blue. "Ocean Azul" was written in a bright turquoise blue vertically down the front. There was a small bar and restaurant in front with tables on either side of the entryway. It was perfect, and Kate loved it.

She found Nicole and Derek sitting at the table closest to the door. They looked deep in conversation and didn't appear to have notice she had arrived. Then again, they never did. That's how it had been since they met. Their worlds started and ended with each other. Deep down, Kate hoped that one day she may be lucky enough to find a love like that.

She walked right up to the table and didn't get their attention until she sat down next to Nicole. They screamed at each other and hugged, like they always did.

Derek got up and gave her a welcoming hug as well. Nicole was relieved to finally have Kate there. She loved their monthly weekend visits, and she was excited for her to see the hotel.

"How was the flight?" Nicole asked.

"That part was wonderful, as usual. The cab ride smelled like shit, but I'm glad to finally be here." Kate crunched her face at the memory and leaned back in her chair, excited for her mini-vacation to begin. Derek hailed the server and ordered Kate a dirty martini without even asking her. She loved that he knew her almost as well as his wife did.

"Thank you," she smiled at him. She really had come to love him like a brother.

"I'm going to leave you two to catch up," he returned the smile, before wandering inside the hotel.

"The place looks amazing, Nic," Kate said, looking around.

"It is great. Wait till you see inside! What shall we do first?" Nicole asked, taking a drink of her wine. Just then, her martini arrived, and Kate was ready to savor it.

"I don't think I've been here since college," Kate confessed. "I'm not sure what to do."

"Did you think about the tattoo idea? We could do that tonight." Nicole loved tattoos, and Kate had always teetered on the edge of getting one. This time, she was prepared to do it.

"I decided…yes!" she smiled, waiting for Nicole's response.

Nicole was ecstatic. "Yes, finally! You can't back out now. What are you getting?"

"I'll show you a picture." Kate pulled out her phone and opened it to a screenshot of a tattoo, a simple drawing of a little girl reaching for a red heart-shaped balloon.

"You have this on the wall of your apartment. What is it?" Nicole took the phone from her to get a better look.

"It's the *Girl with Balloon* stencil from Bansky, the street artist. I love that there can be so many interpretations. What does the balloon represent, and is she reaching for it or releasing it?" Kate mused. "Depending on my mood, I see it differently. I'm thinking of getting it on the inside of my wrist or the back of my shoulder. I have to think of work, after all."

Nicole wasn't surprised at Kate's choice. Kate had been an art history major in college before she decided to change her major to pre-law. So a tattoo involving artwork made perfect sense.

"I love it," Nicole said. "There's a tattoo shop that Derek suggested just down the street."

"Great. But first, I want to get into the room and take a quick shower and change." After that cab ride, Kate was a bit concerned that she could still notice that weird smell on her.

The lobby was beautiful and inviting, decorated in the art deco style. Large lamps offered soft lighting that warmed the stark white space, while the turquoise front desk created a splash of color that echoed the blue sections of the hotel's exterior. They didn't need to stop at the desk. Nicole already had Kate's key. At the Stones' properties, Nicole always had a key ready for Kate, and the room was always excessive for one person.

This place was no different. The door opened into a sitting area with two comfortable chairs and a huge TV on the wall. There was a small wet bar with mini-fridge and microwave. (Nicole always made sure Kate had a stock of tiny bottles of alcohol with a martini glass, vermouth, and shaker tin. It was a personal touch that Kate always appreciated.) The sitting room opened up to a bedroom with a king bed, side tables, dresser, and another large TV. The entire exterior was wall-to-wall windows with sliding glass doors that accessed a balcony. The windows were already opened, and the sounds of people talking and eating drifted up from the sidewalk below.

Nicole grabbed the remote and sat down in a chair, saying, "I'll wait for you to get ready." Since Kate's trips were always just weekends, Nicole already knew she wouldn't want to waste time relaxing in the room.

Kate turned on the shower and stared at herself in the mirror while she waited for the water to heat up. She was about 5'5" tall, with striking black hair that angled toward the front, dark brown eyes, and a little button nose. Her mouth was big, with a wide smile that made everyone in a room want to know what she was so happy about. Her skin was fair enough that she always expected to return home from these weekends with a freckled nose.

She could see Nicole through the reflection in the mirror. Her friend was sitting sideways in the big chair, her long legs flung over the arm rest. Kate loved that woman like a sister, but they looked absolutely nothing alike. Nicole was tall and tan, with long blond hair. Kate had never wished she was a blonde, though. She honestly liked the way she looked.

That brought Ethan back to the front of her thoughts. Was that the problem? Was he into tall blondes? He seemed to genuinely like Kate, but maybe she wasn't his physical type. They laughed at work and hung out and had drinks with everyone. She just seemed to be stuck in the friend zone, and she wasn't sure why. She had never brought it up with him; the very idea made her cringe.

"Girl, you need to get laid," she said to the reflection in the mirror.

"What, babe?" Nicole asked loudly from the next room.

"Oh, just telling myself I need to get laid this weekend," Kate laughed. She could always tell Nicole anything. There was no reason to feel self-conscious with her.

Nicole practically spit out her drink of water. "We'll get right on that, honey," she called back.

Kate showered and put on some makeup. Being an attorney, she had to dress rather conservatively at work, so she used these visits to have some fun with her clothes. Nicole was wearing a bright orange summer dress, so Kate chose a green backless number that stopped just above the knee and tied around her neck in a halter-style, with a little bow at the base of her back. When she was ready, she came out and turned around to show Nicole.

"I love it," Nicole smiled at her.

"I'm thinking about the tattoo as well. If I decide on my shoulder, I figured this gave good access."

"Plus, you're bound to get laid wearing it," Nicole joked.

"Perfect. Let's go."

CHAPTER TWO

Kate had forgotten how much she liked South Beach. It was like an adult playground, with its white sands, bright sun, and colorful buildings. April in Chicago was still rather dreary and the warmth of the Florida sun was exactly what she had been looking for this weekend. Kate closed her eyes and leaned her head up towards it as she walked, soaking the heat into her face. Turns out, that probably wasn't her smartest move, as she ended up almost swerving off the sidewalk. Once back on track, she and Kate walked toward Ocean Drive and the waterfront to grab some lunch. A love of food was one of the many things they had in common. Kate was glad to be so close to the ocean as well. She had been a vegetarian for practically a decade. Technically, she was a pescatarian, since she ate fish along with the occasional egg or dairy. She was excited to get her hands on some fish that tasted like it was caught only moments before.

Nicole had been in Miami for a few weeks already and so had tried most of the restaurants in the area. They stopped at one of her favorites. The stainless-steel tables were bar-height and the barstools had rounded backs. The waitress came over wearing the tightest and tiniest little dress Kate had ever seen. She was breathtakingly gorgeous and had a Hispanic accent that would melt most men- the way she rolled her "r"'s would get them thinking. She handed them menus, and Nicole ordered a pitcher of mojitos, promising Kate she wouldn't be disappointed.

"I forgot how beautiful everyone is here. Why on Earth is that woman not modeling?" Kate asked.

"I know!" Nicole agreed, "Maybe it's because they all look that perfect. It's the same in Rio; they breed beautiful people. Even the men are gorgeous here."

"This whole place reminds me of the old *Miami Vice* show. I half expect to hear that famous opening credits song," Kate laughed.

For a second time that day, Nicole almost spit out the water she was drinking. "Oh God, with the boobs bopping to the beat of the music." She had to stop and laugh more before she could continue. "Crocket and Tubbs walking down Ocean Drive with their Plastelle t-shirts under white suits. Neon lights everywhere."

"So, I'm not the only one that remembers that show so well?" Kate replied, still laughing.

"Just us old ladies," Nicole giggled.

When their mojitos arrived, Kate was happy with Nicole's suggestion. They were fresh and crisp, exactly as they should be. The women ordered some ceviche to start and then the grilled fish filet special. Kate caught her up on the news from their Chicago circle and listened to the Stones' plans in Miami Beach and where Nicole thought they'd go next.

When they were sufficiently full and tipsy, they decided to go shopping. South Beach had some of the greatest little boutiques, filled with clothes that required Kate to have some liquid courage before agreeing to buy. She had made sure to set aside an entire paycheck for exactly that purpose. They were in and out of the first boutique rather quickly; everything was far too revealing and skimpy. Kate was getting braver with options while she traveled, but she didn't want to look like she was trying too hard or pretending she was still in her twenties. She was thirty-five and comfortable with that fact.

The next shop looked far more promising. Kate discovered a very short but airy dress with long sleeves and numerous straps crisscrossing the back. It was the same turquoise color as the dress she was wearing. It must be a popular color for the season. She grabbed it, plus a few others, and hauled them into the dressing room. When she came out in the strappy number, Nicole stopped in her tracks. It was shorter than Kate would usually choose, but since the fit was so loose, it was still classy. It did show off her legs nicely.

"Wow," was all she heard from her friend. Nicole was a writer and extremely articulate, so Kate had learned through the years that a one-word response was her highest compliment. For Nicole, that was basically speechless.

"Really? Is it too short?" Kate asked as she turned back and forth, checking herself out in the mirror from all angles.

"No, it's perfect. And if you could wear that to work, you'd definitely get your Ethan's attention," Nicole smiled slyly.

"Oh God, he's not *my Ethan*, and I don't know about that. He treats me like I'm one of the guys when we hang out after work. I wish I'd get over this stupid crush I've got going."

"Maybe you need to invite a few people from the office down here sometime," Nicole suggested. "We'll put everyone up in the hotel. Then it won't seem obvious that it's all for him."

"Oh good Lord, Nicole," Kate laughed. Her best friend must be on a mission to her laid as well.

Nicole wondered sometimes if Kate realized what a catch she was. She was one of the smartest people Nicole knew and gorgeous to boot. She made jeans and a sports jersey look adorable, but also looked as though, if she put on a sexy pair of glasses, she could be a naughty librarian. That thought made Nicole smile to herself. She didn't think Kate would ever do that. Kate was comfortable with her appearance and intelligence; she wasn't the type to flaunt it or try to act sexy. She was far too down-to-earth.

But maybe that was because no one had given her the motivation to act that way. Nicole was much more adventurous with Derek than she had been with anyone in her past. It was as if you lose that bit of self-doubt when you're with the right one, she mused. Kate was clearly crazy about this Ethan, but was she playing it safe? He fit the exact role of what Kate went for. Clean cut and successful. There wasn't anything wrong with that type at all. But Kate just wasn't getting the attention from him that she wanted, and that bothered Nicole.

Kate bought the dress, while Nicole decided on a pair of strappy heels. They continued shopping for the next few hours, laughing and enjoying their time together. They dropped off their bags at the hotel and headed toward the tattoo shop, figuring that they'd be brave and then treat themselves to a wonderful dinner as a reward.

For some reason, Kate had expected the place to be dark and smoky. But she knew that smoking wasn't allowed in tattoo shops, and she had accompanied Nicole to a few of her sessions as well. So she wasn't sure why the vision in her head seemed to have a smoke machine in the corner. This shop was a bright, clean, open space. There was small waiting area with tattoo books to browse and a desk in the front. Behind that, the tattoos stations were set up like half-walled office cubicles, so that clients could keep their personal belongings within easy reach.

The stations were bordered by a wide aisle. The walls were covered with pictures of tattoos.

How many drunken people had come into this place and thrown a dart at the wall to choose their tattoo? It seemed like such a strange concept to her. This was something that would be on their bodies forever. Wouldn't they want to choose something meaningful? It had taken Kate a long time to make her decision. Though she was a bit scared now, she knew it would be worth it.

Nicole chatted with the guy behind the counter, who introduced himself as Jax. Kate found herself staring at his arms and legs, which were covered in tattoos. Most were skulls, demons, and naked female devils. Not appealing to her at all. She didn't mind tattoos on men, especially when they could be covered by clothes, but she thought they should be more artistic and expressive. Then again, maybe this guy was a Pagan. She silently scolded herself for her hasty judgement.

Nicole finished, and it was Kate's turn to talk. She opened her phone and showed Jax the picture.

"I'm 99% sure I want the back of my shoulder," Kate said as Jax looked.

"Nice spot. What else are you thinking?" he asked.

"I do like the idea of the inside of the wrist, but I'm an attorney. Thinking it's not such a good idea for the courtroom." Why was she going into such detail? Kate figured it was because the guy was easy to talk to.

"Good point. This drawing can't be shrunk down too small either. You'd lose the detail that's there." Jax was used to helping women decide with their first tattoos. At least the woman hadn't stumbled in drunk like some did.

Kate's eyes followed Jax's as he looked around the shop to see which artists were available. And then she saw him.

Strands of dark hair, cropped short in the back, were left to fall just so over intense dark eyes and the creased brow of a deep thinker. Below the eyes was a strong pointed nose and a delicious mouth curved into a sexy smirk. He could have walked out of a 70s rock concert, with tattered shorts, a heavy leather belt, and a fitted t-shirt. He looked like a model, one of those half-naked men who leave the shirts they're supposed to be selling balled up behind them. But the effortless ease with which the clothes hung off of him told her that he had probably thrown them on without a second thought. He was, in so many words, the epitome of the handsome mysterious stranger.

He was in the corner station, leaning back on a stool, legs resting on the client table in front of him. A book lay in his lap, forgotten when something had caught his attention. That something appeared to be Kate, the sexy smirk turned in her direction. Kate found herself unable to pull away from that smirk, those eyes. He was the complete opposite of her usual type and somehow also the sexiest man she had ever seen. She felt an undeniable sense of exhilaration, like she was a kid stealing a piece of candy.

Mr. Dark and Mysterious motioned to Jax, who jumped to go see what was needed. Mr. Dark and Mysterious spoke briefly to him, his eyes maintaining the connection with Kate's. He broke the gaze for the briefest moment to nod to Jax, then snapped back to hers, as though unable to restrain himself.

Worried that her face was turning bright red, Kate forced herself to look at Nicole. Nicole was glancing back and forth between the mysterious man and her best friend, clearly noticing whatever this connection was.

Kate wanted to hide, to bury her head into Nicole's shoulder. She never felt this way. What in the world was going on?

Jax returned. "You've caught the owner's interest," he told her, sounding surprised. "He never tattoos random people."

"He's the owner?" Kate asked, feeling surprised herself.

"Damn, he doesn't like it when I tell clients," Jax said, looking a bit concerned at his slip. "Pretend like you don't know, will ya?"

"I won't say a word," Kate smiled to him.

"Thanks," he replied. "Head on back." He turned his attention to Nicole. "In my experience, women don't usually get tattoos simultaneously. They like to hold each other's hands during the whole thing. Would you like to wait to do yours until she's done?"

Without thinking, Kate spoke up, "Oh, I'll be fine. Go ahead; I don't want you to have to wait."

Nicole knew full well why Kate would be okay with the hot tattoo artist that just happened to own the shop. "You heard the woman, lead the way," she said and followed Jax, smiling at Kate all the while.

What was it about this guy? Kate knew how to pull it together and look confident. There had been plenty of times in the beginning of her career where she hadn't felt very sure about a case. Nevertheless, she'd always gone into the courtroom and faked it. So, Kate took a deep breath, found her center, and walked toward the corner work station. Luckily, the guy wasn't watching her. He was busy setting up the area, making sure it was a sterile environment. Jax came up to him with a print out of her *Girl with Balloon*, before walking away and leaving them alone.

When he turned to her, the rest of the world instantly disappeared. It was only Kate and her mysterious man in the corner. The small station shrunk in size while everything around her blurred.

"I'm Dominic." He had one of those voices that another man might fake in order to sound sexy. But not this guy. This was the real deal. It fell off his tongue like velvet, with a bit of rasp from the back of his throat. The hair on the back of her neck stood up as she imagined him whispering sweet nothings into her ear.

"I'm Kate." Unsure what to do with herself, she sat down on his client table and waited, trying to calm herself by finding amusement in the situation. What the hell was wrong with her? She'd been around hotter guys. Ok, well...maybe not. Actually, no. This was by far the most appealing man she had ever seen.

Dominic was mesmerized. This woman was beautiful in a way that was completely different from all the girls in South Beach. Then again, everyone in South Beach was the "typical model type". For one thing, she was shorter than the women he usually dated. At 5'10", he wasn't exceptionally tall for a man, but most of the women he entertained were his height or taller, especially when you added a pair of their ridiculous heels. And most of them were tan and blonde.

Kate was fair skinned, with jet black hair. However, her face could grace the cover of a magazine over any of the generic, tanned, plastic women that usually appeared there. Her smile was infectious; it made him smile along with her, without knowing why. Part of him wanted to paint her, part of him wanted to talk with her all night long, and then there was the part of him that wanted, almost *needed*, to ravish her. He wanted to ensure that, somehow, all three things happened.

Refocusing on the task at hand, he said, "I'm all set up here. Let's just check the size of this. Where's it going?"

Kate nudged one shoulder forward. "Back of this shoulder."

She sat there, looking back over her shoulder, an image that would be burned in his brain forever. Something about that bare skin of hers was irresistible. He was going to need to pull it together, or she'd end up with a horrible tattoo fail inked on her. "Nice spot. What made you choose this picture?" he asked, his genuine interest a brief distraction.

"I love Bansky and his graffiti style. I love all the interpretations of it as well." She smiled, thinking of her reaction the first time she has seen the piece.

"You know art?"

She wasn't sure if it was a question or a statement. But she answered, "Yes, I love it. I was an art history major in college, initially."

"Why the change?" he enquired as he placed the stencil on her shoulder. His touch almost sent her over the edge. He swept her hair aside and, in that moment, she wanted him to pull her hair back and kiss her. She snapped back into reality when he abruptly said, "No, too big." Without consulting her, he grabbed a wet paper towel and wiped the stencil away. She was inclined to believe him, given it was her first tattoo, but she was intrigued that he decided for her.

He began resizing the drawing on his computer and asked again, "You said *initially*. So, why the change from art history?"

"Oh, that. Honestly, cost of living in Chicago is pretty high. I was concerned about the employment possibilities." She paused, but he just looked at her, wanting more of an explanation. She continued, "I thought about what industry would always thrive. So, I went into pre-law. I'm a divorce attorney now. Sadly, everyone seems to get divorced these days."

"Does it speak to you?" he questioned, as he began to rub the new stencil drawing on her shoulder.

"What?" Kate said, surprised at the question.

"Does it make you happy the way art does?"

Her surprise grew. "How do you know art makes me happy?"

"You're getting a tattoo of *Girl with Balloon*," he smirked at her. She already loved his smile, so mischievous and suggestive. And he had a good point. Art had always been a part of her.

"I'm very good at what I do, and I can still have a love of art," she pointed out. "Even if it didn't end up as my career choice."

"That's true." He seemed happy with her response, which, in turn, made her happy. Why did she care about this stranger's opinion of her?

Dominic turned his head at the tattoo option on her skin. In the mirror, she saw the creases between his eyes grow deeper.

He motioned for her to stand up and look. "What do you think?" he asked.

She looked in the mirror and immediately fell in love. The girl was about two inches high, and the small red heart balloon was just out of her reach, maybe half an inch on her shoulder. "It's perfect," she smiled at him. They stood there for a moment, staring into each other's eyes.

There's a saying that the eyes are the window to the soul. It had never really meant anything to Kate. Not until now, when she felt like she could see right inside of this man. She felt something familiar, something she couldn't put her finger on. Unlike what she had with her brothers and far more intense than anything she had ever had with past boyfriends. She didn't even get this feeling when she yearned for Ethan across the office. It was indescribable.

Finally, Dominic spoke, breaking the trance. "Are you ready? Is this your first tattoo?"

"It is, and yes, I'm kind of scared," she admitted.

"It'll be alright. The pain is temporary." It was indeed the pain that concerned her. Yet somehow, this man, who looked like he'd certainly hold his own in a bar brawl, suddenly looked sweet and sensitive. He took her hand in his and led her over to the table. Who was this man? He could only be in his late thirties, maybe early forties, and he owned his own tattoo shop in the middle of South Beach. She could only assume that the rent alone had to be astronomical. Then again, she was going to be a partner at Murphy and Simmons before she was forty. Maybe Dominic was as ambitious as her?

When Kate took his hand, Dominic's head filled with visions of her writhing in ecstasy between his sheets. He wanted to lead her straight into his bedroom to strip that little dress off of her body and kiss every inch of her.

Just as she was about to lay down, Kate scanned the shop, looking for Nicole. She was already sitting with her foot up on another artist's leg, a tattoo gun drilling into her skin. Her nose was completely scrunched as she typed on her phone, most likely texting Derek throughout the ordeal. She wasn't looking away from the phone, so Kate laid down on the table and took a deep breath.

"Please, trust me. You're in good hands." Dominic's voice was somehow the perfect combination of coarseness and soft velvet all mixed together. If only he knew what she wanted him to do with those hands.

The tattoo gun came to life, and she practically jumped at the sound. He put a reassuring hand on her back, thumb slightly rubbing back and forth in a calming manner. She wondered if he was doing that on purpose; it felt like a mindless habit, something he might do to a girlfriend.

It was the moment of truth. He gave her a quick warning as the needle touched her skin, though it honestly didn't hurt as badly as she was expecting. Not like a cut, but more like a fingernail digging into her skin. As he continued tracing the shape of the girl, it began to sting more and more. Just as the feeling was turning from stinging to real pain, he stopped to wipe away what was probably blood. And he began again. That was the pattern for the next half hour of her life: stinging, pain, and then a break, stinging, pain, and break.

Dominic was impressed with her reaction. He could tell she was hurting, but she stayed strong. He didn't usually tattoo random women that came into the shop. Typically, he either wasn't impressed with their choices or that it meant three friends giving moral support and crowding into his tiny little work station. But the second

21

he saw Kate, he knew he wanted to be the artist that tattooed her. To him, there was a connection between a client and the artist, who was going to visually change them forever. He wanted that connection with Kate. And, for some reason, he didn't like the thought of another man touching her.

Kate's tattoo choice, and the fact that she didn't need her blonde friend with her, only made him fall that much harder. He secretly pictured what one of his paintings would look like on that perfect milky skin. He had some of his art tattooed on himself, but until now, he had always preferred to see it on canvas rather than other people. He wanted to immortalize her on canvas, and he hadn't wanted to paint realism in years. Maybe she was his muse. But he wouldn't hang those pieces in a gallery. If he painted her, he'd want it to be for his eyes only.

"How are you doing?" he asked periodically. She answered with barely audible sounds that he found completely adorable. Maybe he could get her to be a bit louder in bed. He was going to have to try.

"I'm hanging in there," Kate said, the last time he asked. She liked that he tried to keep her mind off the pain.

Finally, it was done. She stood and looked in the mirror. Her skin was red from the invasion, but she knew that would subside. She practically cried after seeing the artwork she was so connected to emblazoned on her shoulder. Now it seemed silly she waited so long to do it. Once she got to see the final product, Dominic covered it with some plastic wrap to protect it from the elements. Nicole was already on her way over, walking slowly as she tested her ankle for pain.

Nicole began to pick up the pace as she saw Kate stand up to take a look. "Ahhhh, I love it," Nicole almost screamed as she reached her. "I'm so proud of you!"

Kate looked down at the little compass on the top of Nicole's foot, put there to represent all the travel now in her life. "I love yours, too. Now where should we go for dinner?" Kate asked. "I'm starved."

"There's a great restaurant I heard about. It's just down the street, so we'll actually be able to hear each other talk. Then we can party on Ocean Drive," Nicole smiled. "Derek can meet us there. He's ready when we are."

Dominic didn't want Kate to walk out of the shop without him. He'd probably never see her again. He had to say something. Without another thought, he interjected, "Would you like to make it a double date? I'd love to take you to dinner." He looked at Kate, hoping she'd agree, though he cringed internally at his "double date" remark. He couldn't have come up with something a bit more suave? Still, dinner was a start.

The expression that crossed Kate's face could have been relief. Could she be thinking the same thing about him? Lord, he hoped so. She smiled at him and looked at Nicole. "Let's make a reservation for four people."

CHAPTER THREE

As the sun started to set, the three of them walked the short distance to the restaurant. It was quite small and very trendy, with neon lights shining bright pink around the patio. There were only three small tables outside, and two were already taken. Kate had become accustomed to Derek knowing everyone and pulling strings, but it still surprised her when Dominic told them to each have a seat at the open table and went inside. A moment later, servers came out, carrying another small table and two chairs. They quickly set up the table next to the women, doubling its size to accommodate four. Dominic took the seat next to Kate. She and Nicole stared at him.

"We needed a table for four," he stated simply, resting his arm on the back of Kate's chair.

"My husband, Derek, should be here any minute. I think you'll get along great," Nicole smiled.

"I look forward to meeting him."

Just then, Derek walked up and claimed the chair next to his wife. "You've made a friend, ladies?" he asked, half-joking, half-wondering who this stranger was.

"I'm Dominic. I had the pleasure of tattooing Kate this evening. She's allowing me to treat her to dinner." He reached across the table to shake Derek's hand.

"Hello, I'm Derek. That is very nice of you." He turned to Nicole. "Let's check out your ink." Nicole swung her leg into his lap, and he lightly ran his finger over the plastic wrap protecting his wife's new compass. "It's beautiful, Love." Then he stood and walked over to the other side of the table. It didn't escape him that

Dominic had his arm on Kate's chair. He wondered what the man's intentions were for his wife's best friend.

He inspected Kate's tattoo through the plastic wrap, taking care not to touch anything. "It is very nice work. I'm proud of you, Little One," he said, using the nickname that Kate had grown so fond of. He kissed the top of her head before going back to his seat.

Dominic wasn't quite sure what to think of Derek. He could tell the man had money, if the watch on his wrist was anything to go by. Dominic had a particular interest in watches and, since he had that same brand in his collection, he knew that the sporty red piece on Derek's wrist ran around $20k. And yet, Derek seemed casual and unpretentious. Dominic liked that. But even with his laid-back attitude, Dominic could tell that Derek, protective of his wife's friend, was sizing him up. He was okay with that. He had nothing to hide; his interest in Kate went far beyond the bedroom.

After the waiter delivered the menus and took their drink orders, Derek began to ask Dominic questions. He appeared truly interested in Dominic's answers. Maybe he was, Kate thought to herself, but she also knew Derek well enough recognize that he was checking out this man who was interested in her. She appreciated the thought, but she was a grown woman with two older brothers. She had seen her dates go through the song and dance with them before.

As they spoke, a man approached the table. "Ah, hello, Mr. Price," he said to Dominic. "It's very nice of you to join us this evening."

Derek was surprised. Could this man be part of the famed Price family, who owned half the Port of Miami? He saw Dominic's subtle displeasure at his family name being mentioned. He clearly wanted to keep his wealth a secret, unlike most men, who would use their money and power to get into a woman's pants. Derek liked that Dominic, apparently, had no intention of Kate knowing who he was, not yet. Before Nicole, Derek had always done the same. Dominic glanced over and saw the look of recognition on Derek's face. Derek gave Dominic a quick nod to let him know that, for the time being, his secret was safe.

Dominic appreciated the unspoken gesture. He wanted Kate to be herself with him, not to think of him as some modern-day Miami royalty. Although, Kate knew art, and he had made quite a name for himself in the art world. He didn't plan on mentioning that tonight, either.

That was, until she spoke. "Dominic Price…the artist?" Kate asked, extremely interested.

Derek's eyebrow rose at the question. He had figured that Dominic was only known for his family.

"The one and only," Dominic replied, trying to keep the mood light. With luck, she would be more interested in him as an artist than the piles of money that most women saw. He hoped he hadn't misjudged her.

Kate was practically giddy. "You're one of the new greats, along with Godard and DeRubeis! I can't believe you're *that* Dominic. Your work is influential. Oh my God, Dominic Price tattooed me!! What the hell are you doing in a tattoo shop?"

Her reaction was sweet and genuine, making Dominic relax the muscles he had unknowingly tensed. He was inwardly smoldering, hoping that the owner didn't start talking about his family as well. If the Gods smiled on him and something real formed between them,

Dominic was determined to trust that Kate wasn't influenced by the Price name.

"Thank you, Alberto, we're looking forward to a wonderful meal." The dismissiveness in his voice was enough for Alberto to go check on the other table. Dominic laughing to himself at Kate's reaction to him tattooing and thought quickly about an answer. "Tattooing is a change of pace," he told her. "Painting is a rather isolated job. This way, I get to be around people for a bit."

"Makes sense," Kate answered, still trying to process what she had just learned.

Soon their food arrived. Kate had ordered fish, which pleased Dominic. It wasn't a deal breaker for him, but it had become less appealing to watch his date eating meat since he'd become pescatarian a few years ago. He had always been an extreme carnivore his entire life until, while exploring different types of art, he had attempted a landscape. Wanting a change from the Miami view, he had gone to a cow pasture to capture that farm feel. When he painted the cow's eyes, he felt like he saw into the heart and soul of the animal. He hadn't had a piece of meat since that day.

Kate, meanwhile, had a million questions for Dominic, but didn't want their date to feel like an interview. She was crazy about the man sitting next to her. She had always been attracted to a clean-cut man in a nice suit. Her boyfriends had always been the preppie type- they golfed, drank microbrews, and had steady employment. This guy...this guy looked like he could be a rock star. He looked dangerous and mysterious, and she loved it. There was something in him that she was completely drawn to. On top of all of that, he was on his way to being one of the best artists of the century. She loved his work, how it was so modern and abstract. The splashes of light he'd create could take her breath away. As Kandinsky believed, colors provoke emotions, and Dominic Price's work had done that in her, prior to meeting him. She wasn't exactly sure how to act. This time, she was definitely going to have to use those fake confidence skills.

Fortunately, the conversation was much easier than Kate had anticipated. She was worried she wouldn't be able to take her mind off of the fact she was technically *out on a date with Dominic Price*. But the conversation flowed easily from topic to topic, without any awkward silences. She was having such a great time that she was eventually able to push the fact of who he was to the back of her brain. Everything was comfortable. They joked and laughed and learned about each other. Like the fact that both were picked on by two older brothers. When Dominic talked about his siblings, they seemed much closer to the type of guy Kate usually found attractive. But when she stared into Dominic's mysterious eyes, she couldn't imagine wanting someone more than him.

...

Kate couldn't quite figure out the time. Somewhere between midnight and morning. That didn't narrow it down very much. Everything was a bit fuzzy. How many drinks had she consumed?

She could see the blurry vision of Nicole and Derek walking in front of her, could feel a heavy arm around her waist. Looking through the fog, she realized it was Dominic's. They were definitely on Ocean Drive. The blaring techno music and crowds of people trying to fit along the small walkway between the endless restaurant tables told her that. Flashes of the night came to her. The four of them did shots of tequila at one bar. No doubt that was Nicole's brilliant suggestion. Then she remembered being surrounded by black lights and dancing with Dominic. Their bodies were so close... She searched the corners of her brain, trying to remember more. Her arms around his neck. His hands on her hips. The feeling of him hard and ready for her. In that moment, all she wanted was her hotel room. She was not in her right mind. She didn't care. She wanted to drag him into bed with her. She wanted him to make her scream.

It was almost 2am, and Kate had had far too much to drink. Dominic wanted her back safely in her hotel room. She had begun to stagger a bit more, but he could carry her if needed. He didn't care what kind of spectacle he made of them. Something inside of him wanted to make sure that she was always safe and protected. He looked down at her dark hair and hazy eyes, trying to picture her in the court room. He had no doubt she could handle herself there, but all he saw now was an adorable creature that he wanted to watch over.

"Turn here. We're off Collins," Derek yelled over his shoulder. From this angle, Nicole looked like she was asleep on his shoulder. *Thank God*, Dominic thought to himself. He didn't want the Stones getting the wrong idea if he took Kate back to his place.

There was something special about her, something that made him want more than just a one-night stand. She was a divorce attorney from Chicago. You couldn't get much further from an artist from South Beach. He remembered being in Chicago once for an art auction and signing. He had loved the city, so Midwestern, so completely different from Miami. Maybe he should travel there to see her again.

The group reached the hotel, and Derek was at a crossroads. Did he try and handle getting both women settled to sleep by himself, or did he trust Dominic to take care of Kate? He had watched him throughout the night and so far, was impressed. He wanted to talk more with him tomorrow. There was a look in his eye that Derek recognized, the very one he had had when he met Nicole. The man walking with Kate was not a man that only wanted one thing from her. On the contrary, he looked like a man that was scared to death of how much he wanted.

"Derek, I'll take care of her," Dominic told him, recognizing his worry, even though they had known each other for a mere few hours.

"I'll see you in the morning before you leave," Derek replied. He knew then that Dominic had no intention of leaving Kate's side that night.

Kate fumbled in her purse for the key and let them into the room. Dominic had gathered from dinner conversation that Derek and Nicole had some small ownership in multiple hotels and that this was one of them. He remembered the grand opening a few weeks back.

Kate staggered toward the bed and began to try to untie the strap of her dress behind her neck.

"Oh, slow down," he told her. "Why don't we find your pajamas, and you can go change in the bathroom?" He wanted nothing more than to peel that dress off and taste her, but she was far too drunk.

"I don't sleep in clothes," she said to him, her tone flirty.

God, she was so adorable and sexy, all at the same time.

"Okay, let's look for comfy clothes then." He had her sit down on the bed to rest while he went searching. He found a little pair of shorts that looked like cut-off sweatpants and a white fitted V-neck t-shirt. That would have to do. He turned back around to see Kate curled up on the bed already asleep.

"Oh, fuck it," he said out loud and dropped the clothes back into the drawer. Kicking off his shoes, he sat on the bed with his back leaning up on the headboard. Kate instinctively curled her body up into him and rested her head on the crook of his shoulder. How did she fit so perfectly there?

"Will you stay with me?" she muttered, only half awake.

"Until you send me away," he said quietly and kissed the top of her head.

He lay there watching her sleep for as long as his eyes would stay open. Whenever she stirred, he wanted to pull her closer to him, to snuggle her deeper into his body. What was she dreaming about? Was he part of the subconscious story being told in her head?

As he listened to her breathing, he reflected on his life, wondering how it had seemed whole before this. He had come from a loving family that happened to be very successful in business. Both of his brothers had joined in the family profession. While his parents had been disappointed that he hadn't followed them, neither of them could deny his artistic talent. His father had taken longer to accept it, but came around once Dominic's first painting sold for thousands. When it turned into a print series, the man knew his son had made a name for himself.

The tattoo shop had shocked them, but the family still stood behind him. Especially his mother, who loved him dearly. He was her little baby, a thought that made him shake his head and laugh. She had been pressuring him to get married for the past fifteen years, ideally to Amanda Martin, the daughter of one of their business associates. Amanda looked the part of a Miami Beach wife: tall and tan, thin and blonde, half her body the product of plastic surgeons. Amanda liked him, but he sensed that was chiefly because of his money. The match would have made sense for their business, if only Dominic could love her. He had never understood his mother's pressure, until now. Looking at Kate, he got a sense of what his mother wanted for him.

He awoke in a haze sometime later, unsure whether he was awake or dreaming, his hands roaming over far too much of Kate's body. He must have been dreaming, since now they were fully clothed, and Kate had definitely been naked on top of him a moment ago. The whole thing felt like a fantasy. This woman was lying next to him, fully clothed. So how could this be the most erotic thing that had ever happened to him?

CHAPTER FOUR

Kate woke with a killer headache that made it hurt to open her eyes. She looked around and realized that she was still with Dominic. It felt oddly natural, curled up into him, almost as though she was alone. That seemed strange. How had she not initially noticed a man in her bed? Yet how normal it felt to have him there. She peeked up at him. His eyes were still shut, his breathing slow and quiet. She stretched her body up and kissed him on the cheek. Other than that, she wasn't sure what she was prepared to do. Did she really want to sleep with him? Though she absolutely wanted to, she wasn't sure that she should. They had only met yesterday, after all.

Dominic's eyes slowly opened and met hers.

"You stayed," she said sweetly.

"I wasn't going anywhere," he assured her. "How do you feel?"

"Ugh," was about the only way she could explain it.

He brushed a dark lock of hair out of her face and rested his hand on her cheek. It was the most sensual feeling she had ever experienced. He leaned in and tenderly took her mouth. (Why did she feel like a teenage girl being kissed for the first time?) His lips felt like fire.

With the first taste of her, he could barely breathe. He wanted to know every part of this woman, had never wanted someone more. She leaned back into the bed, pulling his body with hers.

This was exactly what she needed- a weekend fling with a sexy artist. She had never done anything like this before. But she was a thirty-five-year-old woman. She could do something spontaneous every once in a while.

The feeling of him on top of her sent vibrations through her body. She reached down and grabbed his t-shirt and began to pull it over his head, revealing his bare chest and arms, covered in tattoos, all strategically placed to be hidden underneath the short-sleeved shirt. She could tell right away that most were in the style of his art; he must have drawn the pictures that were now a permanently part of his body. She reached her hands up to his chest and lightly touched the swirls and smears of paint.

Feeling her hands over his chest made him instantly hard. He wanted to be inside of her, wanted to make her scream his name. He looked into her eyes, a smirk creeping onto his face. Then he kissed her again. He couldn't get enough of her. He took her face into his hands while he kissed her chin and her neck. He wanted to rip her dress off of her.

Kate couldn't wait anymore. She could feel him hard and ready and that was all she wanted. She reached behind her neck and untied the straps of her dress. Dominic sat up on his knees and pulled the dress free, slipping it over her hips, down her legs, balling it up, and tossing it across the room. Kate laughed and pulled him back on top of her.

Dominic loved her small, perfect breasts. He had known the entire night that they were bare underneath that dress, and it drove him crazy, imagining them with only the thin layer of material as protection. He had felt them against his body while they danced and had wanted to take her right then and there. Now, he softly kissed each one before taking a tighter grip on her nipple until she pushed her head back into the pillow and moaned. Again he kneeled, and she leaned up to eagerly help him undo his belt and shorts. He climbed back on top of her and kissed her neck. She grabbed ahold of his shoulders and searched for his mouth. Then he was inside of her.

The sensation was exhilarating. She hadn't been with a man in almost six months. She wanted this feeling to last forever. She remembered another flash of them dancing, her knowing he would be good in bed. Their bodies fit and moved like they had always been together. He held the back of her neck and whispered into her ear about her beauty. He told her wanted to paint her. It felt like a dream. She wanted to remember his smell for the rest of her life. She wrapped her legs around his back and put her hands over her head as he took her body over the edge again and again.

When it was over, her body was sated and shattered and she was breathing as heavily as Dominic. She curled up into him again and they laid together in silence, catching their breath. Kate couldn't wrap her head around the passion she felt with Dominic after knowing him for less than twenty-four hours. But she wasn't one of those stupid girls that would think they were now in love. She knew this was just for the weekend, and she wanted to soak up every minute of it.

"Would you believe me if I said I've never done this before?" she asked sweetly.

"You were far too good for that to be your first time sweetheart," he smiled at her.

Kate laughed. "You know that's not what I meant. I've never 'hooked up' with someone before."

"Ahhhh," he said, pretending to realize what she meant. "Well, I'm glad you decided to try it out." He leaned over and kissed her head. "Should we get up? I need to run home and shower and change. But can I see you later?"

"I'd like that," she replied.

He took out a card from his tattoo shop and handed it to her. "My cell phone number is on here. Give me a call." He leaned over the bed and kissed her on the lips, and they said a quick goodbye.

When he walked out the front door of the hotel, he found Derek sitting at one of the tables, reading a newspaper.

"Good morning. Coffee?" Derek said, smiling. Nicole had already warned him that if he scared Dominic off, she would have his head. He wanted to know more about this guy, but was determined to be nice for the girls' sake.

"Sure." Dominic took the seat across from him. He had gotten a pretty good feel for Derek the day before and figured they could become good friends. He welcomed a chat with him.

"Thank you for staying with Kate," Derek said sincerely. "A lot of times she and Nicole go all out the first night seeing each other and then relax the rest of the trip. You were lucky enough to experience an *all-out* night with them."

Dominic laughed from his memories of the night. "They were a lot of fun," he smiled.

"Man-to-man, do I need to worry about you breaking her heart?" Derek asked bluntly.

"I think you'll need to worry about me crying on your shoulder when she leaves," Dominic responded, only half-joking.

"There is something special about the two of them. I could immediately see why they've been best friends since college," Derek told him. "They have an unbreakable bond."

"That's great." Dominic thought about his past. "My dance card was always full growing up. I was always surrounded by friends and girls. But, deep down, I knew that a lot of the attention I got was based on my last name and all the perks that came along with hanging out with a Price. Especially when I hit my twenties, girls were always looking to become Mrs. Price and join the Miami dynasty."

"I was raised under quite different conditions, but I made a name for myself. I understand exactly where you're coming from," Derek told him. "Nicole was the one that I finally let in and it was the best thing I ever did." He was a bit surprised at how well he and Dominic got along, given their opposite upbringings. Dominic was a trust fund baby, and yet it sounded like he became a famous artist and business owner in his own right as well. Derek respected his choices in life and truly liked the man sitting across from him.

Dominic enjoyed the chat with Derek. They were both forty, so it wasn't like Derek was going to try and tell Dominic what was allowed with Kate. Dominic wouldn't have tolerated it, even if he had tried. They discussed Kate briefly, but the remainder of their conversation involved their respective businesses and lives in general. They ended up chatting longer than either of them had expected.

...

"Well, when you set out to do something, you just go and get it done, huh?" Nicole joked with Kate while she lay on the bed next to her.

"Shut the fuck up!" Kate laughed. Nicole was right, though. She had told herself she needed to get laid; now she could mark that off her to-do list. Still... "It was so much more than *getting laid*." She took a deep breath, remembered Dominic on top of her. "Nic, it was amazing."

"You have that look in your eye, girl. I had the same look with Derek."

"Oh no, this is the weekend fling I needed. This is not the insta-love thing that happened with you two."

Nicole didn't believe her for a second. She knew Kate probably better than Kate knew herself. Kate was head over heels. Nicole didn't blame her; Dominic was great. "If you say so," she smirked.

"I do say so." Kate dragged herself off the bed. "I need a shower," she said with a smile. "And then let's go get some coffee and breakfast."

Dominic had exchanged contact information with Derek before he left. He did fully intend on forming a friendship with this man. He liked how well they understood each other. Maybe it would lead to seeing Kate again in the future as well. He wasn't sure how he would say goodbye to her tomorrow. Dominic had his share of women in the past, beautiful women at that. But with Kate, it was an entirely different kind of erotic. Watching her body move underneath him and seeing how he could affect her was maddening.

He wanted to get home quickly so that he could find her again as soon as possible. He wanted to spend every minute possible with her, in and out of his bed.

His phone rang, interrupting his thoughts. "Price," he said, without checking the screen.

"Nicky, dear," he heard his mother's voice. His family were the only ones allowed to continue with the childhood nickname. Random people sometimes called him Dom for short, but Nick or Nicky was off limits to the general public now.

"Hi, Mom, how are you today?" he asked. Somehow, she still talked to him like he was her little boy. It didn't upset him.

"Amanda saw you out last night," she paused, a note of hesitation in her voice. Maybe she was waiting to see if he would respond. He didn't. "She said you were out with a man covered in tattoos."

He cut her off, a bit annoyed now. "Really, Mom?"

"I know, Nicky, but yours can be covered by your t-shirt. I worry that with this tattoo shop, you're going to end up hanging around the wrong crowd. And she said the girl you were with seemed drunk and trashy."

"Enough!" he said loudly. "I don't care what Amanda thinks. You know she thinks anyone I'm with is trash. Though it shouldn't matter, the man covered with tattoos is an international business owner, and his friend Kate, the woman I was with, is much more suited for me than Amanda ever will be. Try to understand, Mom. I love you, but I am not interested in Amanda. The relationship between us and the Martin family is going to have to stay strictly business."

Carolyn Price was used to getting her way. She was determined to get her youngest son to finally see that he and the Martins' daughter would be a wonderful match. Well, it would be wonderful if the two families that owned practically all of the Port of Miami were united. Think of the power of the generations to follow! And it wasn't as if Amanda wasn't a great catch for her son. She was young and beautiful and fit right in with the Price family.

"Dear, what is so wrong with Amanda?"

"Mother, I'm not having this conversation with you again. I am not interested in her that way."

It was never a good sign when any of her boys called her *Mother*. Carolyn needed to avoid upsetting him too much. Perhaps she should go about this from a different angle, get him to spend more time with Amanda. She was going to have to be sneaky to do that without him wising up to the plan.

Amanda had admitted to her that the unknown girl he was with was very pretty. Amanda knew almost everyone in the city; Carolyn figured this mystery woman was a tourist. The convenient thing about tourists is that they leave. So, no matter how beautiful this girl was, she'd be gone soon. Let Dominic have his fun, and then he could think about was best for his future.

"Okay, okay," she soothed, "I just want what is best for you. Love you, dear."

"I love you too, Mom." Dominic ended the call. That woman could drive him crazy. She did want the best for him, but he also knew how much she wanted the Price and Martin families to be joined. He loved his mother, but not enough to marry the wrong woman just to make her happy. It wasn't ideal, since he wasn't even involved in the Port business, but it was her last chance for an advantageous match. Both of his brothers were already married. God help them if they ever got divorced. Then Carolyn would leave Dominic alone, but she would sic Amanda on the poor soul.

Talk about trashy; Amanda was badmouthing a woman she hadn't even met, just for being with a man that Amanda wanted. He couldn't believe he had ever been turned on by her. They had hooked up a few times in their twenties, and he had tried dating her. But after he learned how superficial she was, she had lost all attraction for him. The fact that he slept with Kate after only knowing her for hours didn't escape him. He knew he was straddling the line of hypocrisy. However, the woman he ravished this morning had more class in her little finger than Amanda had accumulated over a lifetime. When he looked into Kate's eyes, he saw sincerity and depth. This bitch, on the other hand, was as deep as a puddle.

Dominic headed toward the crash pad he shared with his brothers. He had a condo further south by South Point Park, where he lived and painted. But he didn't want to waste any time away from Kate, and he had the essentials at his place on Ocean Drive. When Dominic turned twenty-one and came into his trust, the three brothers had split the cost of a two-bedroom condo right on Ocean Drive, convincing their trustee that it was a great investment opportunity. Investment hadn't been their driving motivation, but they weren't wrong about it either. If they sold the place now, each of them would triple their money easily.

Justin was the oldest and did seemed to be happily married. If he did ever crash at the condo, it was with his wife. But it saddened Dominic to hear about how many times the middle brother, Adrian, would have random women spend a few hours or the night with him there. Adrian was married as well, but didn't seem to take it as seriously as Justin. Dominic knew he, himself, wouldn't take the plunge unless he was prepared to stay faithful the entire time. Nothing, other than art, had captivated him enough to do so, not until Kate. Kate was a game changer.

Dominic let himself into the condo, head spinning from everything that had happened. Images of Kate from the night before and that morning danced around in his mind. He couldn't remember the last time he had felt such an intense urge to paint. Whenever he painted, his work mirrored his mood. If he wanted a cooler painting with light strokes and a calming feel, then he would put on linen pants and play a little Frank. If he wanted something strong and bold, he played heavy metal and wore denim and leather. He'd submerge himself into the painting and not come up for air until it was complete. He liked creating larger than life designs, and most of his art was done on enormous canvases.

Sitting outside, Kate nursed a Bloody Mary in hopes of erasing the last of her hangover. Why hadn't she and Nicole learned that they always overdid it on the first night? "He wants to see me today," she said to her friend.

"You want to see him, don't you?" Nicole responded.

"I do! I'm not missing out on a romantic affair with a famous artist. Can you imagine the memories I'll have? It's like the cheesy plot of a chick-flick," she joked.

"You're not at all concerned that you'll get attached?" Nicole sounded sincere.

"I'm not thinking about it. I want to have a nice, fun escape from reality for the weekend and live the fantasy," Kate smiled and closed her eyes at the thought of being in bed with Dominic again. But she was under no illusion that this was going past Sunday.

"You are a smart girl," Nicole said. "Though I wouldn't be surprised if he'd like to keep in touch. He seemed pretty into you last night."

"We were drunk," Kate said flatly.

"It was more than that," Nicole pressed.

Kate rolled her eyes. She loved Nicole, but didn't want her trying to turn this into the love-at-first-sight that she found with Derek. That kind of thing just didn't happen that often. Kate based her life on facts alone. This was getting far too close to a grey area for her. She was happy dealing in black and white. Then again, perhaps the splash of colors across Dominic's arms and chest could brighten her life up a bit...

CHAPTER FIVE

Kate and Nicole were still deciding what to order for breakfast when Kate noticed a smirk forming on Nicole's face. Before Kate could say anything, the smirk turned to a full-on smile.

"What?" Kate asked, but felt a chill on the back of her neck. For some reason, she didn't want to turn around and see for herself.

"Lover boy is walking this way," Nicole replied, still smiling.

"You better not call him that!" Kate ordered, but couldn't help smiling a bit herself now.

Dominic had told himself that he was going to wait in the apartment for her phone call. That worked for all of about fifteen minutes. Then he convinced himself that he needed some fresh air. But he had a handful of windows he could have opened and a balcony, so that wasn't a good excuse. Finally, he decided he needed a walk. That worked.

He told himself over and over that he wasn't looking for Kate. Deep down, he knew exactly what he was doing. Good Lord, what was wrong with him? No one had ever invaded his head like this. He wandered up Ocean Drive, trying to look casual. Dominic had a tendency to look very brooding; his sharp features and intense eyes could barely mask his true feelings. He felt like a hound dog hot on the scent. Every dark-haired woman caught his attention.

As soon as he saw her hair, he knew it was her. After just one night, he knew that he would recognize her for the rest of his life. She was facing away from him, leaning slightly back in her chair. Yet he could tell it was Kate. Glancing away from Kate for a moment, he made eye contact with Nicole as she looked up from her menu. She smiled at him. Crap…busted! Resisting the urge to roll his eyes, he smiled back, knowing he has been caught. Nicole had probably seen his eyes darting around at every dark-haired woman around. Taking a deep breath, he shoved his hands into his pockets and walked up to the table.

"Hope the drink is helping?" he enquired as he kissed Kate's cheek and claimed the chair next to her, praying that his confidence would make him appear less like a stalker.

"Yes, it is!" The smile Kate gave him was genuine. "Everything this morning has helped," she added, blushing just a tad.

Dominic ordered a glass of orange juice and sat back to watch the two friends chitchat about nothing and everything. Observing Kate as she chattered with her dearest friend, Dominic concluded she was the cutest thing in the world. He adored that she seemed to be a little bit of everything- smart and worldly, yet innocent. It made him strangely compelled to protect her. He didn't know how she pulled off the combination, which was fascinating to him. He could sit and watch her for hours.

After awhile, he started quietly pondering why he hadn't wanted to get serious yet. The fear of women wanting him for his family name was a big reason. But deep down, he knew it couldn't be the only one. He watched his two older brothers walk down the aisle with women that wanted them for more than the ticket to the Price dynasty. He had to know he deserved that as well. Did it involve taking care of someone? He had been on his own so long, was he scared of taking care of someone other than himself? He wasn't sure he could answer that question before, but as he looked over at Kate, it dawned on him…that's all he could ever imagine doing from that moment on.

Nicole looked over at her phone, which had been awfully quiet. "Dominic, would you mind if I left Kate in your hands? Derek has just asked me to join him in a meeting. I'm so sorry," she said, her fake apologetic smile all too obvious.

Kate knew Nicole well, could see her trying to hide her real smile. She knew Derek hadn't text her at all. At the same time, she loved her for it. The women looked forward to their monthly visits, but Nicole wanted Kate to explore her true feelings and, at this point, it seemed like Kate could do with a gentle push. They would see each other again. For this trip, she wanted to make sure Kate had every second she could with Dominic.

"I'd love to," Dominic beamed. "What do you say? Wanna hang out with me today?" He smirked and gave Kate a wink. Winks are supposed to be fun and playful; somehow Dominic's looked sexy and sinful. Kate knew just how she'd like to stay busy with him.

Nicole didn't even want to wait for Kate to respond. She jumped out of her seat and took off down the street, grinning from ear-to-ear.

"What would you like to do?" Dominic asked, in the voice that made Kate's thighs ache.

"Let's order food first. You will come to learn that I'm always hungry." Immediately, she felt a little weird saying that. No, he wouldn't. Why would he "come to learn" that? She would be gone tomorrow.

He just smiled at her and grabbed the menu from Nicole's spot. Kate kind of liked that he stayed sitting next to her. She had always thought it looked ridiculous when couples sat on the same side of the table, but right now, she could see, or more specifically *feel*, the advantage. He kept his arm casually flung over the back of her seat as he had at dinner the night before.

"You've got it. Food first," he agreed as he perused the menu.

They both ordered omelets with a variety of fresh vegetables inside. While they ate, they casually chatted more about their lives. Kate was still very tempted to ask him more about his art work and how his success had changed his life. But she held back, not entirely sure why she was being cautious. She wasn't stupid; she had to know there would be women throwing themselves at him. Even if he wasn't the sexiest man alive, she was sure the paintings came with fat paychecks. That didn't matter to her. But how could he know that?

After they were both sufficiently satiated, Kate had the urge to get up and move around. "Come on, Nicky, let's go do something," she said.

Dominic stopped dead in his tracks. Had he heard her right? "What did you just call me?" he asked, utterly shocked.

"Oh, sorry…" Kate replied, "I usually shorten everyone's names to their first syllable. You don't look like a Dom for some reason. And Nicole already took Nic. Nicky just came out. I'm sorry, I can call you Dominic. I didn't mean to presume. Some people hate their names shortened, which is totally fine." She felt like she was back pedaling, but she couldn't get a take on his reaction. He didn't seem upset, more confused.

Dominic hesitated before he answered. No one, other than his family, had ever called him Nicky. For some reason, he liked hearing her say it. Liked it to the point that it kind of scared him. His father always called him Dominic, and his brothers dropped Nicky when they hit puberty. Now, it was only his mother that had continued with that term of endearment. "My mother calls me Nicky. Please…it's okay. More than okay. I kind of like hearing you say it, too."

"Nicky it is then," she said with a smile. "Maybe I'll only use it in private." Kate laughed at that thought.

"I don't mind where you use it, but…it's reserved only for your lips." His sexy eyes were fixed on her mouth. "Nicole and Derek can stick with Dominic," he added.

"Sounds like a deal," she agreed.

Dominic helped her out of her chair. He kept her hand in his as they walked, to her delight. They were two grown adults. Why could something so simple as hand holding seem like such a big gesture? *This is just a weekend fling*, Kate reminded herself over and over.

"Where shall we go?" Dominic asked.

"I'm enjoying this," she said sweetly. "Just walking, with no destination in mind. Let's cross over the street and walk along the beach."

…

Dominic felt like a teenage boy. He wanted to pull Kate into the sand and ravish her in front of every person on the beach. But as much as he wanted her body, he didn't want their walk to end. He wanted to learn all about her life, to know everything that made this woman tick. What had turned her into the woman that walked next to him? Again, he tried to picture her in a courtroom.

How could any man win against her? She was so mesmerizing; she must disarm all of their defenses.

"When did you know you could paint?" Kate asked him. It seemed like they had talked about everything else. She figured it was a good time to finally ask a few questions about his work.

"I actually know the exact moment I wanted to become an artist," he looked over and smiled at her, remembering the exhilaration he felt. "I was in business school and was absolutely bored to tears. But that's what we do in the Price family. My grandfather, father, and brothers all work with the Port of Miami." He left the details vague, though he wasn't sure why. "I flew through the undergrad work in three years and was in the MBA program. I tried talking with my father about how I felt no passion for it." He paused and thought about that conversation. "He didn't understand where I was coming from at all. He thought I was being too impulsive. We fought." He paused again, deep in thought, and kicked the sand under his feet. "We rarely fight... I was still living with them at the time." He left out that it was in a guest house. "My mother was having the house painted. One side was primed white, and it was just calling to me. I took any paint I could find in the house. I grabbed one of the painter's brushes and, without a thought in my mind, I just started to paint…to create...to live. It was about fifteen feet wide and reached as high as I could stretch myself. Apparently, I was yelling and swearing and had music blaring. I honestly don't remember that part at all. I just remember release. I remember feeling alive. Finally, I felt that…that…feeling. That release that only painting could give me." He put his arm around her and squeezed her for a moment as they walked. He had told very few people that story.

"Was your mom mad?" Kate had chills down her arms. What if she had been an artist? Would she have changed to pre-law? Kate loved art, but wasn't the one that created it. It had to be quite a different experience to be an artist yourself.

"At first," Dominic laughed. "She broke my trance with all of her yelling, but then she stopped. Literally just stopped, speechless. She backed up in awe. She stood silently for a moment," he smiled. "She's a very smart woman. She told me to sign it and kissed my cheek. I would like to think that she'd want me to paint even if I wasn't successful at it, but honestly, I'm sure she originally saw dollar signs for me."

"She wasn't wrong, considering you're wearing what could be sold for a studio apartment on your wrist," she joked, pointing to his watch.

"You know watches, too? Good lord, woman, you're perfect for me." He kissed her head.

"I do love them, but don't collect them," she explained. "I've learned about the very expensive items that couples try to slip through the cracks during divorce proceedings. I helped a man keep a Harry Winston just like yours from his cheating wife. It is a Harry Winston, Histoire de Tourbillon Two, right? I like them so much better than the Threes."

"Good eye," he smiled. "Me too."

"Like I said, I'm good at what I do," she joked, hoping to keep the subject light. The last thing she wanted was for him to feel like she was after his money. Wearing a quarter of a million dollars on your wrist was risky, but she liked that it was very obscure. Most people would have no idea of its value. She always thought that that must be the thrill for people that wore them- having something so valuable hidden in plain sight.

During their walk, there were times when they talked excitedly and times when they walked silently together, watching the people around them. Both scenarios were completely comfortable. But finally, Kate couldn't help herself asking, "Where's your place?" She held her breath, hoping she didn't sound too forward. Still, they had already slept together and had such a short amount of time together. Why waste more time?

Dominic's heart skipped a beat, nervously excited all over again. "My condo is at the southern tip of the Island, but I do share what we call our 'crash pad' with my brothers, up just a few blocks."

"Really? Can I see it?"

"Thought you'd never ask." Instantly, Dominic swooped down and scooped her up, as flamboyantly as possible, and began to run down the beach.

When he put her down, Kate kept her arms wrapped around his neck. He leaned his forehead into hers. "How am I going to let you go tomorrow?" he whispered. His eyes were closed, so she grabbed ahold of the back his hair, jerking him alive, and kissed him deeply.

If she wasn't careful, she would be in danger of allowing him to ravish her right then and there in the sand. Luckily, there didn't seem to be many children in South Beach, so she didn't need to worry about taking it a step too far. Who cared if these strangers were grossed out by their public display of affection, anyway? She wasn't going to miss a second with Dominic.

He lifted her up off her feet while he explored her mouth. Suddenly, he knew that they needed to go, or he wasn't going to be able to go anywhere for a little while. He leaned his head back and took in a huge breath of air. He gave her that sexy smirk and said, "Let's get you back to the crash pad."

CHAPTER SIX

They barely made it through front door, especially since Dominic almost broke through it when the key didn't make it into the lock on the first try. Once inside, Kate practically pulled him onto the floor of the long entryway. It felt like she was in a scene from a movie. They fumbled as they moved, insisting that they didn't lose grip of each other. Dominic kicked the door closed behind them and, dropping to his knees, lifted her sundress up to reveal her stomach. Everything had been frantic and thrilling, but for a short moment, he stopped and sweetly kissed her hips and belly button. He glanced up at Kate and gave her that deadly smirk. Full of life again, he ripped the dress over her head. Next, she was undressing him as they found their way to the first piece of furniture that would support them- a white stone sofa table that ran along the back of the couch in the middle of the room. He lifted her up onto the table, and the shock of the cold against her butt and thighs startled her into a laugh.

Again, she found her hands running along the tattoos of his artwork splashed across his muscular chest. She leaned over and kissed along the swirls of paint. She loved his work. Seeing and touching it in real-life on the artist himself...it was an indescribable feeling. She wanted him inside of her now. She laid back on the table while her head rested on the back cushions of the couch. Dominic knew just what to do to take her over the edge.

With each thrust, she moved further back on the table. Finally, she leaned her head back and saw the comfort of the huge white couch behind her. She reached up and grabbed his shoulders. He knew what she wanted.

They maneuvered over the table together and landed safely on the couch, which was deep enough to comfortably hold the two of them.

Dominic climbed on top of her. He had had other women on this same couch over the years, but nothing compared to this moment with Kate. No other woman in his past had ever excited him this way. He reached through her pile of hair and found the back of her head, lifting it up to meet his so he could take her mouth again. She let out a sweet moan in response.

Dominic had always loved it hard and fast, and now was fighting to keep himself in check. Earlier that morning, he had been just barely awake, and she was so perfectly sweet. Their first time felt more like some kind of dream. This time, he wanted to savor the moment with her. He didn't want it to feel like a random fuck with a woman he had picked up. Kate was too special for that. He slowed his pace. She spread her legs wider to take him in deeper. With that one simple move, his eyes rolled back inside his head, and he lost any sense of control he thought he had obtained.

Afterwards, Dominic slid between Kate's body and the back of the couch, and he spooned her up against him. "Is it too early for a nap?" he asked.

"After that? Not at all. I could lay like this forever," Kate replied with her eyes still closed.

…

For the second time in as many days, Kate wasn't sure of the time. This real-life fantasy was playing tricks on her. Dominic was still out like a light. They had moved around while she slept; she was now curled on his shoulder with her leg flung over his. He must have gotten up to open the windows while she was sleeping. She could hear the sounds of the waking world down below along Ocean Drive. She could pick up bits and pieces of overly excited conversations between the sounds of glasses clinking together and plates being gathered. The sun was shining brightly through the window. She snuggled into Dominic's chest, savoring the feeling. She adored being tucked away in their own little existence while the rest of the world went on without them. She continued to doze in between states of sleep and wakefulness for maybe another hour.

Without any warning, Dominic spoke, his voice rough and sexy from sleep. "What would you like to do?"

"You know those huge martini glasses that are all over the place downstairs?" She looked up at him with a sinful smile.

Dominic laughed at her inquiry. "Well... let's do it." He was up on his feet swiftly, ready to take on the day again.

"Did you enjoy your nap?" she said, giggling.

"Naps are wasted on the young. Every adult should be required to take a daily nap as well."

"I couldn't agree more," she said through a yawn, stretching her arms up over her head.

...

Dominic led her again through the narrow walkways of Ocean Drive. Kate loved how alive she felt. Was it South Beach? Was it Dominic? As she gripped his hand tighter, she smiled at the bizarre twist of fate. What if she hadn't decided to finally get her tattoo? This weekend trip would have ended up far differently.

As Dominic led her to one of the few open tables along the street, his phone rang. It was the shop. He put up one finger, giving her an apologetic smile as he stepped away from the table.

"Is this important?" he asked into the phone. He wasn't usually short with the employees, but he wanted to focus on Kate.

It was Jason, his manager. "We're short again…" The dreaded words came from the other end of the phone.

Fuck! Someone was stealing. Dominic took a moment to narrow down the options of who could be the culprit. The first time they were short, he thought it could possibly be a mistake. The second time, he could have pulled all the artists working that shift aside and dealt with it then. But he preferred to bide his time and see how much further this was going to go. All except one employee had been with him for quite a while. A few of them had been there for years. This shop was like his second family. It was incredibly disheartening to know someone could do this. It wasn't exactly chump change, either. Jason hadn't told him the amount this time, but the first two thefts had been around five hundred dollars each. It wasn't the money though; he didn't need it. It was what the money represented.

"Thanks, Jason. Leave the information for me in the office. I'll come by later and look into it." With that, he ended the call and turned back towards the table. Kate was all smiles, a gigantic martini glass twice the size of her head sitting in front of her, filled with a bright red frozen drink. Two beer bottles rested upside down on the sides of the glass.

"Save some for me," Dominic joked, taking the seat across from her.

"No promises, Nicky," she smiled slyly. He still couldn't wrap his head around the fact that she called him Nicky. That had to mean something.

Dominic took a large pull on the straw. "What am I drinking?" he said with a contorted face, leaning back from the strength of the alcohol.

Kate almost spit out her mouthful in response. "I have no idea. I saw their drink over there and told the server, 'Bring me one of those'." She laughed, her own contorted face matching his.

"You said you're always hungry, right? Want an appetizer?" he enquired, picking up the menu in front of him.

"Yes, I am – just no meat," she said between sips. Dominic wasn't sure how she hadn't given herself brain freeze at this point.

"I like that about you," Dominic told her and grabbed ahold of her hand.

"I hadn't realized you didn't eat meat, either. Well, land animals at least." Kate cocked her head to the side, thinking about their past two meals together.

Dominic told her the story about the cow that changed his outlook on it. "What's your reason?" he asked.

"I worked in restaurants throughout college, and we were given a chance to visit the meat slaughterhouse." She paused, remembering the experience. "I'm telling you, if those places had glass walls, no one would eat meat."

"I would bet you're right. So, let's have some wild caught seafood then?" Dominic tried lightening the mood. He had brought up the subject, but he wanted to keep the day light and happy. They had such limited time together.

He already had to find the time to break away at some point and deal with the money shortage at the tattoo shop.

As they waited for their food, Kate indulged her love of people watching. She glanced at the tables around her and the people walking by hand-in-hand. Nicole was right. This place bred beautiful people. She felt like she could tell immediately who were locals and who ones were tourists. It wasn't like the visitors wore Hawaiian shirts and fanny packs, they just didn't hit the same level of gorgeousness. Of course, there were beautiful people all over the world, but there was something different about the ones from South Beach. Or maybe it was Miami altogether.

Kate couldn't help but notice how different she looked from all the other women around her. Sure, she was pretty, but she was short, with fair skin and dark, straight hair. These women were breathtaking. Most were very tall, thin, tan, and seemed overdressed for an afternoon out on Ocean Drive. There were many that were shorter, more ethnic looking, and had flowing dark hair that seemed to go on for miles. They came with fabulous accents as well. But all seemed very different from her. She even saw a handful of couples that looked like a sugar-daddy situation.

All of a sudden, everything around her seemed the complete opposite of the Midwest life she was used to. She didn't think she would fit in here for any longer than a weekend. Did women morph into South Beach beauties when they moved there, or was it only the ones lucky enough to be born in Miami? If she lived there, would she end up looking unbelievably beautiful herself? Should she test the theory, see if she became some kind of super model? Maybe she would grow eight inches, too. Kate laughed to herself, wondering why she was even thinking about this. Then she shrugged it off, remembering that she liked both the idea of an escape to something different and also returning to the world she knew.

She looked across the table at this insanely sexy man, who was watching her watch everything around her. His face was inscrutable, his dark eyes still searing into her soul. With all of this beauty surrounding her, what seemed to make her different in his eyes?

"Have you ever been to Chicago?" Kate asked, trying to bring them both back to the present. She figured he had; most people have found their way there for one reason or another.

"I have, but only once," Dominic admitted. "I was there for an art auction and signing at a gallery." He usually felt uncomfortable talking about art with women. The business side of art, at least. "When I come visit again, will you show me around?"

Kate's heart jumped in her chest. She wasn't sure how to play it cool with him. Then again, she apparently did a fabulous job at it with Ethan. She didn't want to seem uninterested in the idea. She smiled at Dominic. "Of course. Please come. We would have such a great time."

"Where would you take me? Other than your bedroom." He gave her that deadly smirk again, and she practically melted.

"Well, if we did in fact make it out (and I'm really not going to make any promises) then we could be tourists for the day," she said sweetly. "There are quite a few obscure and interesting things to see."

"For example?" he asked, an eyebrow lifted.

"My bathroom is pretty nice, my living room…I have a kitchen," Kate joked. "I would take you to the Tribune

Tower. There's a wall that has rock fragments from all over the world. There's a rock from the Alamo, one from the Great Wall of China, the Colosseum, and they added the World Trade Center. There is even a moonrock in there."

"Wow, what a great concept. I bet that's a piece of art in itself."

Kate loved how Dominic's mind worked. Immediately, he looked at it as a beautiful thing, not only historical, but a form of artwork, too.

Would he really come visit? Kate tried brushing it off as just talk. This was just her weekend fling. Still, she loved and hated that she could imagine walking down Michigan Avenue with him.

CHAPTER SEVEN

"Gael is coming?!" Kate excitedly stated more than asked.

Nicole laughed, thinking about how close Kate had grown to Gael in the past year. Gael was technically Derek's business associate, though in actuality the two were as close as brothers. A Mexican with an American college education, Gael had started as Derek's right-hand man at the beginning of his company. In this last year, had become something much closer to a partner, taking on more responsibility as Derek focused on his new bride.

Gael was absolutely brilliant and, Nicole had to admit, pretty hot as well. The Stones' had tried to set Gael up with Kate, but the two had ended up much more like brother and sister. Their brains worked in such similar ways; Gael was always showing up with some brain teaser he had found, determined to finally stump Kate. It wasn't Nicole's cup of tea, but Gael and Kate certainly found it fun.

"Yep, tonight," Nicole finally answered, coming back to reality. "He'll only be here a day or two. He's got an idea to pitch to Derek and wants to do it face-to-face."

"Must be a far-fetched idea then," Kate joked. Derek trusted Gael's opinions and decisions; he had given him far more control of the company over the course of the past year. If Gael needed face time, he must be expecting to have to do some convincing.

"We'll see," Nicole answered with a smile.

They were hanging out in Nicole and Derek's hotel apartment. For the most part, Derek had stopped negotiating apartments into his land deals with hotel companies. But he made an exception if the location was one where the couple thought they would visit often. They had both immediately agreed that they could spend a fair amount of time in South Beach. Including the time they had spent in Chicago this past year, it was the most time Derek had spent stateside in almost a decade.

Each Stone apartment that Kate had seen exhibited its own style, though they were all incredibly extravagant in their own way. This apartment was perhaps twice the size of Kate's room and extremely open. A partial wall separated the living space from the bedroom area, with a huge piece of contemporary artwork hanging on each side. The wall didn't continue all the way to the exterior of the building, which, as it happened, was entirely made of windows. The view of the water was breathtaking.

They were lounging outside on the balcony while they waited for Derek and Dominic. Derek was meeting with some of the hotel owners who had come for a visit. Dominic had told Kate that he needed to do some business at the tattoo shop.

"I think there might be a problem at Dominic's shop," Kate said, unsure she should even be talking about it.

"Why?" Nicole asked, her head tilting to the side in curiosity.

"He took a call...I wasn't trying to listen, but I could tell he was upset about something. He was fine the rest of the day but just seemed preoccupied when he left to go by the shop." Kate thought for a moment and then continued, "Then again, I barely know this guy. Who knows if he was really preoccupied." She wanted to laugh, but suddenly the idea didn't seem so funny.

"You're going to miss him, aren't you?" Nicole asked sympathetically. She remembered thinking about leaving Derek when they first met in Puerto Vallarta.

"Ahhhhhh," Kate let out a groan of frustration. "Damn it, of course I'm going to miss him. Is that what you want to hear?" Suddenly, she was practically yelling and she didn't know why.

Wow, Nicole thought to herself. Out loud, she said, "Settle down, I didn't mean anything. I know how you're feeling is all."

"I'm sorry, babe. I don't want to miss him. I need this to be my weekend thing. I need to go home and focus on becoming partner." Kate tried to be firm. "I don't want to be pining away for a sexy artist that lives twelve hundred miles away."

"You know we'd fly you down here whenever you wanted."

"Don't do that, Nic. You're trying to make this an instant marriage again. We're not you and Derek!" Kate protested.

"Dominic makes you happy," Nicole pointed out, "Happier than the Ethan I've heard about. I want you to be happy."

"Ethan has nothing to do with this. I know you're just trying to help. I love you, but stop!" Kate didn't mean to sound angry, but she has seen so many relationships that started out perfectly…yet ended with visiting her to get a divorce. Kate was sure that would not happen to Nicole and Derek, but it certainly made her very skeptical that lightning could strike twice. She felt something for Dominic. But that was just because they were in this beautiful place, having this magical time. Once life returned to normal…so would her emotions.

"Done." Nicole knew when to let up. She knew Kate was mad at the situation, not with her. If she kept going, then they ran the risk of things being said that could really hurt each other.

"You may not be on vacation, but I am. I don't care what time it is or how many I've had today. I want another drink." Kate tried to force a smile. Maybe another drink would lighten things again.

"When have you ever known me to turn down a drink?" Nicole joked.

"Good. Then let's go down to the lobby bar. I want a big, dirty martini." Kate swung her arm around her best friend, and they headed for the door.

…

Five hundred even was missing. *What the fuck?* Dominic thought to himself, as he sat at the desk in the little shop office. *Does someone want to get caught?*

His mind raced a million miles an hour, trying to think of every possibility. He hated this part of the job. What had he been thinking, buying this place? He loved to paint or, more accurately, he loved to create art. He didn't like the business side. When he had his first piece of artwork tattooed on him, something had resonated inside of him. As he had watched the ink become a part of his body, he looked around at everyone in the shop. All of their bodies each becoming living canvases. In that moment, he was hooked. He turned out to be a natural with a tattoo gun and, within a year, was known throughout the South Beach area, not only for his paintings, but also for his tattoos. When he had found this shop five years ago, it was becoming run down, and Tom, the owner, was ready to get out of the game. When Dominic offered to invest, Tom suggested he buy the shop outright. The old man still came by to visit now and again. Maybe Dominic should give him a call. Perhaps this type of anomaly had happened before?

Dominic did have a conversation with him about theft while he was learning the ropes. *Follow the money.* That's what Tom would say. Who had the chance to get five hundred cash from clients? The fact that most of their transactions were by credit card made it a bit easier to narrow down. As long as Jax wasn't in on it, he could figure this out rather quickly. He didn't think there was a chance anyone else had access to the money besides the manager, Jason. Who had alerted him to the problem in the first place.

Dominic's phone sprang to life, vibrating along the desk beside him. He looked down; it was his mother, yet again.

"Yes, Mother?" Dominic snapped into the phone.

"You're calling me 'Mother' already? What's wrong?" Carolyn questioned.

"Oh, nothing. Sorry, Mom." He tried to softened his voice. "How are you?"

"I'm well, Nicky. Thank you for asking. I'm wondering what you're doing tonight?" She sounded like she was plotting something, with that scheming tone of hers. Throughout the years, he and his brothers never understood how she didn't hear how obvious she sounded when she was conspiring. Plus, Dominic knew his mother never called just because she was wondering what he was doing. What was she up to?

"I have plans with my friend in town today." He waited for her response, ready for it to be catty.

"Oh, is she still here?" Carolyn feigned confusion.

"Mother, we only spoke this morning. Of course, she's still here." He was already back to calling her *Mother*.

"Well, darn. I was going to be in your area for a while tonight. I thought you could meet me out for a quick drink." She waited, as if he was going to suggest bringing Kate to meet her.

"I'll have to take a rain check. I need to be somewhere. I'll talk to you later. Bye, Mom." He hung up the phone before he could hear an objection. He was forty years old, wasn't he? He couldn't remember the last time his mother had hovered like this, and he wasn't sure what it was all about. But he didn't have time to worry about it. He needed to get out of the office and meet up with Kate and her friends.

"Why are you here on a Saturday night?" Jax asked, as Dominic walked by the counter.

"Signing some papers; nothing exciting," he answered casually, wondering why Jax would care. He didn't want to start over-analyzing his employees but maybe he'd need to in order to solve this problem.

"So how'd it go with the little hottie you left with yesterday?" Jax asked, pushing the boundaries of their friendship a bit, in Dominic's opinion. Though he knew he was being a bit sensitive, given the situation. Jax was a nice guy; he didn't mean any harm.

"Great, I'm off to meet her again. Thanks," Dominic smiled. He put on his sunglasses to signal that the line of questioning was over and headed out the door.

It was a quick walk to the Ocean Azul, where the two women were sitting at one of the outside tables. Kate had her signature martini in front of her. It was a little scary how quickly Dominic had begun to know such details about her. Her dress was a burnt orange color, an amazing contrast to her dark hair. It was low cut in the front, but flowed loose from the arms and waist. Good lord, she looked amazing. She somehow pulled off the perfect combination of sophisticated and sexy, her dresses walking right up to the line of too revealing without ever crossing it.

He slid into the seat next to Kate and kissed her cheek hello. Her eyes lit up as she said hello and went in for a kiss on his lips. Just that quick taste of him excited her beyond belief.

"Derek should be here any minute, and then we can go," Nicole said by way of greeting.

"Where are we off to tonight, ladies?" Dominic asked with a smile.

"To one of the new rooftop bars. I forget the name," Nicole admitted.

"I bet I know which one you're referring to," Dominic replied. "Need me to get us a table?" he asked, trying not to sound cocky.

"Thanks, but Derek said he's got it under control," she assured him.

"I would bet he's got us the best view in the place," Dominic added, and Kate laughed, knowing it was probably true.

They chatted while they waited for Derek. It wasn't long after Dominic arrived when he glanced up, and his face went blank.

"Fuck," he looked over at Kate, "I'm sorry in advance."

"Sorry?" she questioned and followed his eyes to the two women walking towards them. One was older, but looked like a million dollars or rather that she paid a million dollars to look that way, at least. The other was younger, maybe late twenties, in a teeny-tiny hot pink dress and blond hair that was clearly not her natural color. She was tan and pretty, but very made up. What would Dominic be sorry about? Kate went to ask, but then the older one spoke and...ahhh, there it was.

"Nicky, dear. Fancy running into you here." Carolyn Price smiled and looked from her son to Kate and then Nicole. She gave each woman the head-to-toe once over.

"Hello, Mom...Amanda," Dominic replied coldly, looking only at his mother. He couldn't believe she had the nerve to show up when she knew he was with Kate. And with Amanda of all people.

"That's right, you did say you were entertaining someone while she was here on vacation." Carolyn tried to sound confused again. She looked at Amanda and then sent Kate a smile that could pass as genuine, if Kate didn't know better. Luckily, she did.

"Let me introduce you to my friends," Dominic interjected. "This is Kate, and this is Nicole." Both Kate and Nicole said a friendly hello to both women. "Ladies, this is my mother, Carolyn, and a family friend, Amanda."

"Oh Dominic, you won't call me Mandy anymore? And aren't we past family friends?" Amanda enquired, trying to sound flirtatious. Dominic only rolled his eyes.

Kate couldn't help herself. "Oh, you mean like brother and sister?" she said, in her best obviously-fake sweet voice. "How nice." She ran her hands through the back of Dominic's hair and stared straight into Amanda's eyes, waiting for her reply. She wasn't usually rude, but this woman was on a whole new level of bitch.

God, I love that woman… Dominic thought and then…*wait…love? Oh shit!*

His own reaction to Kate's action threw him a bit, but he still couldn't stifle the laugh that came out of his mouth. Nicole smirked at the entire situation, not really giving a shit about how the whole thing went down. She was enjoying the show and she knew that Kate could handle herself.

Carolyn lifted an eyebrow at Kate, not sure how to take this. Was she appalled or impressed at Kate's willingness to get down and dirty with the stranger in front of her? She wanted to lean towards appalled, but she wasn't sure that she was.

"That's not what I was implying…" Amanda stated rudely, but she knew the only ally she had at the moment was Carolyn. And right now, she couldn't read Carolyn's reaction to Kate's remark at her snide comment.

"I'm pretty sure she knows that," Dominic snapped at her and took ahold of Kate's hand. "Always a pleasure. Mother, we'll talk soon."

Mercifully, Carolyn took the not-so-subtle hint. She smiled at her son and chivied an annoyed Amanda down the street. Dominic could tell that his mother wasn't looking forward to that talk.

"Uh oh, Mom's in trouble," Nicole joked, as the two women walked away.

For a split-second, Kate was glad to be leaving the next day. She had seen her fair share of family drama with divorce, and she knew the issues families could cause in relationships. She was glad that, as of tomorrow, she wouldn't have to worry about any of it. "Your mother seems to have an agenda," she said, trying to make it sound like a joke.

"You have no idea." Dominic said, deadly serious.

CHAPTER EIGHT

Gael arrived just as the two couples were finishing dinner. Dominic stood when the other three did, each of them giving Gael a hug. There was an initial twinge when he saw how exited Kate was to see this mystery man.

It only took Derek seconds to formally introduce the two men. "Dominic, this is my business partner, Gael. I've known him almost half of my life." He put a hand on Gael's back. "He may also be *almost* as smart as your girl over here."

"*May be*?" Kate joked.

"I think it's a certainty," Gael retorted.

"Nice to meet you." Dominic shook his hand and said his name to clarify that he had it right. "It's Gael?"

"Guy-el," Gael repeated the name slowly, emphasizing his Hispanic accent.

Kate took ahold of Dominic's hand as she sat back down and told Gael to pull up a chair.

"Derek likes to pit us against each other. But really, he's harmless." Kate made a funny face at Gael, like a little sister to her brother, which made Dominic feel better. The connection between the two did seem more like siblings than lovers.

"That's only because you've never had to go up against me in negotiations, little girl," Gael said as he leaned in.

"Oh, shut up, you two," Nicole interrupted playfully, rolling her eyes. Dominic got the feeling this was normal interaction between them. "Now, how was Todos Santos?" Nicole asked. "Is the resort beautiful?"

The resort at Todos Santos, Mexico was Gael's first solo project to finally come to fruition. Derek had wanted to let him have his moment to experience the grand opening before they went for a visit.

"You will love it, Mrs. Stone. When will you be visiting?" Ever since Derek and Nicole's rather shotgun wedding a year ago, Gael had been so thrilled that his friend had found the perfect woman to marry that he liked to celebrate it by using her formal name.

"Wanna go there next, Love?" Derek asked Nicole.

"Gas up the jet, baby," she replied excitedly, getting a laugh from the whole table.

"Are you working with port authorities at all this trip?" Derek asked Gael. Derek privately wondered if the Price family had had any interactions with Gael in the past. It surprised him that it hadn't occurred to him before.

That piqued Dominic's interest. "You work with the port authorities as well?"

"*Sí, amigo,*" Gael told him. "From time to time, I am a liaison between the port and Mexican authorities. I worked to unite the *Policía Federal* and the private security companies in Mexico in the past. I have helped them throughout the years on a contract basis. With my time in the States, I began helping the port authorities as well. We're working to slow the importation of drugs as much as possible. They are always finding a way in," he explained.

"He's quite the jack of all trades," Kate added.

"We should exchange information; I'm sure my family would love to discuss some things with you," Dominic told him.

"I'm not sure you were aware. This is Dominic *Price*," Derek stressed the last name, knowing full well that Gael be aware of the family.

"Ahhh, yes, let's talk more in the future." Gael replied simply, before turning the conversation to another topic. This kind of talk should not be done in public.

...

After dinner, the Stones stayed out with Gael while Kate and Dominic opted for a night in. As they walked back to her hotel room, it felt oddly comfortable, like they were a long-term couple. They wandered silently down Ocean Drive, hand in hand. Kate reflected on the evening. The dinner was fabulous. Half of the time, Derek and Dominic chatted together as if they were the connection between the two couples, instead of Kate and Nicole. After Gael's arrival, the three of them talked and joked, laughing like old friends. Kate and Nicole smiled to each other over their drinks as they watched the males bonding in front of them.

Then there were moments when Kate had caught Dominic looking at her as if he was trying to figure everything out. What was she going to do if he wanted to make some kind of long-distance relationship out of this? She wasn't ready to get into any of that. She was crazy about him and loving every second they had together, but she was determined to keep this what it was: a weekend fling. These feelings were just confusing her. She was leaving tomorrow, damn it.

"Now that we're alone, please don't tell me my mom and Amanda are going to scare you off," Dominic said hesitantly.

"Not that it ultimately matters, but who is Amanda exactly? And why did your mother want to make sure I met her?" Kate asked, glad they were still walking. She didn't want to look him in the eye while they discussed this. In the grand scheme of things, a meddlesome mother and bitchy girl weren't really important, but they were definitely an annoyance.

"Our families are in business together. Combined, they would have a large majority ownership in the Port of Miami." He glanced down at Kate, but she was looking straight ahead, listening. "As I mentioned before, my mother is shrewd. She has tried to get either me or one of my brothers together with the Martin's only daughter for a long time. Justin and Adrian are both married now, but she hasn't let up on me yet. Honestly, you're a threat to her plans."

"Well, lovely. Good thing for her that I'm leaving tomorrow. What kind of threat is that?" Kate joked half-heartedly.

"I don't want to think about that right now," Dominic told her. "I want to take you upstairs and ravish your body and then talk till the sun rises."

With that statement, she couldn't help but glance up at him. There was that deadly smirk again. How was he always able to break down her walls just as she was remembering to put them back up? He laughed as she picked up the pace. When they reached the lobby of the hotel, she stopped and ordered a dirty martini for herself and a nice scotch on the rocks for Dominic.

"Let's make my last night here interesting," she teased.

Back in her room, Kate felt like they were all too comfortable together. The way they moved around each other, the way their bodies neatly fit together on the oversized chair. She leaned her body into the crook of his shoulder, holding her martini glass while they talked. Why were they learning everything about each other? She was asking as many questions as he was. It wasn't smart. Yet she couldn't help herself.

As the martini began to work its magic on her senses, Kate slowly began to play with the buttons on his shirt. It was a tattered plaid thing and, with each button she undid, she began to reveal more and more of the artwork on his chest. Dominic watched her examine the streaks and swirls, the colors splayed over his defined muscles. She traced a red circle over his left side and onto his shoulder. His body was already irresistible, even without the splashes of color everywhere. She pushed the shirt further off of him, exposing the entire design. She glanced up at him with sinful eyes and began to slowly kiss every part of the tattoo.

"I love your work," she said to him quietly, between kisses. "I love that I get to kiss it on your body."

Dominic lifted her chin up so that they were face to face. "*You* are the work of art," he said to her, his voice velvet. He took her mouth in his, savoring every part of it. He grabbed her hair and pulled her head back so he could kiss along her neck. He loved the way it made her moan. She pushed the shirt further back until he could free his arms. Wearing only a pair of beat-up jeans, he stood and scooped her up into his arms. Keeping his lips on her, he carried her to the bed and set her down. He lifted the orange dress over her head and there she was, with gorgeous matching lingerie that could have been straight from France. He ran his hands across the delicate lace of the bra. She was the true masterpiece in the room.

Kate smiled up at him while she unhooked her bra and tossed it aside. Dominic's desire came to life. He pushed her down on the bed and climbed over her. He looked into her eyes as he slowly removed her panties. Kate helped him push his jeans off. She wrapped her legs around his back, pulled him in close, and, once again, she was his.

Each time they were together was more intense than the time before. Dominic never truly understood the connection that was supposed to happen between two people during sex. He loved to fuck, from the time he was old enough get a girl, but...this. This was indescribable. What he was feeling was so tangible, he could paint it.

As Dominic's excitement grew, he pulled Kate up from the bed and led her over to the exterior wall. There was a small ledge below the windows, the perfect height for her to lean forward and support herself. He kissed the side of her face and her neck as his body pressed flush against hers. She could feel how hard he still was. He lifted her arms up and around the back of his head. She grabbed his hair while his hands explored every part of her body. Dominic pulled her hips into him and leaned her forward so that she could see the city below her as he took her body over the edge. Legs like jelly, she turned around to face him. Kate took his mouth in hers, walking him back towards the bed. After pushing him down, she climbed on top of him. Dominic rolled their bodies together, and again, he was in charge.

Even Kate's wildest dreams about Ethan had never been this good. Nothing from her past had ever been like this, either. How could this bad boy on top of her be filled with so much passion? When Dominic looked at her, she couldn't pull her gaze away. With each thrust, he would kiss her sweetly, never taking his eyes off hers. She could have sworn that at one point, he whispered in her ear not to leave tomorrow.

What the hell was she going to do?

They were back in the chair again, naked and sprawled over each other. Sitcom reruns played on the TV in the background while they talked more. Dominic was serious; he didn't want to lose any of their last night together by sleeping.

"Can I drive you to the airport?" he asked out of nowhere.

"No one ever wants to drive people to the airport," Kate laughed.

"I want to soak up every moment with you. So I do want to drive you."

"I'm sure Nicole and Derek will survive not seeing me off at the plane. Thank you," Kate said sweetly.

"Will you let me see you again?" he asked cautiously, not sure how to handle this part of the conversation. His feelings for Kate were intense and had come on immediately. He could tell she felt something for him, too, but she was holding back for some reason. He didn't want to push her, to risk scaring her off. Dominic was prepared to take what he could get over losing her completely.

"Who else would I let give me my next tattoo?" she smiled.

"Ahhh, addicted already, are you?" he said as he kissed her nose.

"I could see how they can become that way. If I find another perfect option, I'd get one on the inside of my wrist. I do still have to think of work. I love the back of the neck, but it's not realistic for me."

"Let's see how yours is doing. We've been a little rough on it."

She leaned forward while he inspected the tattoo on her skin. Most of the dried ink had flaked away from their bedroom sessions. He had made sure she was putting ointment on it to help with the healing. "It's looking great," he said and kissed it lightly.

"Will you ever get any tattoos that aren't your art?" she asked.

"I'm considering getting *KATE* tattooed right across my ass," he laughed.

"Oh, that'll look fabulous!" she laughed with him. But inside, Kate was scared of how much she could hurt the amazing man in front of her. It wasn't his fault that she was such a cynic. That personality trait was just one of the perks of her job. Knowing she was her own worst enemy when it came to love, Kate begged herself to trust in both of their feelings.

"Honestly, as long as it's meaningful, yes, I would," he said thoughtfully.

Kate yawned and closed her eyes while she leaned her head against his chest again.

"Let's sleep for just a little while…." she said, drifted off without waiting for a reply.

CHAPTER NINE

Standing outside the Ocean Azul, Kate hugged and kissed her friends.

"Todos Santos next month?" Kate guessed.

"Definitely!" Nicole replied. "Want me to make sure there is room for two of you?"

A tear began to form in the corner of Kate's eye. "Stop it!" she protested, "I don't know what I'm capable of with Dominic. I'm scared Nicole. This guy could damage me beyond repair. I see so much heartbreak at work. Maybe I should have stuck with art history. Who knows, maybe we would have met that way," she smiled sadly. *Why couldn't she let herself give this a shot?*

Nicole answered with another hug.

Luckily, Dominic was putting Kate's bag in the car when Nicole made the comment. Kate still hadn't given him her phone number, and she wasn't planning on it. She needed to be in control of what happened next with them. If anything even did.

Dominic walked up and shook Derek's hand and gave a friendly hug to Nicole. "I hope to see you two around," he said, though his tone was sad.

"Let's have a drink later. Come by the hotel." Nicole smiled at him. It would seem weird to be with him without Kate there. But she was hoping it would keep a connection going between him and Kate. She knew Kate could be her own worst enemy with this sort of thing. If there was any way Nicole could help Kate see that Dominic was perfect for her, she was going to try it.

"Sounds like a plan," he said, before putting his arm around Kate, leading her to the car, and holding the door open for her.

They drove in silence for the first few minutes. Kate's mind was in a haze. Was she doing the right thing? How could someone she just met screw with her mind so much? She needed some time and distance to think.

Dominic couldn't make himself form any words, his brain holding his tongue hostage. He wanted to tell her to stay. He wanted to turn the car around and beg her, but he knew both of those things were impossible. Finally, he found a way to start the conversation without sounding like a crazed psychopath.

"I know we just met, but it will be weird here without you." He picked up her hand and brought it to his mouth. He held it there for a long quiet kiss while he soaked up the smell of her skin. "I wish you could stay longer."

Kate took a deep breath and held it in. This was exactly what she didn't want to think about. "I have a huge client meeting tomorrow." She paused to figure out how to continue. "I know it sounds like an excuse, and a bad one at that, but I chose this weekend to travel because I wanted to be well rested, to be fresh for tomorrow. I wasn't expecting this to happen. I wasn't expecting you." She gave him a half-smile, internally panicking that she didn't have the answers for how to make their situation work.

"Am I a bad thing?" Dominic probed, not sure if he was insulted or not.

"Nicky, no…" Her heart grew heavy. "This weekend was amazing. I meant that I need to go back to Chicago and work tomorrow, without you in my head." She knew this was coming out wrong, but she couldn't find the right thing to say.

Why did she have to call him Nicky? He hadn't let go of her hand yet, so he squeezed it tighter. "Well, I hope I find my way back into your head again at some point."

They drove again in silence. This wasn't how she wanted their last moments together to be. Why did she have to meet him right now? Why couldn't he have just been a sexy guy that didn't amount to anything? She tried to lighten the mood as best she could.

"This is an impressive car," she said, looking around at the luxurious details of the interior.

"Well, you know me. I was trying to impress you to get into your pants," he glanced sidelong at her, giving her his smirk.

"I do know you. And I know that you choose things that are not obvious and well-known. I guarantee there are plenty of women that have no know idea what a Saleen even is."

"You are good," he said.

"I told you, I'm good at my job," she smiled. "A cheating spouse can't just say, 'we each keep our own cars', when one is worth a single-family home in Chicago."

In what seemed like a flash, they were at the airport. Dominic got out and walked to Kate's side, helping her from the car. When the door closed, he pushed her up against the side, leaning his body into hers. He was wearing the same heavy leather belt as the day they met, and all she wanted to do was rip it open so she could take his tattered shorts off him. *How can a belt be sexy?* she thought to herself. Kate couldn't care less about the employees milling around the small executive airport. She wasn't sure if this was goodbye for good, so she wanted to savor it, savor him. Dominic was breathing heavily while he leaned over and nuzzled his head into her neck. Even in his vulnerable state, he still had that tough, bad boy look to him. She half expected to feel a gun tucked in that belt as she rubbed her hands along his back.

She wanted to be brave and whisper that she loved him. Tell him that they would work this whole thing out. What was holding her back? She held back tears and relished the feeling of being in his arms. If they were meant to be, time and distance would tell her. Then maybe she wouldn't be so scared.

Dominic finally pulled his head up and looked into her eyes. He held her face in his hands and kissed her. It was slow and gentle at first. Barely separating her lips with his tongue. Then without warning, he reached his hands back into her hair and pulled her head back while the kiss grew deeper. Dominic was trying to memorize everything about her kiss. The way she felt, the way she smelled and tasted. The memory of her in his tattoo shop, looking over her shoulder, flashed into his mind, and he growled with excitement. He leaned back and picked her up off her feet, planting kisses all over her face and neck. He was frantic, the passion growing even higher than it had been the night before. Kate wrapped her legs around his waist while they continued with their goodbye.

Her mind wanted to explode right along with her body. How could she have found this wonderful man and yet get on a plane without him? Was she crazy to risk losing him? Her heart and brain needed to get on the same team. Though she wanted to pull him onto the plane and join the mile-high club with him on the way back to

Chicago, she fought every urge in her body and ended the kiss.

"I have to go. The plane is waiting," she said through heavy breaths and his continued kisses.

"I can't put you down." He sounded so helpless.

"Nicky, babe. I have to go. I promise I don't want to, but I need to," she said as sweetly-yet-sternly as she could.

Dominic slowly lowered Kate to her feet, took her hand in one of his and her bag in the other. They walked toward the plane's staircase. She grabbed his cheek and quickly kissed him on the lips. "Thank you for the ride. I will talk to you soon."

"I don't have your number." Dominic said, not believing he hadn't realized it until just now.

"I will call you." She hoped he wouldn't fight her on this one. "I need this to go at my pace."

With that, she turned and walked up the stairs and onto the plane. Dominic watched as the employees pulled away the rolling staircase and closed the door to the jet. He stayed in that exact spot, frozen like a statue, until he saw the plane take off into the sky. He watched it until it was swallowed up by the clouds. He may have stayed like that even longer. He wasn't sure.

The flight attendant brought her a dirty martini with a spear of olives. (Nicole always thought of everything.) With a barely audible thank you, Kate accepted the drink and downed it before handing it back to the woman.

"He was gorgeous," the flight attendant smiled and winked.

"Yes, he was," Kate replied, reflecting back on her weekend.

...

Dominic hadn't been back to his condo at South Point Park since he met Kate. Now, he needed to go somewhere that didn't have memories of her. He went directly to his building, eyes straight ahead as he went down Ocean Drive, avoiding the memories of her everywhere. He made it up to his condo, threw his keys, phone, and wallet on kitchen counter as he walked by, and fell back onto the huge grey couch.

The place was rather minimalistic- dark wood floors with a large white area rug, coffee table, and deep chairs across from the couch. There was a dining table behind the couch, one he never used. Beyond that was a plain white wall. He had never created the right painting for that space, so it sat vacant, waiting. He looked out the floor-to-ceiling windows that lined both exterior walls. No painting he could hang would ever compare to the views those windows provided.

There was a large bedroom for himself. The other was his studio. Should he paint? Should he draw from his state of emotion right now? He wasn't sure what would end up on the canvas if he did. He closed his eyes and hung his arm over his head. He only wanted Kate.

He tried to sleep. It never came.

…

Kate was back in her own apartment in the River North area of Chicago. She needed to be home, even though, half a dozen times, she stopped herself from telling the pilot to turn around and go back. She reminded herself that this client meeting could be huge for her career.

Being home was going to help. Her place was small, but it was hers. She walked into her tiny living room, which had a small breakfast nook off to the side. The kitchen was made to hold only one person inside, so it was a good thing she was small. She walked past the bathroom and dropped her bag and purse on her bed. Grabbing her computer from the nightstand, she curled up into the pillows. Work always helped her escape. She hoped it would this time, too.

She opened her computer, and her email immediately popped up. She had about a dozen to read through, but the name *Ethan Wallace* practically jumped off the screen. There was nothing in the subject line, so she opened it with her heart beginning to pound. She wasn't sure if she wanted it to read "I've been a fool, marry me now" or "get over it, we'll never happen". Just leaving Dominic made her feelings for Ethan all the more confusing.

The thing took an eternity to open, but she finally read:

Hey Kate,

Everyone from the office is going out to the bar Monday night to celebrate my big win in the Thompson case. Wanted to let you know since you had Friday off work. Good luck at your meeting Monday morning.

Best,

Ethan

It always annoyed her a little bit that he used "best" as the salutation in an email between friends. It seemed extra formal after the weekend with her bad boy. That thought made her smile.

Kate was able to stay focused on work for the rest of the evening. But she made herself shut the computer down at a reasonable hour so that she could have a good night's sleep. Most of that was spent dreaming about Dominic in her bed.

The fantasies throughout the night were almost as good as the real thing. Kate woke up feeling exhilarated. She formulated a new plan over her morning cup of coffee on the balcony. She was going to attempt to remember her time with Dominic as what she went looking for: a wonderful weekend. Though she wasn't fully convinced it would work, she knew she had to try.

She was going to focus on work and her life in Chicago. She was prepared for her meeting and ready to take on the day, in a fitted olive green dress and jacket that went great with her dark hair and slightly tanned skin from her trip.

Kate walked into her office feeling like she was walking on air, smiling ear-to-ear. *Maybe I really did need to just get laid?* she thought to herself and laughed. She stopped by the kitchen and poured herself her second cup for the day. She turned around and almost spilled her coffee when she practically walked right into Ethan.

"How was the trip?" Ethan asked.

"Mmmmm," she said, rolling her eyes in the back of her head. "It was amazing."

"I've never been to South Beach. Maybe I'll have to go sometime."

Kate thought he was trying to act a little too casual, making her laugh inwardly. She loved the place for a far different reason than he would. She didn't think Dominic was quite his type. Then again, she really wasn't sure what Ethan's type was. In the moment, she didn't care. She wanted to focus on herself for a little while.

"You're coming out after work, right?" he asked, sounding genuinely hopeful.

Really? Now you care if I'm around? Kate decided not to overthink it. "Oh sure, I'll stop by."

...

The day flew by. Kate landed the case she had been working on. The high-profile Chicago couple's divorce would make a great addition to her resume. Thankfully, she felt like she could win this for the husband. She could usually tell rather early on how much the judge would side in her favor, and when she could push the envelope on how they requested the assets to be divided.

After work, she walked across La Salle Street with Anne, another woman from the office. They made their way through the crowded bar to the back room that Ethan reserved for the group. She ordered a martini from the bartender. Most of the office had become acquainted with the bartenders there, since it was common for them all to stop by for a drink after work.

"Thanks, Blake," Kate said, smiling.

"Anytime, babe. You look gorgeous tonight," the bartender flirted back to her.

"Well, aren't you sweet," she said before turning back to her friend.

"You do seem like you're on cloud nine. You're kind of glowing," Anne told her with a laugh.

"The weekend away was just what I needed." Kate closed her eyes, remembering Dominic on top of her. Was she going to be able to pull this off? Keeping him as a memory? Kate wasn't sure, but she had to try to stay focused on the present.

"I think Ethan can tell," Anne smiled, clearly thinking this would make Kate ecstatic. A few of Kate's female coworkers knew of her feelings for Ethan. "He's watching you."

"Why is it that when you truly stop worrying about it, they notice?" Kate shook her head at her own question.

"Did you meet someone?" Anne pressed.

"Just a weekend thing, nothing serious," Kate lied a bit. "But he sure got Ethan off my mind."

"Good for you. I need one of those," Anne joked.

Kate almost spit out of drink. "You're married!"

"Yep," was all Anne said, and gave a laugh. Kate couldn't tell if she was just joking.

When Kate looked up, Ethan was walking towards her. She cocked her head to the side, examining him. He really was handsome: tall and slim with light brown hair, styled over to the side front, with just a hint of product keeping it in place. He had a clean-shaven face. She had always liked that before, but now she was hoping he'd get lazy and let some scruff grow in. He was wearing blue pants and a blue sport coat with a tan shirt underneath. He had unbuttoned the top button, most likely at the bar. All in all, he looked very put together. She tried to remind herself that this was what she had always been attracted to.

She smiled up at him as he approached her. He set his drink down on the bar behind her and left them in a position where his arm was almost around her. She eyed him, wondering what the sudden change in his behavior could be.

"Thanks for coming to help me celebrate." Ethan was leaning in a bit close, but then again, it was loud in the bar.

"Of course. I landed the Preston couple today as well," she said, lifting her glass.

"That's good for the firm, too. Great job," he told her. His tone seemed almost flirtatious. "Will you let me take you out to dinner after this to celebrate your accomplishment today?" He tried looking deeply into her eyes, but it didn't have the same effect as when Dominic did it.

Kate wasn't going to let herself do that. She wasn't going to compare them.

She thought for a moment. If it was Friday morning, she would have jumped at the chance to get Ethan one-on-one. She would have suggested they have dinner in her apartment. Not now... now she needed a little bit of time away from Ethan as well. She didn't want to lose her chance completely, but she figured she could postpone it a day or two to get some breathing room.

"Oh, tonight? I'm sorry, but I can't," she faked disappointment. "Could we try tomorrow?"

"Sure, I look forward to it," he smiled. "I'll get us reservations at The Station down the street for after work."

"Perfect." *Seriously... why now?*

"I'm not sure why we haven't done this before," he remarked casually.

Are you fucking kidding me?? Kate luckily said this to herself rather than out loud. "I'm not sure either," she said to him, almost laughing.

The whole thing was absolutely ridiculous. It brought to her mind the scene from the old movie *French Kiss*. The one where the heroine's ex-fiancé wants her back. The heroine, Kate (wow, they even shared a name!), asks why he couldn't be the one that turned on the "Kate-light". The real Kate wanted to ask Ethan that same question: "Why couldn't you be the one? The one who turned on this big shiny Kate-light that burns so bright?"

Kate knew she was being ridiculous. The world was funny like that. Nothing ever seemed to be easy. Why would she think this would be?

CHAPTER TEN

Sleep barely came. Dominic wasn't ready to paint yet either. That was a first for him. Painting had always been his escape. But he was scared to bring his feelings to life on canvas right now.

It was 10am. He had a client scheduled (one of his regulars) to finish up an Aztec design that would ultimately cover the man's entire back. He set aside four hours to get it done. These longer appointments were the only time that he went into the shop so early. The shop didn't usually open until noon. Most people don't want their skin attacked by a needle first thing in the morning.

Dominic walked through the front door and saw that the light was on in the office at the back of the shop. He didn't think much of it, figuring Jason left it on after closing up. As he walked further through the main floor, he heard the wheels of a chair move and the file cabinet door opening. He stopped in his tracks. *Why is Jason here so early?* He picked up his pace.

Dominic quietly walked in to see Jax sitting at the desk, looking through some paperwork. *Not Jax, I really liked him...*

"What can I help you with, man?" Dominic said, trying to sound casual.

Jax's neck stiffened, and he straightened his back. There was a noticeable pause before he turned the chair around to face Dominic. Most likely trying to come up with a story. "You're here early," he replied, clearly not sure what else to say.

"You shouldn't be here at all," Dominic said as he walked up and grabbed the papers that were so interesting to Jax. It was the information sheets from all the clients from the day before. Dominic knew that he must have been looking for one to slip through the cracks. Sad thing was that there were such easy ways to pull this off, and no one would be the wiser. Jax apparently wasn't that smart.

"Listen... I was..." Jax was trying to come up with something to say.

Dominic wasn't about to hear him out. "You need to get the fuck out of here," he said rather calmly.

"This won't stop, Dom. If it's not me, it'll be someone else." Jax's eyes looked crazed. "I can give you the money back, but it won't help. It won't stop anything."

He wasn't making any sense. Won't help with what? Won't stop what? "I don't give a fuck about the money. And YOU were the one stealing from me, not the others!" His voice rose to practically a yell. He took a breath and continued. "Wherever you got that key, you might as well throw it away. It won't work in about an hour. NOW LEAVE."

Jax must have realized there was no more to say. He just dropped his head and walked out. Dominic watched him walk through the main room and out the front door. He attempted to slam the door shut, but the hydraulics in the hinges slowed it just as it reached the frame, and it closed quietly behind him. Dominic couldn't help himself. He let out a small laugh, even though the situation wasn't funny. He had discovered who was stealing, but now he was down a counter person at the front.

He immediately pulled out the stack of applications he had filed away from random people showing up, hoping for a job. Maybe there was an artist that wanted some extra hours or something. He looked first for someone that wasn't an artist. He didn't have the need for one and didn't want to promise something for the future. He found one with bubbly handwriting. He half expected to see full circles as the dots on the i's. She listed her desired position as "Counter Girl." Most likely she was one of those girls that just liked to fuck tattoo artists or guys covered in ink. He'd come across it before. Someone must have thought she was cute enough to keep her application, just in case.

Desperate times call for desperate measures. He dialed her number, and a voice that matched the handwriting answered. He glanced down at the application. Of course, her name was Tiffany.

"Tiffany, this is Dominic Price from South Beach Tattoo. Are you still interested in the counter position?"

"Oh my God, absolutely!" She was obnoxiously happy. "When do you need me to start?"

"Today. Just caught my counter guy stealing from me. You won't be trying that, right?" He gave a very serious tone to the question.

"Never! What time should I be there? Do I just wear something cute?"

"We open at noon, so whenever you can get here would be great. I'll be with a client until about 2pm, so hopefully it'll be slow when you get here. Grab anyone free if you have a question. We'll go through everything once I'm done. Oh, and yes," he didn't want to come across like an asshole, so he tried lightening up a bit, "wear whatever you like, as long as it won't distract my artists."

She giggled in response. "See you at noon." She hung up the phone, still giggling.

Time to regroup. Nate, the client, would be here any minute. Dominic pulled out a stack of information sheets, since Tiffany wouldn't know where to get them herself. He'd have the artists all run their own cards and collect their own cash for the day, before he could sit down and walk Tiffany through everything. He went to his corner station and got everything set up to be sterilized for his morning session. He was relieved to see Nate walk in. He needed to disappear in his work for a while.

…

When Nate left, Dominic felt revived. Creating art really did help. He still wasn't sure if he'd go home and have a go at a canvas yet. But the Aztec design had come out well, and Nate was thrilled to have it completed. Dominic glanced up at the counter. Luckily, it had been slow. A few artists had stopped by his station to ask what happened to Jax, but he wasn't going to tell anyone except Jason about the events of that morning.

It was a unanimous decision among the artists that Tiffany was much easier on the eyes than Jax. Even Slone, the woman that did the body piercing, was looking at her like she hoped Tiffany swung both ways. *Fresh meat*, Dominic rolled his eyes as he thought to himself. At least Tiffany seemed to be able to keep her young girl craziness in check. She was talking with a possible customer, acting very professional. He had flown through her application so quickly that he didn't even check her date of birth.

As Dominic watched her, he guessed that she was maybe in her mid-twenties? She sounded so young on the phone. At an average height, maybe 5'6", with long, wavy hair, she wasn't exactly a natural beauty, but in her little dress with her makeup done, she could turn a few heads. She was a brunette, of course, which, after Kate, was a new favorite for him. *Oh, Kate!*

Just as that thought went through his mind, Tiffany looked over at him with a smile. He didn't date his employees, so that smile better not mean what it looked like. Plus, his heart was still aching for Kate. Tiffany had sent the client over to one of his artists and was standing there alone. This was as good a time as any to show her the ropes.

…

Kate sat on her bed, staring at her phone. She had Dominic's card in her hands, but she just couldn't pull the trigger. Instead, she called Nicole.

"I can't call him, and I don't know why," she stated as soon as Nicole picked up the phone.

"Hey, babe, what are you scared of?" Nicole asked, concern in her voice.

"I don't know that either. And, to add to my confusion, guess who asked me to have dinner tonight?"

Back in South Beach, Nicole's blood pressure rose. She realized that she had never met Ethan, so she shouldn't have formed an opinion of him, but she had, and it wasn't good. She had heard too many stories of Kate's longing and of him showing no interest. "Ethan? Seriously?" was all she could say.

"Yep…"

"Why did you say yes?" Nicole didn't want to sound like a bitch, *but really??*

Kate almost started crying, something she almost never did. "I don't know, because he's here and Dominic isn't. Maybe because I'm not willing to risk the heartbreak that could happen with Dominic. Maybe Ethan will help erase my feelings for Dominic!" Her voice rose.

"Why are you fighting this with Dominic so much? You're crazy about each other! He didn't show up for drinks the other night. Derek got ahold of him yesterday, and he said he slept the whole day. Couldn't get out of bed..." Nicole's voice trailed at the end. She didn't want to make Kate feel bad.

"Oh God!" Kate sighed. "I was at a bar with Ethan hitting on me, and he was home sleeping? Depressed? Heartbroken?"

"Probably a little bit of both, to be honest," Nicole said, matter-of-fact.

"I don't know if some of this is the long-distance thing," Kate admitted. "If he lived in Chicago, of course I'd give this a try."

"Why does the distance scare you?" Nicole questioned. "Are you worried he'll cheat on you?"

"Maybe. Do you know how many couples I see where one is divorcing the other for infidelity, and the guilty parties always regret their actions, never meaning to hurt anyone?"

"Are you worried you'd cheat?" Nicole couldn't believe Kate would, but maybe that could explain her conflict.

"God, no, I could never cause the kind of pain I see every day at work."

Kate's reaction made Nicole breathe a sigh of relief. She'd love Kate regardless, but being a happily married woman herself, it would be nice to have a best friend that was the faithful type. "There are no guarantees in life, but I'd be willing to bet that Dominic wouldn't do that to you." Nicole tried to soften her voice.

"I think I need a little bit of time to let my heart believe that," Kate replied.

"To add to your misery, guess what I saw in a magazine today?" Nicole's voice lightened.

"What?" Kate sighed.

"Justin Bieber has the *Girl with Balloon* tattoo on his arm!" Nicole could barely finish the sentence before cracking up.

"What? Are you fucking kidding me? I have the same tattoo as Bieber?! He isn't even into art!" Kate practically yelled to her friend. This could be the information that pushed her over the edge, though it was, ultimately, meaningless to her life.

"You and the Beebs been hanging out lately? He told you he's not into art?" Nicole teased.

"You know what I mean." Kate went from wanting to cry to laughing. "I needed that, Nic, thanks."

"That's what I'm here for."

They finished their conversation, but Kate still couldn't call him. She didn't want to send a text message, either. She knew how impersonally that would come across. Time and distance, she reminded herself.

Dinner should be interesting. But the thought of Dominic sleeping all day was not what she wanted in her mind when she was out with Ethan. She wasn't sure what she wanted to be thinking about, but Dominic wasn't it. Just as she was trying to push the man out of her thoughts, she caught a glimpse of her tattoo in the bathroom mirror. Would she ever be able to truly forget him, with this permanent reminder? Why couldn't her weekend fling have been truly that? Casual sex and no emotions? These pesky feelings were causing her all kinds of problems. She finally had a chance with a guy she'd had a huge school-girl crush on for years. This was finally her chance to get Ethan to see her as more than just a "work friend". And yet...

Kate showered and chose a perfect first-date dress: black, with a flared skirt and halter top. The straps came out from the same point in the middle, almost crossing in the front. She kept her makeup light and simple, not wanting to overdo it, but accentuated her dark eyes and styled her short hair so that it curved around her chin a bit more than usual. She had asked Ethan to meet her at the restaurant, wanting to come home after work to wash the day off of her and regroup for dinner. When the preparations were complete, she stared at herself in the mirror, not sure if she was doing the right thing. Turning to the side, she could see the girl reaching for her balloon. That's how she saw her today- reaching for something, not releasing something. She wondered what that meant. Maybe she wasn't ready to let go of Dominic just yet.

CHAPTER ELEVEN

The date with Ethan was perfect in every way, technically. He looked extremely handsome in his sport coat. But she couldn't help wanting him to have a big leather belt and to give her a look like he wanted to spank her bare ass with it. But the conversation flowed great, and he was a complete gentleman. So what was the problem? Oh, yeah, *he's not Dominic*.

She was determined to give this time, though. Maybe he'd slowly leave her every waking thought and dreams at night. She wanted to see if Ethan could be everything she'd pined for over the past few years. Kate knew she'd need to take it slowly with Ethan, too. It wouldn't be fair to either of them if Dominic still occupied her heart.

…

Still feeling energized from the tattoo session, Dominic walked in the door with a little extra swing in his step. He tossed his keys onto the breakfast bar and walked into the living room. Out of the corner of his eye, he saw the white wall behind his dining room table. Without a second thought, he started moving chairs and pushing the table out of the way. He stood there, only a few feet from the wall, looking at it. His breathing picked up as his chest began to heave. This felt like the first time he had ever painted. The wall was calling to him, and he knew what he needed to do. He put on some loud music to drown out his thoughts. Then, he grabbed paints and brushes from his studio, dropping everything on the floor in front of the wall. He stepped back again for one final look. And then he dove in.

The next thing Dominic knew, he was lying on the couch, barely able to catch his breath. His phone was still blaring music. He couldn't remember painting anything. He looked up at the wall and saw Kate looking back at him. He had somehow painted her so that she was looking perfectly into his eyes from where his head usually laid on the couch. How did he manage that? Searing, dark eyes were looking straight into his soul. Almost black and white from the dark shades that he chose, she was turned to the side looking at him over her shoulder. It was an exact replica of her in his tattoo shop, the first time they met. Strands of almost-black hair fell in front of her face, and her button nose was perfect. Her large mouth was almost pursed into a smirk. He had definitely found what that wall had been waiting for. Her face.

. . .

"Honey, you need to go see him," Carolyn urged Amanda. "Before Tiffany gets her claws in him."

"I can't believe this. What are the chances that Tiffany Simmons got a job at his shop? She'll land him for sure; no one ever refuses her." Amanda was not ready to give up without a fight. "She did say he looked rather depressed, even though she's never met him before."

"This is your chance. If he's upset about the brunette being gone, he'll want someone to turn to." Carolyn tried to point out the obvious.

"So I should try the friend route?" Amanda questioned.

"Well, it's better than nothing." The older woman looked at her watch. "He'll be done working now. Go by his place, and tell me what happens. You know what is at stake. I'm counting on you."

"I know, Carolyn. I want us to be family, too. Wish me luck," she said in a cheery voice and hung up the phone.

She had better pull this off. Carolyn thought to herself and pursed her thin lips. She wasn't going to let Tiffany land Dominic. Her family was trash, and she just wasn't going to allow that to happen.

Carolyn sat in her luxurious living room, considering her options to help the situation. She knew herself well enough to know that she couldn't just sit there, waiting. Maybe she needed to find some dirt on this girl in case he couldn't get over her. How could she find out who she was? She could go snooping around the hotel where she stayed. Maybe she could pay off an employee to find out something for her. Taking a liking to the idea, she called to have her car and driver downstairs immediately.

A loud knock at the door woke Dominic from a (finally) sound sleep. Painting Kate must have settled his soul enough to allow him to nod off. It took everything in him to force his body up and off the couch. His arms were still covered in paint, but it had dried by now, scattering flakes all over the couch.

He opened the door to see Amanda looking back at him. *She has some nerve*, he thought to himself. He wanted to slam the door shut, but he didn't want to be an asshole.

"What do you want?" he asked, expression blank.

"Tiffany Simmons called me and told me you hired her today," she paused for effect. "She said you seemed sad and thought I could cheer you up." She paraphrased the last part. Well, okay, she lied.

"That may be why she seemed familiar," he said. "You two are friends?"

"Well, back in the day, we partied together. But she remembered you and I were always somewhat of a couple."

That's a stretch.

"Well, I'm fine. Thanks for stopping by." He started to close the door, but Amanda held up her hand, looking down at his arms.

"You've been painting. Oh, please, let me see what you're working on." She was smiling, but her true nature always seemed to show through. Amanda never gave a shit about his paintings. She never understood them, or even wanted to try.

She walked past him into the living room and stopped dead in her tracks. "Well, it certainly looks like her," was all she could think to say. All of a sudden, Tiffany was no longer her worry. This stupid bitch that was supposed to be a weekend fling was now her major concern. "Did she have to sit long for the portrait?" Amanda tried to sound aloof.

"I just painted it, actually." Dominic ran his hand through his hair and his heart stopped again as he looked at Kate's face on his wall. It felt very odd to see her with Amanda in his apartment. What the hell was Amanda doing here?

"You did this from memory?" she said, her tone more confirming than questioning. This was even worse than she thought.

"Apparently. I don't really remember painting it." This time he rubbed his eyes, hoping to see if he was in the middle of some horrible dream, and he'd wake to find Kate curled up in his arms. No such luck. "Really, Amanda, I'm fine. You should leave."

"Can't I still be your friend?" Amanda walked over and put her hand on his shoulder.

Maybe if he fucked her right now, it would erase some of the memory of Kate. Maybe he could use Amanda to help him get over her. It's not like she wouldn't know what he was doing. She would be a willing participant in it. The small problem was that he wasn't an asshole. Even though he really didn't care about Amanda's feelings, and no matter how much he wanted to get over Kate, he wasn't willing to sleep with Amanda to do it.

He walked silently toward the door and opened it. "This is not a good time. Thanks for checking on me." Again, his face was blank. Amanda couldn't believe he was so distraught that he wouldn't take advantage of her being in his apartment. How easily they could have hopped into bed and fucked all night long. As much as she wanted to storm out on him, she heard Carolyn's twisted voice in her head, telling her to be nice. It was weird, imagining his mother pushing for her to sleep with her son. Amanda stopped in front of him by the door, leaned in and kissed his cheek lightly. "You know where you can find me. Let me know if there's any way I can help," she smiled, before leaving.

...

It had been three weeks since she left. Dominic tried not to count the days, but it was hard not to. In that time, nothing had helped. He filled his days with painting and his evenings taking on more clients at the shop. His plan had been to stay busy, but it wasn't working.

He couldn't believe that Kate had really moved on. Why didn't she ever contact him? His curiosity was getting the better of him. One day, he finally headed to the Ocean Azul. He knew that Derek and Nicole would be leaving soon, and he wanted to see if they'd heard from Kate. He didn't care if he came across like a love-sick idiot, it was his only option. He had warned Derek this would happen.

"Wanna grab a drink?" Tiffany asked in a flirtatious tone, as he walked by the front counter. "I'm leaving, too."

Here was another opportunity standing in front of him. A beautiful woman that could take his mind off of Kate. He could take her back to his crash pad and spend a few hours trying to make Kate disappear. For about two seconds, he considered it. Really considered it. With his luck, he would do that and then find out from Nicole that Kate was in love with him. He'd feel awful. He needed to find out what Nicole knew first.

"I'm sorry, doll, I have plans." Dominic didn't offer to reschedule. He didn't want her thinking this was an option...not yet. Maybe he'd take her up on it if Kate really was over him. He walked out the door without waiting for Tiffany's reply.

Dominic sent Derek a text on the way and, luckily, they were at one of the tables outside. Nicole practically jumped out of her chair and hugged him when he arrived. Derek shook his hand firmly. Dominic sat, not knowing exactly what to say. Nicole must have known, though, because she started first. And she wasn't going to beat about the bush.

"Have you heard from her?"

"No... Have you talked to her?" Dominic wasn't sure if he was hoping for a yes or no.

"Of course. She misses you. I know that. She's her own worst enemy. I don't know why she's fighting her feelings." Nicole shook her head. "Maybe it's the long-distance thing."

"That can always be worked out," Derek added. "Look at us," he said to his wife.

"She doesn't think she could be this lucky, too," Nicole replied sadly. Of course, Kate could be. She already was, and she was fighting it for some stupid reason.

Dominic looked over at Derek. "Is your plane here?" he asked hesitantly. The question came as a surprise to him; he hadn't truly considered going to Chicago until just then.

"It can be in a few hours," Derek told him, with a smile on his face. He knew that sooner or later, Dominic would go fight to get her back. They were alike in so many ways.

"I don't want to take the Price plane. My mother would catch wind of it, and I don't need her knowing where Kate lives." He felt like a twelve-year-old defying his mother's house rules. "I don't trust her; she's crazy when she sets her mind to something."

Nicole was bouncing in her seat. *Finally!* she thought to herself.

Derek noticed her excitement, "Not a word, Love," he said sternly. "My boy needs the element of surprise on his side."

"Oh, boo!" she smirked at him. "I understand, I won't say anything."

"How fast can you be packed and at the airport?"

"I'll be there when the plane is," Dominic answered, doing the math in his head. With the time change between Florida and Chicago, he could be at her place at maybe

9pm. That was far better than showing up uninvited at 2am. "Make sure to text me her address," he added.

It was the longest plane ride of Dominic's life. He was about to show up on her doorstep...what if she turned him away? Not wanting to think like that, he tried to focus on the right words. Going there with a script wasn't an option; he lived his life more off the cuff. That's how this needed to be handled as well. He'd go there and bare his soul to Kate and hope that she'd be willing to try to make this work.

His heart was leaping out of his chest as he got out of the cab and stared up at her building, a modern combination of slate and marble, twelve storeys tall. She lived in what looked like a fun area of Chicago. The cab driver said it was called River North. He noticed that they had gone over the Chicago River only minutes before the cab came to a stop.

He saw a woman manning the desk in the lobby. This was going to be interesting. How was he going to get upstairs past her? He could try paying her off? Maybe just explain the situation, appeal to her sensitive side? He figured he'd try both and then move onto begging and pleading if needed. He wanted to surprise Kate at her door.

It wasn't that hard to get he woman to agree. She seemed hesitant at first, but when he offered up his watch as collateral to prove that he wasn't a stalker there to kill Kate (and after a quick internet search to confirm its value), she had allowed him in. *It's the moment of truth*, he thought to himself on the way up in the elevator.

CHAPTER TWELVE

Kate wasn't sure she should have invited Ethan to her place for dinner. She didn't like the message it probably sent, which was: *expect sex*. The past few weeks had gone relatively well or, rather, as well as she could expect. At this point, there was a small part of her that wished she hadn't met Dominic. Kate hated admitting that to herself, but she knew she was holding back with Ethan because of him. She had allowed him to kiss her once, but that was all she was prepared for right now. It had been nice, but nothing like what she felt with Dominic. That same level of intimacy and connection just wasn't there. She had to remind herself that she might not find that immediate passion again with someone, that often it took time to grow. Comparing the two men wasn't fair for anyone.

But one thing was for sure. Whoever said that time heals all things was full of shit.

She made them both a martini to calm her nerves. Ethan looked rather confident, probably because he thought he was finally going to get laid. So why wasn't she? This was such an odd situation. She had spent the last two years dying for this chance, and now she was dreading the whole concept. Why did she feel like she was cheating on Dominic? She shook her head quickly back and forth, trying get him out of her head, at least for the night.

"It smells wonderful." Ethan was trying making conversation; he could tell she was uneasy. Kate had invited him over, so he figured she was comfortable enough to take this to the next step. She had always been incredibly comfortable around him as friends. He wasn't sure why she now seemed slightly on edge all the time. He had begun to wonder if she was only platonically interested in him, but dinner at her place was a solid sign towards the romantic.

"Thanks. I hope you like it." Kate was making a large wok full of stir fry veggies. She knew that he would have preferred chicken or steak in it, but she wasn't going to cook it for him. He'd have to get that when they ate out. She figured it was a good sign that her mind was still including him in the future.

He walked over and kissed her softly on the lips, testing the waters. She tried to return the kiss, but her heart just wasn't in it. She smiled at him and turned her attention back to the wok.

As she was trying to find something to say, there was a knock at the door.

"Shall I get it?" Ethan asked. He answered the door before she gave him permission.

Dominic stood there, staring at a strange man. He glanced at the apartment number to make sure he was at the right door. Just as he confirmed it, Kate came into his view. Kate had a man over. His heart dropped and his blood pressure shot through the roof at the realization. All he wanted to do was rip this guy's head off and drag Kate back to Florida with him. *That's rational*, he thought sarcastically to himself. She looked more beautiful than ever before. He loved and hated her all at the same time. How could she be with another man? In her apartment? He could tell immediately that she had gotten her hair trimmed shorter since she had been back. He hated that he noticed something so small.

As soon as Kate saw him, she dropped her spoon, her hand coming up to cover her mouth. Ethan looked back and forth between the two, not sure what he was witnessing. Kate's eyes filled with tears. She walked right past Ethan and threw her arms around Dominic. She had started to cry, and she wasn't sure why. All she could do was whisper "sorry" in his ear over and over. He returned the hug, relieved to have her in his arms again, but he was still extremely hurt at the situation. He glanced over at Ethan with a questioning look.

"Oh my God… wow…." Kate was fumbling for words. Dominic was standing at her front door. In front of Ethan. She was exhilarated and terrified at the same time. Ethan didn't look very thrilled himself.

"Mandy, is it?" Dominic tried to joke dryly, motioning to the other man she was with. It was lost on Ethan, but Kate caught the reference to Amanda's nickname. She didn't blame him for it either. She'd hate to walk in and see Dominic with another woman, Mandy or otherwise.

"I know how this looks," she said to him, but knew she needed to explain to Ethan as well. After everything, Ethan didn't do anything wrong and didn't deserve to be hurt. She couldn't believe what a mess she had created.

"Ethan, this is the man I met when I was in South Beach. We spent the weekend together, and I've been trying to move on since I've been back," she sighed, looking between the two men, different in every way. With Ethan's clean appearance, he looked the part of an attorney. Dominic…her bad boy artist, with his sexy long locks along his forehead and overgrown scruff on his face. "If you had asked me out the day before I left, the three of us wouldn't be here today. I'm not trying to put this on you at all."

"It kind of seems like it," Ethan retorted.

"Didn't sound that way to me," Dominic stated defensively. Kate appreciated it. Even in their situation, he was still protecting her.

"It would have been nice to know there was another guy out there. That you were using me to get over him," Ethan shot at her.

"Ethan, I'm sorry you feel that way. I had a *HUGE* thing for you for *years*." She balled her fists. "Now, after meeting Dominic… He changed me somehow. I think you noticed it, too, because you didn't notice me before."

Ethan didn't have a reply for that. He hadn't asked her out before South Beach. He wasn't sure why. "I did notice you," he tried. "I never knew you have a thing for me, though."

"*Had* a huge thing," she clarified. "But now I need to see this through with Dominic. I wasn't using you to get over him. I was finding out if there was anything to you and my crush. I think it's too late; I can't seem to forget Dominic." She smiled sweetly at Dominic, whose heart melted. Turning back to Ethan, she said, "Ethan, let's talk over lunch tomorrow at work." She was trying to keep the situation from escalating out of control.

"You're going to have lunch with him?" Dominic questioned, like she was planning a murder or something.

Kate shot Dominic a glare and pointed at him. "You stay out of this!" She raised her voice. "I may love you, but you showed up at my door, so let me handle this, my way!"

"Love?" Both men questioned in unison.

"Oh, damn it! I don't know, maybe? But that doesn't change the fact that this is between Ethan and me and has nothing to do with you."

"Fair enough," Dominic said with his hands in the air, surrendering. It was just lunch; why was he freaking out?

"I'm sorry for the interruption," Dominic said to Ethan and held out his hand to shake. "But this thing between Kate and me isn't over yet."

Ethan reluctantly took his hand. "I'll see you at work tomorrow," he directed to Kate.

Whew! Kate thought. "Thank you. I'll see you tomorrow. And, again, I'm sorry."

"Whatever! I'm interested to hear what you have to say," Ethan said without looking for a reply. Then he walked out the door, slamming it behind him.

Kate walked Dominic over to the couch. She flopped down and put her head in her hands. "I can't believe you're here!" She looked up at him and smiled. "And I can't believe how happy I was to see you. I should never have thought time and distance could change what we have." She curled into the crook of his shoulder, and they sat there, silently enjoying being in each other's presence again.

This felt like all of the dreams Dominic had had in the past few weeks. Not lust, not sex, just being with her. He looked at the little black coffee table in front of them and saw two dirty martinis neatly placed on coasters. "You had martinis with him?" He wasn't sure why that hurt him so much. It was just a type of drink. They very well may have been sleeping together during the past few weeks. He didn't want his mind to go there, either.

"It's just a drink, Nicky. It's not like you showed up with us in bed together," Kate pointed out, but it had sounded much better in her head.

"Oh, that's not a visual I want!" He put his hand over his eyes, trying to block the image.

"We haven't done that!" she exclaimed, feeling bad that that's what he thought. She tried softening the mood. "I know I jumped into bed with you right away, but he's not nearly as tempting as you are."

"Funny," he quipped, still not sure how he felt.

"I was trying to find normal again. How could I know that one weekend would change my entire life?"

He found that that helped, knowing exactly what she meant. If he was honest with himself, he could admit that he considered fucking both Amanda and Tiffany to help erase Kate from his memory.

"Babe, is something burning?" Dominic asked.

"Oh God, dinner!" She hopped up, grabbed the spoon she had dropped, tossed it into the sink, and pulled the wok off the flame. When she lifted the lid, out came a billow of smoke with a scent that resembled a charred version of what would have tasted fabulous.

Dominic sauntered up behind her and peered over her shoulder into the wok. "That would have been good, too."

"That wasn't even made for you," she reminded him.

"Let me take you to dinner then," he said as he kissed her cheek.

She turned to face him, putting her arms around his neck and leaning into his chest. With her eyes closed, a thought entered her mind. "Nicole told you how to find me," she stated more than asked.

"Yes, and I swore her to secrecy. She knew I needed the element of surprise on my side."

"And my doorwoman – does she need to be fired?"

"Thank you for reminding me. She's holding my watch hostage until I show her that you're alive."

That made Kate laugh and not just a little. She practically doubled over in a belly laugh as she released all the tension of the evening. "We'll grab it on the way out," she told him, still laughing.

...

Well, the hotel knew nothing. Carolyn thought to herself. She couldn't believe that they didn't even have a listing for a Kate Whatever-her-last-name-was. No Kate at all. She gave a man at the front desk a hundred-dollar bill to see what he could find. He came up empty and kept the money.

She wasn't sure what her next move should be. She didn't want to talk about it with her husband; Sean would tell her to stay out of it. He was brilliant, but he didn't have her foresight. This union needed to happen with a marriage. The heads of the Price and the Martin families disagreed far too much to try and merge their companies peaceably. They were the equivalent of modern day school-girl frenemies. They would insist that one buy out the other and neither would back down. *Men are never any help.* Dominic wasn't taking her calls either. She was ready to go by the godforsaken tattoo shop pretty soon. She had already stopped by his condo, and his doorman hadn't seen him since the day before.

...

Kate and Dominic laid in her bed together, their legs intertwined. Dinner was wonderful, and christening each room in her apartment was even better. "I like your place," he said, breaking the silence. "It's cozy."

"Code word for 'little'," Kate joked.

"No. Well, yes, it is little. It's the feel of the place I was referring to, not the size," he clarified.

"Thank you. I've always liked it," she said, snuggling in closer.

"I could get used to it here, being in the same city as you again," he said with a sigh.

"It is nice. How long can you stay?"

"Tomorrow is Friday… Any chance you could take last minute vacation time at work?" he looked down at her with the sinful smirk that he knew always got to her.

Kate thought through her week. She wasn't expected in court at all. She had some things she needed to follow up on, but honestly, she could pass that on to her legal assistant. Kate tended to be a control freak at work and that wasn't fair to Michelle, who could use more experience. Or maybe that was just what Kate was telling herself to make her feel better about taking the time off. "Probably. Why?" she asked cautiously.

Dominic's heart practically leapt out of his chest. "Please come back to South Beach with me. Nicole and Derek are still there. I want more time with you."

She twisted her mouth around, contemplating whether she really could be gone that long. She hadn't taken a week off all year, though she missed a few Fridays here or there when she traveled to see Nicole. And her company did have the use-it-or-lose-it policy with vacation days.

"Oh, we have to surprise Nicole then. This could be fun! Tit for tat, right?" she laughed. "I have to go into the office tomorrow. You can hang out here or do some sightseeing, and then we'll head straight to the airport."

...

There wasn't much to talk about with Ethan. Lunch was rather awkward, but Kate was glad she faced him. She had always been prepared to be honest with him, which was why she didn't ever let things go too far, physically. She explained the unfortunate timing of everything. Since she knew now that he was interested in her, she didn't mind admitting how she felt the past few years. They ended the conversation on somewhat of a good note. Ethan apologized for not asking her out sooner, and she agreed to let him know if this thing with Dominic ever ended.

She said the words to be nice, but she wasn't sure if it would change how she felt. She still liked Ethan. She wouldn't have had a crush on him for the past few years if she didn't. It was just that Kate knew now that Ethan was not what she was looking for in a man. The bad boy sitting in her apartment was the one for her.

CHAPTER THIRTEEN

"You remember your lines, right?" Kate wanted payback, and she knew, ultimately, that Nicole loved surprises.

"I'm more of an improv guy," Dominic joked. "Don't worry, I'll have her convinced."

The plan was to have Nicole and Derek meet Dominic out front of their hotel for a drink and to hear the story of his trip to Chicago. Nicole had tried to call Kate a few times during the day, but Kate had dodged the calls, which, fortunately, wasn't suspicious. After all, it was still a weekday, and Kate could easily be in court or in a meeting.

"I can't believe how excited you are about this. You're kind of diabolical," Dominic smiled and kissed her hand while they travelled down Ocean Drive. Dominic had hired a limo so that Kate could hide in it for a few minutes while he did some acting.

As the car pulled up to the Ocean Azul, Kate could barely contain herself. She knew how much Nicole wanted Kate and Dominic to be happy together. She was jumping around in her seat trying to stay calm.

"Okay, crazy lady, get back there and hide," Dominic smiled at her, opening the door as soon as she was out of view.

It was time for the show. He did his best to put on a sad, defeated face and slowly walked up to the Stones' table.

Oh, no! Nicole thought to herself. She had expected a happy ending. "What happened?" she asked.

"Well, I saw her." Dominic paused for effect. "With another man…"

"What?!" Derek said, shocked.

"With Ethan?!" Nicole's voice went up several octaves.

Oh, what an opening to mess with her! Kate thought. *She walked right into it.*

"You knew about Ethan," Dominic was saying. "And you let me go there! She opened the door half-naked, fresh from his arms." He did his best to sound shocked.

Nicole's face was priceless. Her jaw literally dropped. She fumbled for the right words to say. "I knew she liked him before you, and I knew he asked her out right when she got back. I had NO IDEA it had gone that far! I promise I wouldn't have let you go if I knew."

Dominic was starting to feel bad. She looked so upset. She leaned her head into Derek's shoulder, and he rubbed her back and kissed her head. Dominic sent a glare in the general direction of the tinted limo window, hoping Kate would emerge. She wasn't budging, so he continued, "I'll be okay. It isn't your fault. Oh, I left something in the limo. Good thing he hasn't left yet."

Dominic walked out to the limo, stuck his head in the door, and whispered sternly, "Stop laughing and get out here!"

"SURPRISE!" Kate jumped out, smiling, and threw her hands in the air.

"You bitch!" Nicole raced over to her best friend and practically knocked her to the ground as she hugged her, laughing and crying while she kissed her cheek repeatedly. Then she looked up at Dominic, scowled, and hit his arm. "You had me going! If this painting thing doesn't work out, you should try acting," she joked.

Derek slowly walked over to them, laughing to himself. He knew how happy this had just made his wife.

"It was all Kate's idea." Dominic said, throwing his arm around Kate, incredibly relieved to have her back in South Beach, and for an entire week at that.

"Now sit and tell me what really happened," Nicole ordered.

"I did show up when Ethan was there, that wasn't a lie," Dominic confessed. "I may have just exaggerated how Kate was dressed." He looked over at her sitting next to him, glad the other scenario hadn't happened.

"What??" Nicole yelled. "Spit it out. I want to know everything."

...

Carolyn had caught wind that Dominic was no longer in hiding. Her sources also told her that he was most likely with the same girl from before. *Kate, is it?* Carolyn thought to herself.

When Justin married himself off to someone other than Amanda, Carolyn had taken it rather well. Amanda was a bit young at the time anyway. Plus, Justin still seemed head over heels about his wife, Carrie, to this day. When Adrian got married, Carolyn was annoyed. Adrian and Amanda would have been perfect for each other. Instead, Adrian had eloped in Vegas with Natalie and, if she was being honest with herself, Carolyn is a bit surprised that their marriage has lasted. She was pretty sure Natalie was knocked up at the time. They both swear it happened on their honeymoon, but no one bought the story. Adrian and Natalie just never seemed happy, and Amanda's personality always seemed much more suited for Adrian.

But now, Dominic was her only hope. Amanda was a lovely girl. A little promiscuous, she had to admit, but what man didn't like a woman that was fun in the sack?

Carolyn loved her husband, but really, that had come after the wedding. It wasn't an arranged marriage, per se, but both came from influential families in Miami. Their marriage made sense. This one did, too. Dominic needed to see that. It may be hard; he'd always been her black sheep. This was going to take some meddling, and Carolyn didn't mind doing it. Everyone said that no one turned down Tiffany Simmons. Maybe she could take advantage of that fact to get little Miss Kate out of Miami. Carolyn may need to pay a visit to Dominic's new counter girl...

…

Dominic and Kate took the limo back to his apartment. The fact that there was a huge painting of Kate's face on his living room wall hadn't occurred to him until they were almost there. It certainly reflected the dark place he had been in when she left, but he was hoping it would come across as adoring rather than stalker-ish. He wasn't exactly sure how to warn her about it, so he figured it was a day for surprises.

Kate loved the building. It wasn't the tallest around, but definitely grabbed her attention. It resembled a big block of glass, with glass balconies jetting out of it everywhere. It could have been a massive ice cube in the middle of the scorching heat. It looked extremely modern, and she couldn't wait to see inside.

Kate had expected it, but she was still taken back from the amazing views as soon as she walked in. She didn't realize that the corner of his living room was going to be windows, too. She walked straight up to it, feeling a little dizzy, looking down with windows practically surrounding her. She turned around, smiling and looking for Dominic, and saw the painting on the wall. She almost fell back into the window in shock. Her face took up the entire wall behind the table. It looked just like her, but somehow Dominic had been able to make her more beautiful than she considered herself to be. How did he manage that?

"Don't freak out," Dominic said cautiously, walking up and grabbing both of her hands in his.

She wasn't exactly freaked out. More a combination of a little freaked out and flattered at the same time. "I can't believe you did this from memory. We didn't take any pictures together."

"It was like the first time I painted, on my parents' wall. I didn't remember painting that, and I don't remember painting this."

"Sounds weird saying it, since it's me, but it's beautiful," Kate admitted.

"You are beautiful; this merely shows the truth." He walked around and stood close behind her, wrapping his arms around her little waist.

"You have an amazing place," she said, looking around and taking it all in. She glanced through the open door into his bedroom. She loved that even more. It had a huge canvas leaning up against the wall. Partially hidden behind his modern low black bed, it had to be at least ten feet wide and, with his signature look to the swirls of paint, she was sure he created it. The darker colors of the painting were emphasized by the dark slate of the sheets and the thin comforter on the bed. A very minimalistic bedside table and dresser completed the room, allowing the focus to remain on the art. It was simple, very clean, and incredibly masculine.

"I love it here," he told her. "And I'm going to love it more with you here. The real thing is much sexier than your two-dimensional twin over there." He leaned over and kissed her sweetly on the lips.

"Do you have any wine?" she asked, wandering toward his kitchen area.

"You drink things other than martinis and tequila shots?" he smirked at her.

Kate laughed. "Shocking, isn't it? The tequila is all Nicole. I do love my dirty martinis, but I don't discriminate."

"Red or white?" he asked as he walked around the breakfast bar and into the kitchen.

"You have both?" Kate was surprised.

"I like wine. It's not just here for the ladies," he winked at her.

"A red would be great."

Dominic opened one of his favorite bottles of Pinot Noir. He bought the stuff by the case so that he always had a bottle when the mood struck.

Kate recognized the label immediately. "Meiomi is one of my favorites."

"Me, too. It's a great wine for its price point. Why pay hundreds for a bottle when you can get this stuff for twenty-five bucks?" Dominic said as he pulled the cork from the bottle.

"Exactly."

Dominic handed Kate her glass and took her hand in his, walking them silently to the patio door. The patio was enormous, covering almost the entire length of his condo. There was a wet bar at the far end, with a white couch and coffee table in front of it. Living in Chicago, it would never occur to Kate to have such a comfortable setting on her balcony. And her balcony was tiny in comparison to this one. On the other side stood a large white table that was big enough to seat six comfortably. Dominic led them towards the couch. Kate sat and looked out over the water, sipping her wine.

"I can't believe you're here," Dominic said, shaking his head slightly, like he wasn't yet convinced it was real.

"I can't believe you came and found me." Kate lifted her legs and rested them in his lap. He instinctively started rubbing her leg slightly with his thumb. She recognized the feeling immediately. He had done that when they first met, as he tried to calm her during the tattoo session. Her life had changed incredibly in just under a month. She was starting to understand a little bit more how Nicole felt when she met Derek. Length of time didn't seem to matter when a connection was this strong. Her feelings for another man had never been this deep.

Neither of them had noticed it before, but there had been a sheet of tension over them the last time she was there. They had such a short time together--less than 48 hours--that they couldn't completely relax. Not that a week was much longer, but there was a level of comfort that wasn't there before, perhaps because they knew that they could try and make this work. They could each take a breath and fully enjoy their time together.

They talked about everything as they finished the bottle. It had been quite a day. They woke up in Kate's bed together in Chicago, and now they would be falling asleep together in Dominic's bed in South Beach. At one point, Dominic leaned his head back on the couch and closed his eyes, allowing himself to just be in the moment. Kate took the chance to study his face. Individually, his features weren't anything special, but put together, he was the sexiest man alive. Creases ran from his thick eyebrows around his eyes. The skin around his strong nose was tanned from life in Florida. She loved the few long strands of hair that he always let fall into his face. (She lightly brushed them back now.) He had a look like he lived a hard life. Not physically, but internally. His eyes may have seen a lot, or maybe he thought too much. There was something there, and she wanted to understand it completely. Maybe she loved him more than she realized.

CHAPTER FOURTEEN

Kate's first full day back in South Beach was spent in Dominic's condo. Other than the balcony, they didn't make it outside at all. They made breakfast together and ordered in lunch and dinner. (South Beach had by far the best take out Chinese food that Kate had ever had. Who would have guessed?)

It felt like they had so many years to catch up on. Dominic wanted her to know everything about him. Kate's life had been relatively normal, or as normal as any life can be. Dominic's experience had been far different. He explained about growing up as a Price. He always knew deep down that once he fell in love, and trusted a woman's love in return, that it would be with an outsider. He needed someone that loved him without knowing the dynasty he was from.

Kate asked questions about his family, not worried anymore with how they might come across. It seemed odd to remember a time when she was concerned he'd think that she wanted him for his fame or the fortune from his art. Now every question was about understanding him more deeply. The subject of his mother came up again and her wish for Dominic to marry Amanda Martin.

"She couldn't really want you to marry someone you don't love," Kate stated bluntly.

"She doesn't realize what she's asking," Dominic explained as he tried to understand it himself. "I think she honestly believes that we would be happy together."

"She must, because it seems extremely out of left field, considering the way you've talked about your family. It always sounded like you were all very supportive of each other."

"Yes, we are. But one thing I've always known about my mother is that you don't cross her," he said rather sadly.

"Is she involved in the business side of the port operations?" Kate questioned.

"She's not on the payroll or anything. My grandfather founded the company, and she is very protective of keeping what her father, husband, and sons have built through the years."

"She sounds a little scary," Kate admitted.

"I know I'm making her sound like some female Godfather or something. It isn't like that. She likes the lifestyle benefits of what we have, and I think she wants to make sure that never ends."

"Well, I simply cannot wait to see her again. She'll just love me," Kate rolled her eyes to show her sarcasm.

"Don't worry, I won't force a meet-and-greet on you. I won't be surprised if we run into my brothers, though. Especially Adrian, he's always out on Ocean Drive somewhere."

"As long as they don't want you marrying Amanda, too, I think that'll be fine," Kate smiled as he poured her more wine.

...

They ventured out the next day, making their way towards the Ocean Azul to meet Nicole and Derek. As they walked past South Beach Tattoo, Tiffany came running out.

"Dominic... Dominic!" Tiffany yelled, waving her arm. She ran towards them with the tiny steps her high heels required, her fake boobs bouncing under her tight shirt.

"Hi, Tiffany," Dominic said when she reached them. "Kate, this is the new counter girl. Tiffany, this is my girlfriend Kate."

Kate didn't miss the slight questioning tone he had given to the word "girlfriend". She smiled at the term, though, and shook Tiffany's hand. It also didn't escape her notice how gorgeous this girl was. Far better looking than the guy that worked there when she and Nicole went in for their tattoos.

"Dominic, could I have a quick word with you?" Tiffany smiled, throwing Kate an "I'm sorry".

"I'll run into the corner store and grab a water," Kate said casually.

Dominic kissed her cheek. "Okay, babe. I'll be right there." Kate began to walk away, and he turned back to his employee. "Now, what's up, Tiffany?"

"I'm not really sure how to say this, but thought I should..." She stalled for a minute, looking rather antsy in her towering shoes.

"What's going on?" Dominic began to get concerned. After Jax, he was a little on edge.

She took a breath. "Your mother came by the other day."

Oh Lord! Dominic said to himself.

"She offered me a thousand dollars to hit on you and try to get you into bed." Tiffany whispered the words, looking around to make sure no innocent bystanders overheard them.

"WHAT?!" Dominic was unable to stop himself. *Will she stop at nothing?*

"Yes, she said that she'd make it worth my while if I could help get your girlfriend to go back to where she came from." Tiffany waited for his reaction. He stood there, stone faced. "I told her that I'd see what I could do," she went on. "I thought it would be worse to turn down the offer. I didn't know what her next idea would be. This way, I could let you know so you could handle it."

"I really appreciate it." Dominic was fuming, but trying not to let it show.

"Of course. Would you like me to tell her anything if she contacts me again?" Tiffany asked.

"Actually, tell her that you and I slept together. Let her pay you," Dominic said. "Thank you for letting me know."

"You're welcome, and I will. Since I'm telling you about your mother..." Tiffany hesitated again, "but...she did say that she thought your girlfriend was a gold digger and only after you for your money."

"Lovely," Dominic said sarcastically. "Kate had no idea who I was, initially, but thank you again for telling me."

"You're welcome. She's is a lucky girl," Tiffany said as she waved goodbye.

Dominic ignored the last statement. Tiffany was being nice by telling him about his mother. But he wanted to keep things as simple as possible with the girl. Her previous mild flirtations hadn't gone unnoticed.

But what the hell was he going to do about his mother? She had crossed a line this time. Was he going to tell Kate? He had about twenty-seven seconds before he was inside the store, and she'd be right in front of him. It only took about three seconds to realize he wouldn't lie.

He didn't want to start things off with secrets. And this involved Kate, too.

Dominic's mind was racing, and he wasn't paying attention at all to where he was going. He almost crashed right into Kate as he walked through the entrance of the corner store.

"Is everything okay?" she asked as they steadied each other.

"Yes...no. You could have stayed there for that conversation." Dominic sounded rather confused.

"What are you talking about?" Kate asked. "What did she say?"

"Apparently, Carolyn Price has taken things to a whole new level..." Now he was the one that was stalling. "She offered Tiffany a thousand dollars to help break us up. You know, try to get me into bed."

Kate burst out laughing, surprising them both. "Just to clarify… you are forty, right?" She kept laughing. Maybe it was easier than crying. With that realization, she did have a scary thought. In the grand scheme of things, Carolyn Price was more of an annoyance. She didn't matter to Kate. That is, unless Carolyn succeeded at her mission. Kate really was falling for Dominic; she wasn't very thrilled about the mother of the man she loved trying to break them up. Loved? *There's that word again!*

"Yes, I'm forty. I'm not going to let my mother ruin this for us." He put his arm around her.

"I know, but I'm also not going to break up a family." She leaned her head into his shoulder.

"I won't let that happen either," he said lovingly.

"It's always something exciting with us, huh?" she joked.

"Well, when we decide to leave the house, my mother does seem to follow. Let's go hang out with some normal people," he offered.

That made Kate laugh again. Nicole and Derek's life may be far from normal, but their relationship appeared to be as perfect as a marriage could get. Then again, neither of them had any other family. Maybe that was the secret to a successful marriage: no pesky in-laws.

...

During their short walk to the hotel, Kate and Dominic agreed to keep the topic of meddlesome mothers to themselves. This was a day for fun and relaxation. Neither wanted to rehash the story with their friends.

Kate, Dominic, and the Stones went to see the lighthouse at Key Biscayne. Dominic had occasionally spent some time with tourists, but had never wanted to do much siteseeing with them. He grew up in the area; why would he want to visit a tourist site? Although Key Biscayne was rather close to South Beach as the crow flies, the islands weren't connected by any bridges. Getting there required going back to Miami and turning back around before heading back out. It wasn't that it was far, it just hadn't been worth it to him until now.

The day was fabulous. Dominic got the four of them day passes at a wonderful resort in the area. They had a leisurely lunch by the pool, lounging under the cover of a large grass hut-style cover that blocked them from the direct sun.

Dominic considered Nicole and Derek to be friends now, and they felt the same way. In fact, he had been quite the topic of discussion between Derek and Nicole for the past few weeks. Nicole was concerned that, if it had gone badly between Kate and Dominic, the Stones would have had to keep Dominic at a distance. Derek, in particular, had found a connection with Dominic and didn't like the idea of losing that. Traveling around distant properties for fifteen years didn't lend to making new friends very easily. Though he was close with some of the men from his former life as a Mixed Martial Arts fighter, Gael was really the only person in his business life who had become a true friend. And now he had Dominic as well.

. . .

As the day drew to a close, the group headed back to South Beach. Dominic's work was displayed in multiple hotel lobbies throughout the town, which gave him access to some exclusive private rooftop pools and bars. He took them to one of his favorites, a cozy place with a laid-back nautical vibe. Party lights were strung up rather haphazardly, illuminating the rounded furniture that fit into the nooks of the rooftop space.

Dominic loved South Beach on Sunday nights. Everything was much more relaxed, as residents prepared to go back to work on Monday. Sitting up on a small couch on that roof, with Kate leaned into the crook of his shoulder, nursing her dirty martini, he could finally agree with the people who called South Beach, "America's Sexiest City".

Kate was wearing a simple white dress with a rounded neckline and a thin, brown braided belt. Dominic had noticed that the humidity would start to take its toll on her hair the longer the evening went on. Little black hairs were beginning to break free of her smoothed tresses, and the ends were beginning to curl under her chin. He thought it was the cutest thing, an imperfection that made her perfect. The bridge of her nose was a deep pink from spending the day in the sun. Her eyes looked like her mind might very well be a million miles away. He wondered what she was thinking about. Was it him, or was she working through a case for when she went back to work next week? *Ugh, next week.* He hated thinking about that. He liked that he didn't have a nine-to-five job that would require his continual presence. He could paint anywhere, or even take a hiatus. And Jason was a great manager at South Beach Tattoo; he'd be able to leave him in charge for a week or so at a time. He wished Kate had something similar, but he knew she couldn't be pushed into anything.

Kate, meanwhile, was worried about what would become of Dominic and her in the future. Could she handle a long-distance relationship? She had never been the jealous type, so that aspect didn't worry her so much. She was more concerned about how drastically such a relationship might change her life. Nicole's life had changed radically. Probably for the better, but still...lots of change. Was Kate ready for that? What if this worked out, and Dominic wanted her to move here to be with him? Would she? She had lived close to her family her entire life; she hadn't even gone far for college, since the University of Chicago had ended up being the best school for her.

Kate didn't want to say anything about it now. She was getting ahead of herself, anyway. She wanted to enjoy this week together and then see if any of these concerns were even valid. She shook it off as best she could and then realized that Dominic was watching her.

"I didn't get enough of you yesterday." He looked down at her with that deadly smirk. "Can I take you home?"

Oh, that smirk... What was it about that smile of his? Kate would always want him, but after he gave her that look, she was never quite sure they'd make it back to the privacy of his place in time.

"We should leave before I pull you on top of me right here and now." She leaned her body up and kissed him deeply.

"We had better get out of here then." He stood and took her hand.

"Don't you have to pay?" Kate questioned.

"It's fine, I have a running tab here."

"But what about her tip? I waitressed all through college, we have to take care of her." Kate was surprised that Dominic might stiff the waitress.

"Oh babe, I'd never do that. I have it set up so that they get 30% from what we get tonight added as a tip. And, at these prices, she'll do just fine," Dominic told her as he continued to help her up from the couch.

"South Beach is very proud of their alcohol," she agreed. "The prices are outrageous. And I thought Chicago was expensive." If it were possible, Kate fell a little bit harder for Dominic, knowing he took care of the staff when he was out. She loved that he was so generous.

Apparently when you drive a Saleen, it gets parked right by the hotel's front door. Maybe it was because he was Dominic Price? The valet was even able to get a cabbie to pull his car out of the way when they arrived. Kate remembered thinking the little valet in his white suit looked like Moses parting the Red Sea, creating a free space for Dominic to pull in. She admitted to herself that she liked that people watched them as they left and were led to his car. Well, they watched Dominic. If the women did look at her, it was with an envious stare. *You're jealous of me now? If only you knew what we're about to do next,* she said to herself, as she thought about ravishing her delicious bad boy.

CHAPTER FIFTEEN

Luckily, the elevator was empty. Kate didn't think she'd be able to stop herself even if it hadn't been. There was something so delectably dangerous about Dominic Price. It was how he looked at her sometimes. Like he wanted to take her body to a place it had never been before. She certainly wasn't in fear for her heart just then.

They walked from the car to the elevator with perfect composure. As soon as the doors closed, he turned to her with a growl under his breath and grabbed at the back of her thighs. He picked her up and pushed her against the wall of the elevator as she wrapped her legs around him and held on for dear life. Kate knew that, ultimately, he liked it a little rough, and that hunger brought something out in her. She grabbed ahold of his hair and pulled it back hard, exposing his neck. She took in his masculine scent as she tasted him. His growl became louder, and he searched for her mouth.

When the door opened, Dominic kept ahold of her as he walked down to the end of the hall. Somehow he found his keys and got the right one into the locks without taking his lips off hers. He kicked the door open and closed it behind them with another kick from his heavy boot. Kate loved how forceful he could be. He chose to skip the couch and carried her directly to the bedroom. When the bed was in sight, he tossed her halfway across the room, where she landed safely on a pile of pillows. She laughed as he pulled his shirt over his head. She would never get sick of seeing the shock of color on his sculpted chest. She crawled towards him and tugged at his leather belt, the one she dreamt about while she was away from him in Chicago.

Kate wanted him inside of her. Now. She practically clawed at him to pull him on top of her, marveling at the view of his perfect abs and chest as he climbed over her body. Dominic had the most amazing laugh when he was turned on. It was throaty and wicked, and she loved that she was lucky enough to hear it. It sounded nothing like his laugh during the day. This one was reserved solely for the bedroom.

Afterwards, as Kate laid draped over Dominic, she couldn't imagine what it was going to be like without him next week. This feeling was exactly what she had feared. Kate needed to have a serious heart-to-heart with herself. Should she be protecting herself from something that might not happen? Could she really enjoy life completely if she was always scared she'd turn into one of her divorce clients? She knew, intellectually, that she shouldn't be so guarded, but she wasn't sure she could let go of her worries.

As her mind turned, Kate absent-mindedly traced the swirls of paint along Dominic's chest. He loved it when she did that. The rest of the world could disappear with her touch, and somehow, it made him feel completely at peace. He knew he was in love with Kate. He was pretty sure he had been since the moment he saw her. Who even believed in "love at first sight"? Lust, maybe, but not love. But he knew, this time, that it was love. This was the woman he wanted, his mother be damned. They were going to have to figure this out, to find a way to be together. But he wasn't ready to say anything yet. He knew Kate was fighting her own feelings, and the last thing he wanted to do was add to her stress. He had waited forty years for her. He could wait a bit longer.

...

The next day, Kate sat across the table from Nicole, amazed at where they were, in comparison to just over a year ago. They would probably still be doing the exact same thing this time last year, just in Chicago. Now, they were looking out over the magnificent view of South Beach, eating at a restaurant that was directly across from a beach entrance. Kate could see the white sands, with gorgeous bodies laid out on colorful beach towels like an enormous patchwork quilt. The water glimmered in bands of every shade of turquoise.

The women were sharing the most enormous pile of nachos that either of them had ever seen. The tortilla chips were covered with fabulously seasoned black beans and melted chihuahua cheese. Kate couldn't figure out how the piles of tomatoes, onions, and peppers weren't toppling over. The guacamole they ordered to go with it was made at the table side and was some of the best she'd ever had. Everything was perfect. They opted for peach iced-tea with their lunch. (Kate had begun to slow her pace on the day drinking, since she'd be there for the week.)

"I love our version of the 'South Beach Diet'," Kate joked.

"I can't believe how...mmm...strong we are..." Nicole's sentence trailed off as she piled food into her mouth, making Kate laugh.

"What was Gael's pitch to Derek?" Kate asked.

Nicole chuckled at the question. "Derek wasn't sold on the idea initially, until he did some research, that is."

"Well, that tells me nothing," Kate laughed and pushed again. "So, where is it?"

"Colorado," Nicole stated bluntly.

"Colorado?" Kate questioned. Colorado was great, but it was far from the beach resorts where Derek grew his company. Then again, the spa-style place he had created in Chicago was amazing.

"That was my reaction as well," Nicole admitted. "But it's this remote little town called Ouray."

"I've never heard of it." Kate's curiosity was piqued.

"Look it up!" Nicole replied. "It's known as the 'Switzerland of America', and it's adorable! There are no large resorts nearby, and Gael wants to help keep it that way. But he does want to get a rather large chunk of land for the opportunity to expand, if it starts to grow in that direction."

"Is Derek on board then?" Kate asked.

"He is. We're going to take a trip there soon, just to check it out. But he trusts Gael's judgment on this," Nicole told her. "Apparently, Gael likes the mountains. Who knew?" she added with a laugh.

Later, as the two friends walked along Ocean Drive, Kate couldn't help looking out of the corners of her eyes for Carolyn Price or even Amanda. It made her a little uneasy to imagine running into them without Dominic with her. She didn't need his protection necessarily, but it felt like she was on their turf. What if they confronted her? Carolyn saw no problem asking her son's employee to sleep with him. Who knew what Dominic's mom was capable of? It was all just too weird for Kate.

As if Nicole knew what she was thinking, she smirked and asked, "What are you going to do about this possible mother-in-law of yours?"

"That's not funny!" Kate said with an eye roll. "What kind of mother tries to get a woman to sleep with her son, no matter what the reason?"

"It's weird, I'll give you that."

"Exactly. It's just plain weird." Kate went on, "I was just thinking, what if we see her today while we're out?"

"Good question," Nicole smiled. She loved this part of conflict- the unknown, where anything could happen. "Do we try the kill-her-with-kindness approach? Or should we confront her? Or run the other way?"

Nicole was enjoying this a little too much. Kate shook her head, not sure what her natural instinct would be. "I don't want to cause any family problems for them."

"You're being too nice, Kate. The woman crossed that line already," Nicole pointed out, as they wandered into a little boutique shop. "What does Dominic say about it?"

"He doesn't really say anything," Kate paused to think. "I can tell that he's irate with her. But I think now it's more that he's completely shocked that she would do this to him."

"She probably just sees you as a piece of ass that's visiting," Nicole joked.

"Nice, Nic!" Kate shot back. Then she started thinking out loud. "But if that were the case, why wouldn't she just wait for me to leave? Why would she pay to have someone come between us? I know he hasn't told her about his feelings for me, so I'm not sure what her motive is."

"Ooohhh," Nicole said, her voice climbing to a high-pitched tone. "And what are lover boy's feelings?"

"Good lord, can you be an adult for a minute?" Kate laughed as she put her arm around Nicole.

"On occasion," she smiled back.

"The things he says scare me actually," Kate admitted, "But it also scares me because I feel the same way about him, too."

Nicole started to jump up and down in the middle of the store. "Will you finally let me give you advice about this? Doesn't it sound a little familiar? Oh, maybe like something I went through last year?"

Nic's right, Kate thought to herself. At first, she had been so concerned about falling for this man, who could very well be completely wrong for her and disrupt her life. Especially if he broke her heart. She wasn't ready to compare herself and Dominic to Nicole and Derek. But maybe it was time to at least get a little bit of advice.

"I give. Whatcha got for me?" Kate sighed.

"Okay, here's what I learned about myself last year." Suddenly, Nicole sounded like a middle school teacher, and Kate wanted to puke. But she loved her and knew she was trying to help, so she kept her mouth shut and listened. "I ran for miles and miles trying to think about my life and what I wanted," Nicole was saying. "I tried to decide how much I was willing to risk and how much of my heart I was going to trust. Other than the family drama, my situation was like yours, but on crack."

Nicole paused and looked for a reaction. Kate gave her an encouraging smile that let her know she should finish. "I was living with Andrew, and Derek wanted me to stay with him in Mexico. All in just over a week? Ultimately, I couldn't imagine not waking up to him every morning, and I didn't know if that was true love or infatuation."

"That's it!" Kate interrupted her. "That's exactly what I'm worried about."

"But is he asking you to move here? Or could you try long-distance?" Nicole asked.

"He hasn't exactly asked me to move here, but he says all the time that he doesn't know how he'll handle being away from me again."

"In so many words, he'd probably like you here," Nicole clarified.

"I'm not moving here. Nic, I love my job and I don't want to be an attorney in South Beach. I'm on my way to being partner. I'm not losing that part of me for any man!" Kate was starting to sound a little frazzled.

"I get it! Stay calm. No one is asking you to move." Nicole led her out of the little boutique and over to an open table along the street.

"He might ask! He's the artist, though. If this works out between us, he can move." Kate felt like she was starting to hyperventilate. That wasn't a good sign. "Maybe I'm not ready for this to get serious."

"You can't make that call until you've talked this over with Dominic," Nicole pointed out. "You're getting freaked out by something that may not even happen. Kate, what I learned last year was how much I was willing to trust my heart. And I decided it was one hundred percent. You have to decide how much you can trust yours. Because our hearts and heads don't always agree."

A server walked up then. Nicole ordered a glass of wine for herself and a dirty martini for Kate. She knew her friend needed the drink to help level her out.

...

Kate was still a little on edge when she was back with Dominic. She rifled through her clothes, trying to decide what to wear out to dinner that night. Nothing looked appealing, and she realized she was kind of tired. Dominic was sitting outside on the balcony, reading a book. Kate turned and watched him for a moment through the window in the bedroom. How easily would they coexist? She liked that he read, at least. So many people stared mindlessly at the TV these days. Kate had her shows that she loved, but the plot of a good book was far more intriguing to her. She was glad that he felt the same way. In that moment, she could see the two of them, both lost in their own literary worlds, but still connected physically on the same couch. Her head in his lap, maybe as they read? That thought seemed nice, not scary at all. So what the hell was she so frightened of?

She yawned and glanced back at her clothes selection. The future was too daunting to think about now, and he seemed engrossed in his book, anyway. She grabbed a blanket from the end of the bed and curled up on the pile of pillows. She would close her eyes for just a few minutes...

Kate was woken by a loud knock. She was completely disoriented. When her heart slowed, she looked around and realized she was in Dominic's bed, but alone. It had been dusk when she had laid down, and now it was pitch black. She stood up and looked out the window. She smiled at the sight of Dominic's head hung back asleep in the chair, his feet crossed on the table in front of him, and his book fallen against his chest. With the patio door closed, he must not have heard the knock. *Bang. Bang.* There it was again!

Kate jumped up and ran toward the door, and then stopped herself. *Should I answer it?* She bit on the edge of her lip, considering. Worried the visitor would hear her, she tiptoed slowly to the door and looked through the peep hole. The first thing that came into focus was a classic pearl necklace and then, as Kate squinted her eyes, so did Carolyn Price's face.

CHAPTER SIXTEEN

Well, shit! Kate thought to herself, as she watched Dominic's mother standing outside, her lips pursed. Should Kate wake Dominic up before letting Carolyn in? She was still a bit groggy herself after being woken up from a deep sleep. But perhaps she should start the conversation herself and use that to gain the upper hand. Kate took a breath, rolled her eyes, and opened the door.

"Mrs. Price, please come in," Kate gave her a half smile. No matter what happened, she still wanted to take the high road. She didn't want to stoop to this woman's level. Dominic deserved a partner that wouldn't be catty.

"Oh, hello. Kate, right?" Carolyn walked right past her, looking for her son.

"Dominic fell asleep reading. Let me go wake him for you." Kate didn't wait for an answer. Suddenly, she didn't want any conversation to take place between the two of them without Dominic's presence. Things could be twisted so easily in the he-said-she-said game. She knew that from her legal work. So many hours of wasted time because of misinterpreted or misrepresented words.

Kate opened the patio door and looked at her bad boy, sleeping soundly, and so incredibly gorgeous. Sometimes it was sexy, and sometimes it was rugged, but in this moment, he was classically handsome. His strong jawline seemed softened as he slept, his intense eyes lost in the dream world behind his closed lids. She smiled, looking at his heavy eyebrows. How could eyebrows be sexy, too? She lifted the book quietly off his chest and brushed her hand through his thick hair. He let out an audible moan of pleasure as she brought her hand around to the side of his face. He leaned his head in and, just as she was about to speak, his eyes opened.

"Hey, sleepy, we have a visitor," she smiled at him and kissed the tip of his nose. She could handle whatever his mother threw at them.

Dominic loved hearing her referring to the visitor as *theirs* rather than *his*. His mood changed immediately, as he craned his head to the side and saw his mother standing awkwardly in the living room, watching them. The sky was black, and he was slightly disoriented. What time was it? Had his mother showed up uninvited at two in the morning?

"Son of a bitch!" He took Kate's hand and stood up. He didn't hesitate at all. He wanted Carolyn out of his house.

"Mother, why are you here?" he said, as they soon as they were through the patio door, making it perfectly obvious that he wasn't happy about her pop-in.

"Can't a mother visit her son?" she replied in a sickeningly sweet voice, as if she didn't understand in the slightest why he'd be upset.

Dominic realized that he had about two seconds to decide if he was going to rat out Tiffany. He didn't want to lose her as a source for his mother's crazy plans. How could he handle this? He figured he could throw Amanda under the bus. Maybe she would buy that story.

"Amanda told me that you pushed her to come by here and *check on me*."

Kate wasn't expecting that to come out of his mouth. Why hadn't he told her that Amanda came by? What had happened between them? She did her best to squash her immediate feelings of jealousy. She had spent the few weeks she was back in Chicago with Ethan, so she had no right to question what Dominic had been doing.

Carolyn took a deep breath. *So he doesn't know I put Tiffany up to it. Good girl, she must need more money. And Kate hasn't found out yet… interesting.* "She was worried about you. The two of you used to be rather close, dear. She heard whispers about you and your new counter girl. She didn't want you getting hurt again. I merely suggested that maybe you could use a shoulder to lean on." Carolyn looked right at Kate as she said the words. Kate may have looked very sweet with her son while she was waking him. The scene may have reminded her of how she would wake Dominic when he was a boy. Nevertheless, Amanda made more sense for the family business. The next generation would have almost complete control over the port, if the families united. He needed to understand that. Though she wasn't sure she should, Carolyn decided to go for the jugular. "Plus, how do you know she's not after your money?"

Realizing his little attorney was about to defend herself, Dominic held up his hand, letting her know he wanted to handle it. "You have no idea what you're talking about, and it makes you look ridiculous. She had no idea my last name was Price or any idea who the *Price Family* was before she got here. For Christssake mother, she's from Chicago. They don't give a shit about the Port of Miami or the social politics of South Beach, Florida. She's an attorney and a good one at that. She doesn't want me for my money!"

Dominic ran his hands through his thick hair, dark strands falling back into his eyes as he tried to wipe the situation from his reality. His mother was never going to get it; he wasn't ever going to choose Amanda. He grabbed Kate's hand and began walking her to the bedroom. Without looking back, he called out to his mother. "Kate is who I love, and I don't care about your opinion on the matter. See yourself out."

Without thinking, Kate yelled, "Wait!" to his mother. Dominic turned and looked at her, wide-eyed.

"You love me?" she said, with a tear in her eye.

"Yes, I love you. I've loved you since the moment I saw your face. I've been waiting my whole life for you." He leaned over and gave her a quick, soft kiss.

Kate wanted nothing more than to have this moment last forever, but the fact was that his mother was in the other room, and she was not going to be the cause of him fighting with any of his family.

There was no door between the living room and bedroom. Carolyn could easily hear those intimate words pass between the two of them. She needed to know what she was up against, so she slowly moved as close as she could to the doorway to make sure she heard every word.

"Nicky, I love you, too. You know I'm not going to jump into anything crazy. But you need to get out there and straighten this out with you mother."

"Are you defending what she did?" he said, surprised.

Kate knew he wasn't referring to Carolyn sending Amanda to his apartment. This was really about Carolyn paying Tiffany to sleep with him. And that *gold digger* comment. "No, not at all. But what I am doing is telling you to get out there and straighten this out with her. I don't care what she thinks about me. I only care about the two of us. If the situation were reversed, and you didn't push me to talk to my mother, I would know you weren't the right one for me. I love you, Nicky, but your family needs to come first right now."

Carolyn couldn't believe her ears. She was calling him Nicky? No one outside the family had ever done that, and she, herself, was the only one that had done it for the past twenty-five years. Her hand was covering her mouth in shock, though she didn't remember putting it there. Kate stood up to Dominic and put his relationship with his mother before herself. She was brave. It reminded Carolyn of herself. She hadn't expected this woman to be so strong and independent. She made no flinch about the reference to Tiffany or Amanda. She seemed to have a faith in Dominic that, perhaps, nothing could break.

Standing in the middle of her son's living room, Carolyn saw her reflection in the large glass window in front of her. It blended with the view of the water outside, black from the night, and lights from other buildings scattered about. There she was, looking back at herself, wearing a neat white pantsuit with her simple strand of pearls. Her chestnut hair was slicked back in a tight bun at the nape of her neck. She didn't look like herself. She looked old. Had she really not seen herself in her own reflection for that long?

She stood there like a statue, staring. The few minutes that she had been in the condo, she had been watching Dominic. As she looked now, she noticed the wall behind her. It had always been white, but in the window, the reflection looked like swirls of grey. She turned around and found herself facing down a larger-than-life picture of Kate's face. She saw Kate through Dominic's eyes and...she was beautiful.

What had she done? What if Kate didn't know about Tiffany and left him when she found out. Carolyn knew her son, though. If he truly loved this woman, he wouldn't have slept with someone else. Her mind began to sort everything out. Had she been hustled by that little pipsqueak counter girl? She may well have been.

When Carolyn realized that Kate and Dominic were still having their moment, she tilted her head to catch a glimpse of them through the doorway. Kate had her head leaned into Dominic's chest, and his arms were around her. They stood there, silent, united. Carolyn knew she needed to say something. "Kate, may I have a word with you?"

For the first time, the woman in the other room sounded genuine. Her voice was actually nice and sweet, when she wasn't trying to sound like a bitch. Carolyn saw Kate lift her head, kiss her son quickly, and turn to walk into the living room.

"What can I do for you?" Kate tried to sound as nice as possible, but this situation was just awkward.

"Please, sit with me for a moment." Carolyn gave her a genuine smile. As both women sat on the couch, they could hear Dominic open the patio door from the bedroom and close it behind him. They both appreciated that he was giving them some privacy. Somehow, Kate knew she didn't need to be concerned that this conversation would get twisted. Something in Carolyn had changed, Kate just wasn't sure why.

"I owe you a rather large apology. I hope, for the sake of my son, you will accept it." Carolyn put her hands over Kate's for just a moment.

"Of course I will, but I would like to understand a little more," Kate replied honestly.

"This wonderful city is here mainly because of the Port of Miami. For three generations, my family has made it everything that it is today. Yet, still I want more for the next generation. I was determined to gain more for my sons' children by uniting the two families that held the largest stakes here. Since the first time I saw a flirtatious look between Dominic and Amanda as teenagers, I have set my mind to making this happen."

"It's been a daunting process, apparently. He's forty," Kate pointed out with a smile. She wanted to make sure that Carolyn knew that she'd still be a woman that spoke her mind. But she didn't want to be outright disrespectful.

"Yes, it has. Maybe I needed to see my son truly in love to understand that what I was trying to do was wrong." She set her hand over Kate's again. "Please, forget my stupid mention of whispers with the counter girl. There were no whispers." Carolyn tested the waters, trying to see what Kate knew.

"It's forgotten. Dominic told Tiffany to tell you they slept together. Please, don't take this out on Tiffany. She's young, and this is an expensive city. If you take back the money, I will replace it for her."

Carolyn was impressed. "You would do that?"

"Your son is apparently a wonderful boss. He has loyalty from his employees. That's a trait to be admired."

"You understand my son well. I won't be contacting Tiffany again. There is simply no need."

The women stood and gave each other a warm hug. Carolyn had been so terribly wrong about Kate. She should have trusted her son's opinion from the start. Kate noticed Carolyn looking at Dominic while he sat outside, facing the water. Lord knew what was going through his mind. "You know, he's the one that could use the apology more than me," Kate smiled.

"Yes, I believe he deserves one, too." Carolyn said. Her diamond rings clacked together as she wrung her hands.

"Would you like me to go out there with you?"

"Oh no, thank you for the offer," Carolyn said as she headed for the door.

Kate picked up a magazine on the coffee table and tried her best to give the same respectful privacy that Dominic gave to them.

"Nicky, dear, may I speak with you?" Carolyn claimed the chair at the corner of the table, next to him. He kept his eyes on the water.

"What is it?" He sounded more exhausted than angry at this point.

"I'm very sorry for ever meddling with your love life." Unable to look at him, she looked down and fiddled with the rings on her fingers.

"Thank you," he replied plainly.

"Kate is a very lovely woman, and I will never push Amanda on you again. I shouldn't have been doing it before."

"No, you shouldn't have. Mothers need to stay out of their son's lives and what goes on in their bedrooms."

Carolyn didn't miss his reference to Tiffany. "Yes, I know. It will not happen again," she said quietly.

"I am in love with that woman in there. I would never hurt her. Adrian is always running around with other women behind Natalie's back. The entire city of South Beach seems to know about it. I can't imagine you didn't. And yet, you pushed for Amanda and me as a couple. Mother, I know she said harsh things about Kate, but she's the bitch. I want nothing to do with a woman like that anymore. Seems like Amanda is right up

Adrian's alley." What the hell was he doing? He couldn't stop himself. Maybe he was more upset by his brother's actions than he realized. He was always distant from that type of situation before, but now that he had Kate, he couldn't imagine sleeping around on her. Adrian and Amanda deserved each other.

Carolyn's head started spinning with ideas. But she could strategize later. Now, she wanted to make sure everything was fixed between Dominic and herself.

"You'll forgive me, then?" she asked. "I am very sorry, and I look forward to forming a relationship with Kate."

That knocked down any of the defenses he still had standing. "Yes, *Mom*, I forgive you." He smiled at her. "Let's go inside and see Kate."

As they walked in together, Carolyn pointed to the painting on the wall. "It's truly magnificent."

"Thank you. She's my muse," he smiled at his mother as he joined Kate on the couch.

"I am going to leave you two for the rest of the evening. I hope you both could meet me for brunch one day before you leave, Kate."

"We will, thank you," Kate said and took the lead to stand up.

Dominic knew he couldn't push her too quickly, but he loved how she already seemed like the woman of the house. They walked Carolyn out together. When the door closed behind her, they looked at each other with confused expressions.

"What the hell was that?" Kate said, laughing.

CHAPTER SEVENTEEN

"That was interesting." Dominic leaned over and put Kate's face in his hands. "I don't want to question her one-eighty right now."

"She told me she needed to see you in love to realize her mistakes," Kate told him, knowing he'd be relieved.

"No more Amanda, thank God!" Dominic let out a sigh of relief. And then, "So you love me, too?" He kissed her face.

"You caught that, huh?" Kate tried to joke. "I do. I know that now."

Dominic knew not to push the subject. She had already stated that she wasn't going to jump into anything. He heard his stomach start to rumble from hunger. "What time is it, anyway?" he asked.

"Just after 9:30."

"I was worried my mom showed up in the middle of the night. Why did you let me sleep so long? You have to be starving."

"I fell asleep trying to decide what to wear. Your mother's knock at the door is what woke me. Otherwise, you probably would have woken up in the middle of night, outside and very confused," she laughed.

"I actually fall asleep out there reading more than you'd think," he smiled. "I'm starving."

"Me, too. I told you that you'd soon learn I'm always hungry. Should we go out?"

"Do you like to cook?" he asked with a raised eyebrow.

"Hmmm. I haven't spent much time in the kitchen. I work long hours. Other than the stir-fried vegetables you saw burning on my stove, I can order a mean take-out."

"Well, I have lots of time on my hands, and I like to cook. We could search my fridge and throw something together."

"Sounds great." Kate loved the idea of Dominic cooking. There were so many facets to the man in front of her. Some men may think that they can cook because they can throw together a boxed dinner. She was pretty sure that was far from what Dominic meant.

Dominic led her into the kitchen and opened the refrigerator door wide, so they both had a view. "I can work with this."

He began pulling out ingredients. She saw him grab a handful of vegetables- broccoli, asparagus, Brussels sprouts, and onions. Luckily, all her favorite vegetables. Then he grabbed a jar of sun dried tomatoes, a chunk of parmesan cheese, and the milk. She was trying to figure out what he was planning, but since she didn't cook much, she was still in the dark. She didn't dislike cooking; she just never had in the past. Next, he made his way to the pantry and grabbed some flour and pasta.

Kate couldn't believe that, in about twenty minutes from refrigerator to plate, there was a fettuccine alfredo dish with vegetables sitting in front of her. It smelled amazing. It tasted amazing. Maybe she could cook. She didn't realize it could be done so quickly.

"Have you always liked to cook?" she asked between bites. She couldn't stop herself.

Dominic laughed in response. "We had a nanny growing up. She was Italian, and she loved to cook for us." He smiled at the memory of her. "I paid attention."

"Well, this is fabulous," Kate said.

"I did learn that I enjoyed cooking much more when I no longer ate meat. I always thought it was rather unappetizing when it was raw." He contorted his face for effect.

"I'll give you that. Maybe that's why I never started cooking when I was younger," she wondered.

...

Kate woke up with Dominic's arm flung over her waist. The feeling of him sleeping next to her would never get old. She rolled her body slightly backwards to snuggle into him. Without waking, he adjusted his body with hers. The whole simple interaction between the two of them made her smile. She laid there, savoring the moment and listening to Dominic quietly breathe in and out. She said a silent thank you that he didn't snore. How did she get so lucky? Snoring could be a deal breaker for her. If Dominic had snored, this moment would have been ruined by some horrific noise coming from him. Thankfully, this was perfect. He was perfect.

Dominic's phone finally woke him. With eyes barely opened, he answered the call. It was his gallery; they needed his signature on some documents. He usually tried to stop by weekly to see how things were going. With Kate in town, he hadn't thought about it. She loved art; why hadn't it occurred to him?

When the call was finished, he slid back under the covers and curled her body into his. "Good morning, babe."

"It is a good morning," she said, smiling.

"That was my gallery. Would you like to run by there with me this morning? We could make a day of it and visit the other galleries in the area."

Kate turned and looked at him, bright-eyed. "You have a gallery here? How am I just hearing about this?"

Dominic laughed and kissed her. "I'll take that as a yes."

"YES!" She almost yelled and then laughed at her reaction. "Let's run through the shower."

Before Dominic realized what was happening, Kate was out of the bed and turning on the water.

"Slow down, what is the rush?"

Kate came back and sat on the bed. "Sorry. Too much? I'm excited to see your work displayed all together."

"You're sweet," he said and pulled her on top of him. He went from playful to serious in an instant and pulled her face into his.

"Oh, nice try, mister. Get your ass out of bed, and take me to your gallery!" She laughed and wiggled out of his grip before he could stop her.

They went through the same song and dance in the shower. Dominic appreciated her level of excitement. He was surprised at how excited he was himself to show her. He never brought women in with him, so he was pretty sure the staff would be talking about it for days. When it first opened, he did try to take Amanda, but she just checked out her makeup in her little compact and kept asking when they'd be leaving to go to the newest club in town. She glanced at his paintings occasionally, but never truly saw them. He knew it would be a completely different experience with Kate.

To get to his gallery, they had to take the causeway over the water, back to mainland Miami. "You are going to love this area." He looked over, smiling at her. "The entire area of Wynwood is like a huge art gallery, with street art everywhere. There is an electricity in the air that you can't find anywhere else. We'll stop at the local coffee shop after we visit the gallery."

"I can't believe I didn't know about it." Kate's excitement was rising.

"I've been too selfish, keeping you locked up all to myself," he joked.

Kate knew the place as soon as they reached it. There was color everywhere. The buildings, walls, doors, windows – everything was covered with amazing artwork. There were restaurants scattered about, with the outdoor seating so common in the city. The tables looked like they were set in the middle of an art gallery. She could barely contain herself.

Dominic laughed at her, wishing he had brought her sooner. "There's even an app that tells you all about the work everywhere," he informed her.

"Are you serious? I'm putting it on my phone now!"

"Would you like to walk around first?" he asked. With so many things to see, he wouldn't be offended if she said yes.

"Absolutely not! We can check all of this out later." Other than focusing attention on her phone for a moment, she didn't take her eyes off of the street. She wanted to take everything in. There was art everywhere she looked. One building on a corner was painted completely green, before the artist went back with splashes of color to create a gorgeous canvas. She saw a painting of a beautiful woman laying along the length of the building, with an over-accentuated butt. Kate shot her eyes quickly over to the next side and saw faces that looked like they were representing different cultures around the world. She realized she could probably spend the rest of her trip in this one little area, surrounded by its beauty.

"It's known as the 'Museum of the Streets'," Dominic told her, glancing at her quickly before bringing his attention back to the road.

"I can see why. Thank you for bringing me here. I'm rather speechless."

Dominic smiled and took her hand. "Mine is just over here." He motioned with his head and pulled into the spot in front of his gallery. In block letters, just above the reach of the artists, it read DOMINIC PRICE. She smiled wide, seeing his name in a sign on a building. Helping her out of the car, Dominic took her hand and pulled her into him.

"Remember, there's a little piece of me in all of my work. Be kind with any criticism." He was half-joking, half-serious. He loved what he did, so, ultimately, he didn't mind the critics. But he wasn't so sure how he'd take it, if Kate didn't like something. Her opinion mattered.

Kate gave him the best reply he could have ever hoped for. "Nicky, I loved your paintings before I loved the artist."

They walked through the door and, true to the Miami style, it was modern and contemporary. The walls were bright white, and those that held artwork were only about seven feet high. It made the space feel larger. A woman began to walk towards them. She was wearing a simple black dress, and Kate saw another woman behind her also in a black dress, though a different style. She liked that Dominic made a point of noticing the small details. He wouldn't want an employee's outfit to contrast with a painting she was trying to sell.

"Dominic!" the woman said kindly. She was maybe in her fifties, with hair that was so blonde, it could be white. Her gentle eyes and happy smile made Kate feel immediately at ease.

"How are you? Alexa, this is my girlfriend Kate," Dominic replied, keeping his hand at the small of Kate's back.

"Hello, dear. It's so nice to meet you," Alexa said, holding out her hand to shake Kate's. She gave Kate a quick once over and smirked at Dominic in approval.

"It is very nice to meet you," Kate returned her polite smile, but really, she was itching to look around.

Dominic could tell this and so freed her from any further conversation. "Alexa, let's head back to the office and let Kate browse." He kissed Kate's cheek, and she smiled in appreciation.

A majority of the paintings were large, taking up most of a wall partition with one painting alone. Kate was immediately drawn to one across the room. It looked almost like a trail through the woods, but in true Dominic Price style, the colors were vibrant and blended together. Kate loved that there were influences from other artists, but it was definitely a design that was all his own. When she wandered around the corner to the other side of the partition, she fell in love all over again. The color combination was amazing. There was a brilliance of blue, swirled and thrown over a color that Kate had never seen before. Kate couldn't quite figure out how Dominic created something so different; it seemed impossible. It was a kind of yellow that made her feel like she was looking directly at the sun, without the bright light killing her eyes. She couldn't pull herself away. She stood in front of the painting, moving back and forth slightly to see which distance was best. All of a sudden, the lights above her slowly dimmed. As the area darkened, the color of the sun grew deeper, and bands of orange appeared throughout.

"What do you think?" She heard Dominic's voice and turned towards him. He was standing behind her with his hand on the light switch.

"I know I haven't seen everything yet, but this may be my favorite." She looked at him in awe. How did he create something so beautiful?

"Thank you. I'm rather fond of that one, too." Dominic walked up and stood behind her, looking at his own work. "Let's finish looking around and grab some coffee. We can check out the art outside and in other galleries. Then find somewhere to have lunch."

Kate turned into him and reached up to kiss him on the lips. A sweet kiss, she didn't want to be inappropriate in his gallery. "Sounds wonderful."

...

The day couldn't have been more perfect. She wanted to tell Nicole all about it, but was glad it was only her and Dominic experiencing it together. Their lunch was fabulous- a black bean and quinoa salad with fresh vegetables. There was a spice added to certain foods in Miami that she couldn't quite recognize, but she loved it. And she had never before dated a man whose food tastes matched so closely with her own.

Back at the apartment, Dominic watched Kate, as she changed into comfortable clothes. He enjoyed watching her; she was very comfortable with who she was and didn't hide behind outfits when they were alone. He knew she'd change before they went out, but now, she slid on some little boy shorts and a fitted tee, gathered the longer sections of her hair back into a ponytail. No matter what she was wearing, he would never tire of looking at her. She flashed a wide smile at him as she walked past and crunched her little button nose slightly.

He knew that he would always want her with him. How was he going to handle long distance? They had talked about their life goals, and he knew that her career was important to her. He also knew that she loved her firm. She loved the partners and was working very hard to become one herself. He had already asked her to take a week off. Was that the right thing to do? Was he already asking her to choose him over her career for a week? They did need a little bit of time to decide if this was going to move forward. They hadn't had any official talk, but they were both in love now, and they knew it. That was most likely a green light.

He knew Kate could handle long distance. She had already had a long-distance relationship with her best friend for the past year, and their bond didn't seem any less solid for it. The big question was, could he handle it? He wasn't sure. He knew that he needed Kate in his life, so he was quite willing to be flexible. He just wasn't sure how they were going to pull this off. He wanted her all of the time, and she needed to be in Chicago. Did he need to be in South Beach? Maybe not one hundred percent of the time. Maybe that was the best compromise.

Kate had grabbed a book and settled down on the couch. They already knew how to manage spending long hours together. He grabbed his tablet from the coffee table and decide to do some research on Chicago real estate. Maybe something small to start out...

CHAPTER EIGHTEEN

Dominic searched through some condo options in downtown Chicago, close to Kate's place. He still wanted a two-bedroom, as he'd need somewhere to paint. Being with his muse would definitely give him all kinds of inspiration. He suspected that the city itself would inspire its own style in him. He made sure to search without Kate catching on. He didn't want to freak her out. Then again, she may be relieved to learn that he wasn't going to ask her to move to Miami any time soon. He saw how her breath quickened when the subject of their dreams of the future came up. He saved a few places to go back and investigate later, and turned off his tablet. Kate fit right into his life. It looked like his couch was made specifically to fit her little form.

...

Once they were all dressed up for a night out, they dropped the car off at one of Dominic's favorite restaurants on Ocean Drive. Kate noticed again that cars were moved so that his could sit in front of the restaurant entrance. The little hostess recognized Dominic immediately. She was smart, saying a quick hello to him and then turning all of her focus on Kate. "Well, hello, beautiful. Isn't Dominic a lucky man! I'm guessing you'd like to sit outside?"

Someone had taught her well. The hostess knew that a woman who feels like an employee is flirting with her date would not ask to return there again. Kate loved this girl. "Yes, that would be great," she said happily.

They were enjoying their drinks and waiting for Nicole and Derek to arrive. Dominic preordered a large seafood platter, assuring Kate that the four of them could eat for days and still have leftovers. Kate saw a man almost walk past their table, only to stop when he recognized Dominic. "Hey, bro!" he said, as he slapped Dominic firmly on the back.

"Adrian?" Dominic responded. "What are you up to tonight?" It didn't escape him that Adrian wasn't with his wife.

"Gonna stop by the new bar down past 7th Street for a drink and maybe grab a bite to eat," Adrian told him, eying Kate as he spoke.

"Kate, this is my brother Adrian. Adrian, this is my girlfriend," he said, looking between the two of them.

"Girlfriend, huh? Nice to meet you. If my little brother gives you any grief, you come and see me."

Kate laughed. He seemed nice enough. "Thanks, I'll do that," she joked along with him. Adrian appeared a bit taller than Dominic. Standing next to each other, Kate could see the striking resemblance between the two, with the same heavy eyebrows, strong noses, and dark hair, though Adrian wore his shorter than his little brother's. She wondered if Justin looked like the two of them.

Adrian turning his attention back to Dominic. "I've been meaning to call you. Have you heard any of the stories about the new kid on the block trying to gain some street cred?"

"Not a word. But really, art galleries and tattoo shops usually don't get the kind of riffraff that the port can bring in." He wasn't entirely serious, but he also knew that the threat of drug smugglers was very real. The port authority would never be able to entirely stop the drug smugglers, but they did the best they could. The Price family had a no-tolerance policy for any of it, obviously.

Dominic had heard some crazy stories about employees whose greed got the better of them, taking bribes and trying to help sneak drugs through.

"Not sure why you don't want to be on the front line with Justin and me," Adrian said, hitting him on the back again. Kate could imagine them as children, and it made her laugh to herself.

"Too much excitement for me. All of those meetings in three-piece suits."

"Yeah, yeah." The entire family had tried very hard to keep Dominic involved in the port business in some way, but it just wasn't going to happen. The closest he got to the business was paintings done specifically for each of their offices. "Well, let's hope this guy ends up to be a nobody."

Dominic wanted to find out more of what his brother was alluding to, but this was not the time. "I'll call you, and we'll go out for a drink soon," he offered.

"Okay, bro. Nice to meet you, Kate." He took her hand and kissed it lightly.

"That'll do, Adrian." Dominic said, laughing at his brother. Adrian may be a playboy, but there was no way he'd ever set his interests on Dominic's girlfriend. Adrian laughed, said his goodbyes, and continued walking along Ocean Drive.

Within minutes, Nicole and Derek arrived. Kate immediately began to tell them both about Wynwood. She was practically jumping out of her seat as she fought to get all the details out, barely sticking to one subject before bouncing to another. From what Nicole and Derek could tell, the museum area was simply amazing, and they had to go sometime.

"We'll check it out," Nicole said, giggling at her friend.

As one server brought them a round of drinks, another arrived with their food. To describe it as impressive wouldn't do it justice. The large skillet took up the entire center of the table. There were filets of white fish, grilled to perfection. There were crab legs and lobster tails, and Kate noticed scallops mixed in with prawns twice the size of any she'd ever seen before. And they were each given their own portion of drawn butter. For the next few minutes, the conversation ceased as all four friends focused on trying a little bit of everything. Both Kate and Nicole worked on devouring the food as lady-like as possible. The men, unconcerned with how they looked, wolfed it down.

"I forgot to mention it," Kate said, when she came up for air, "I just got to meet one of Dominic's brothers. The middle one, right?" Kate clarified.

"Yes, Justin is the oldest, and Adrian is the middle." Dominic smiled when he spoke of them.

"Do you have any idea who he was talking about? About the one guy looking to gain 'street cred'?" Kate asked, with air quotes for the term.

"No, I don't. They usually know more about the thugs on the streets before the rest of the population here does. Probably faster than the cops as well. There is always someone trying to find a new way to sneak some drugs through. The areas that are Price property are pretty well sealed shut."

"That sounds kind of dangerous," Nicole noted.

"It can be. My grandfather, dad, uncles, and now brothers have all been approached and sometimes threatened that they need to play ball. But if you give in, they own you. It would never be a one-time-thing with these people," Dominic told them, as he remembered some of the stories. "Most of the drug smugglers are gang members as well. Sounds like this new kid might be trying to work his way up through the ranks by finding a new 'in' at the port."

"I hope your family isn't getting threatened," Kate said, concerned.

"Me, too," Dominic said, sounding somewhat distant from the conversation.

"Sounds like you were smart to stay away from the family business," Derek pointed out.

"That's probably the only interesting part of their business, but it's definitely an...*exciting* one," Dominic tried to joke. He was still worried for his brothers. One day, some stupid kid might not take no for an answer and then what?

"Let's go dancing!" Nicole stated, trying to take their minds off that depressing subject. "We could go to the place we did the first night we all hung out together.

"Yes! That sounds fun." Kate loved to dance. Especially this restaurant, which turned into a night club once the DJ clocked in. The entire area was white, and it lit up brilliantly when the black lights were turned on. Kate was wearing the perfect dress for black light- a black tank-style top with a white skirt that hit about mid-thigh in the front and dropped down past her knees in the back. The skirt would glow while she was under the black light.

Dominic was looking forward to getting Kate out on the dance floor again. He remembered the way their bodies moved together, and, this time, Kate was not falling-over drunk. They could dance together and both remember it tomorrow.

Derek got them a private booth in the back. The cocktail waitress had a bar-back help her bring over a large steel ice bin that held pre-chilled bottles of vodka for Kate's martinis, tequila for Nicole's shots, and a very nice bottle of scotch for the men to share. The waitress prepared them each a cocktail and told them she would always be available when they were ready for another.

The DJ had already begun to play, and the music was loud. They stayed seated for a few minutes with their drinks. Kate snuggled into Dominic's shoulder while she sipped her martini. Nicole had her legs flung across Derek and threw back her head with her shot of tequila. Kate loved seeing her so happy. She glanced quickly up at Dominic, realizing again that she may have found the same thing with him. It had always been a far-off dream, but now it seemed possible.

While Kate was appreciating where her love life was now, Dominic took the drink from her hand and set it on the table. "Let's go dance, beautiful." He took her hand and helped her up.

"We're coming, too," Nicole said, as she grabbed Derek to follow them.

Dominic found his way to the middle of the crowd and pulled Kate into him. She wrapped her arms around his neck, and he held onto her little hips. The shoes she chose for the night had a very high heel and brought her closer to his height. No matter how high the heels were, she'd never be eye-level with him, but stealing a few kisses while they danced would be much easier tonight.

Kate looked over at Nicole and Derek, lost in their own world, as usual. Then she looked up at Dominic. She hadn't realized he was watching her. She smiled at him, feeling only slightly self-conscious. Without taking those searing eyes off of her, he leaned in so she could hear him talk.

"You are beautiful," he said, before kissing her lightly on the lips. It was a sweet and innocent kiss. Except…those eyes of his exposed his devilish thoughts.

Dominic was so direct. Kate wasn't used to that. She wasn't sure what to say back. Do men really like to hear how handsome they look? She didn't want to feel like she was giving a compliment just because he gave her one. She thought she'd try going for a flirtatious reply. "Why, thank you, sexy," she said in return and then grabbed onto the back of his hair. She knew how much that could undo him. And when she tugged, he growled into her neck.

"Just wait until I get you home," he said, tasting the small hint of salt on her neck from dancing.

…

As soon as Dominic closed the door behind them, he watched Kate walk slowly and deliberately through the living room. With her back still to him, she took one strap off her shoulder and then the next. The dress needed just a small amount of encouragement from Kate to fall completely down to the floor. She stood still for a moment for effect. Dominic stood there, frozen in time, with Kate in the middle of his living room with only a lacy black thong and high black heels, her dress a pile of material surrounding her on the floor. She was mesmerizing. Her usual milky white body had tanned a bit from her time in South Beach. Finally, he made himself move towards her. Before he could reach her, she turned in place.

He grabbed the back of her thighs and lifted her up. She instinctively wrapped her legs around his waist, not caring where he took her. Dominic chose the couch. In this moment, the bedroom was too far away. He laid her down, and they worked together at removing his clothes. Again, all it took was unbuckling his thick leather belt for Kate to go over the edge. As soon as his jeans were off, she pulled him on top of her and wrapped her legs tightly around him again. Dominic took her hands and held them over her head. He looked into her eyes, and all of the intensity and fire softened momentarily. Leaning in close, he whispered that he loved her. He wanted to tease her tonight. Knowing that she was excited and ready, he wanted to toy with her just a bit. Make her body beg for his.

Slowly, he kissed her all over. Light kisses that tickled and excited her skin and that he knew would give her chills all over her body. He moved himself down, stopping to kiss her belly button and the sides of her hips. He lifted one leg and began tasting her, from her ankle all the way up to her thigh. With one final sinful glance, he grabbed ahold of her hips and lifted them to his mouth. Kate pushed her head back into the pillow, taking in all of the sensation. He knew just how to please her. She grabbed at his hair, and it only made him tighten his grip on her hips. Before long, Kate called out his name as the sensation overtook her body.

Exhausted from pleasure, but still wanting more, she pulled Dominic practically by his hair on top of her. With one glance into her lazy eyes, he knew that the time for teasing was over. Dominic knew sex wasn't always about love, but tonight it was going to be. He wanted this to be another way he showed Kate how much he loved her and how much they needed each other. He knew that no matter how he tried, he would never find another connection like this with another woman. She was it for him.

CHAPTER NINETEEN

Dominic couldn't sleep that night. He laid there next to Kate, watching her dream, hearing Adrian's words play over and over in his head. *The new kid on the block trying to gain some street cred.* Dominic only knew about the family's past experiences with smuggling attempts from overhearing conversations between his brothers and their father. Why would Adrian bring this up to him now? He couldn't shake it; he needed to talk to his brother. This was a very real and very dangerous part of their business. As he watched Kate sleeping peacefully, all he could think about was how much he wanted to protect her, to make sure she was always safe. If there was any way this darkness could spill over into his life, he wanted to know about it.

Dominic slipped out of bed, started some coffee, and showered. He was completely exhausted, but he wanted to paint, to get this nervous tension out of him. Before he headed for his canvas, he sent Adrian a text. He needed to meet him today and find out what the situation was with this kid. He'd see if Kate could hang out with Nicole for a while. There was no reason to worry her, if it turned out to be nothing.

Once the text was sent, Dominic went through his ritual for beginning a new piece of work. He stared at the blank canvas for a minute or so and then closed his eyes for another minute. Usually, he could visualize the completed work before he even began painting it. It was an organic process, though, and sometimes he would take the work a completely different direction as he painted.

This time, a vision came quickly to his mind's eye-dark with streaks of every hue of red, all on top of black. He opened his eyes, grabbed a brush, and dipped it in the black paint.

Adrian got back to him rather quickly: he'd meet Dominic down on Ocean Drive at his favorite breakfast spot. *Perfect*. He'd see if Kate wanted him to drop her off at Nicole's; it was only a few blocks from where he needed to be. Dominic threw aside his phone and went back to work on the painting. It was a rather small canvas for him, only about 4 feet by 2 feet, and wouldn't take long to finish. He had it set horizontally, with the streaks of paint almost the length of the canvas, trying to pour his anxiety into the work. He considered destroying it once it was finished. His paintings always seemed imbued with life to him, and he didn't want any bad mojo hanging around his place. Bad energy was never a good thing.

Later, Kate stood by the studio door, wrapped in Dominic's bathrobe, with a cup of coffee safely in both hands, held right up to her mouth so she could also take in its glorious aroma. She had slept, but somehow, she could tell that he hadn't. It felt like, even in sleep, there was a part of her subconscious aware of Dominic. Even though she didn't really remember it, she knew he tossed and turned all night. Now, she watched him paint, unaware that she was there. She loved being able to see him in his element, wearing only a pair of old jeans and that damn belt of his. His back was to her, but she imagined the look of concentration taking over his face. He was intense while he worked. She could see his muscles in his back and arms tighten when he'd get a surge of inspiration and swipe the paint brush across the canvas. Somehow, this man could make painting sexy. Then again, he could probably read the phone book, and she would get turned on.

Kate watched him for a few more minutes, and then cleared her throat to grab his attention. He seemed lost in his own world, but she caught his attention on the second attempt. He turned around with a smile on his face. "This may be the best way to start my day: painting and you." He set down the brush, and as soon he reached her, he took the hot cup of coffee from her hands and set it down on the table. Then, without warning, he picked her up and kissed her lips.

"Well, good morning to you," Kate said, giggling. She wrapped her arms around him and allowed herself to truly feel happy. It almost didn't feel real. Like something was going to steal this happiness from her.

"Hey, I need to go have a chat with Adrian. Would you like to hang out with Nicole for a bit this morning?" he said, as he set her back on her feet.

"Sure, let me check in with her. Could you drop me off there?" she asked.

"I'm meeting him a few blocks from their place, so that would work great," he smiled and walked into the bathroom to wash the paint from his hands.

"Um, babe. You may need to take a shower," Kate smiled at him.

Dominic looked up at his reflection in the mirror and saw red across his check and by his neck.

"I don't think those are tattoos," she joked.

"What the hell was I doing?" he laughed. "You check with Nicole, and I'll run through the shower."

. . .

"His name is Santino Reyes," Adrian stated bluntly. "He uses his mother's last name, Cruz, occasionally."

"Do I need to worry about this kid?" Dominic asked.

"He may be a kid (he's mid-twenties)," Adrian added, "but he's serious."

"How is this guy any different from the others?" Dominic pressed.

"He's more determined. He's made some vague threatening remarks about how he'll find a way in one way or another." Adrian shook his head. "I've just talked with some friends of mine that work security. They're going to work overtime to watch over Natalie and the boys while I'm at work."

Adrian and Natalie had twin sons, three years old. Natalie was home with the kids or on play dates most days. "What about Justin?" Dominic was starting to get concerned about this. Should he send Kate home?

"He thinks I'm jumping the gun. But there's something about this guy. It seems like there's no soul in him. When you speak to him, it's like he's an empty shell that would have no remorse over anything. He gives me the heebie-jeebies." Adrian paused, thinking. "I'm not sure how far he's willing to go when he says 'one way or another.'"

"I haven't gotten any visits from this guy. What about Mom?" Dominic asked, concerned for Carolyn's safety as well.

"I've already talked to Dad about that. They may go stay at the cabin in Colorado for awhile. We're heading into summer anyway. This is when they usually take an extended vacation. He doesn't want to worry her, so he casually suggested it. You know she'd freak out if she thought any of us were in danger."

For the first time since he met Kate, Dominic was happy she'd be leaving in a few days. Then he remembered the saved condos in Chicago on his tablet at home. This may have given him the final push he needed to talk to Kate about this and look into spending the summer in the Midwest.

…

As Dominic walked up to the Ocean Azul Hotel, he saw Derek sitting outside, relaxing with a cup of coffee.

"They saw some dresses in the window across the street," he explained Nicole and Kate's absence, shaking his head in humor at the two friends shopping together. "They'll be back soon."

"Oh, I bet they could do some damage," Dominic joked as he sat down.

Derek grabbed the attention of a waitress. "Coffee?" he asked Dominic. With a nod, Derek motioned to the waitress to grab another cup.

Dominic ran his hands through his hair, pushing back the locks that hung near his eyes.

"Why the face?" Derek asked.

"Honestly, Adrian, my brother, has got me concerned about that new kid trying to get drugs through the port. He's worried he'll go at this from any angle possible." He leaned back in his chair, trying to relax. "I couldn't get it out of my mind last night. I couldn't sleep, and I'm fucking exhausted."

"I can give Gael a call," Derek offered. "That man knows everyone in law enforcement, even though he wasn't ever a cop in the States. He is often extended professional courtesy when he asks nicely. Want me to find out what they know about this guy?"

"Sure, thanks." Dominic gave Derek all the information he had on him. Tracking him down might not be so simple, since he might not be well known yet, and both of the last names he used were quite common.

...

"I rarely shop in Chicago. I could get myself into some trouble if I lived here," Kate said, looking through racks of dresses.

"I'm pretty sure your bank accounts can handle it, Miss Lawyer," Nicole smiled at her friend.

"Oh my God, I can't believe I forgot to tell you at breakfast." Kate looked over at Nicole in shock.

"What?" Kate's reaction piqued Nicole's interest.

"We used the 'L' word the other night," Kate said, trying to sound cute, like they were teenage girls talking about her first crush. "I didn't have a chance to tell you last night."

"You said *LUST* to each other?" Nicole joked.

"Very funny," Kate shot back. "He told his mom that he loved me, and then I said it back to him later when I was trying to get him to talk to her."

"There's a first for *I Love You* stories- his mother as part of the discussion. Usually it's," Nicole threw her voice up an octave in imitation of a cheesy romance movie. "'I love you.' 'Really? I love you too!'"

"Nope, we didn't have one of those. But it was still kind of romantic," Kate told her. She smiled as she remembered how it all went down.

"I told you that he was the one for you. Remember that? Remember not believing me?" Nicole teased.

"Yes, I do recall you mentioning that once or twice," Kate gave her friend a snarky smile.

Nicole was incredibly happy for Kate. She couldn't imagine anyone making her happier than Dominic did. And no one deserved it more. Nicole looked over at her friend, who was holding up a dress, deciding if she should try it on. She couldn't love Kate more if she was her real sister. She was her family. For a small moment in time, she had been her *only* family. When Nicole's father died, Kate was it. Granted, she met Derek immediately following that. But Nicole remembered lying in bed the night her father died, thinking to herself, *I have no family left*. Then Kate's face had popped into her head. She did have family left. She had Kate. Nicole had always been so thankful to have her in her life. Now, she was thankful that Kate had found Dominic.

...

Dominic saw a smile come across Derek's face, and he followed his eyes to the two beautiful women crossing the street towards them. Both Kate and Nicole had multiple bags in their hands and the smiles on their faces were priceless. "There was an amazing sale," Kate said, as she dropped her bags by the table and sat down next to Dominic. "Everything okay with your brother?"

"Just got an update on everything." He didn't want to lie to her, but didn't want to go into detail just then.

"Guess what?!" Nicole almost yelled to her husband.

"What, Love?" He picked up her hand and kissed it.

"Kate's already addicted to tattoos. We're going to get the Celtic friendship tattoos on our wrists." Nicole eyes were wild with excitement, and she clapped her hands together.

Derek laughed and looked to Kate. "She's tried for years for you to finally get just one, and you're ready for your second one within a month?" he joked. "I love the idea."

"Wrists are good, because I can cover mine with a watch or thick bracelet when I'm in court." Kate turned to

Dominic with bedroom eyes and a pleading look on her face. "Think you could find time before I leave to give us matching tattoos?"

Dominic smiled, "Of course. That'll look sexy, babe."

"Be careful, or she could end up looking like a human doodle pad, if she's hooked and you're her pusher," Derek said between laughs.

"Oh, shut up," Nicole kissed him quiet.

"There's no time like the present?" Dominic looked between the three of them. "We could head over there when we're done here."

"It's only 10:30," Nicole pointed out, without thinking through her statement. Dominic raised his eyebrow at her in question. "Oh, duh, you own the place," Nicole rolled her eyes at herself. "Sometimes I forget that I'm blonde."

Derek kissed the top of her head, trying not to laugh at his wife. "Show me what this Celtic symbol looks like."

Nicole took out her phone and opened it to the picture she had saved. It looked somewhat like a sideways infinity symbol with a swirl through it. "We're going to get it done in purple." Nicole smiled at Kate, as she showed the picture to Derek. "I'm excited to have a tattoo from the famous *Dominic Price*." She over-emphasized the name.

"Do I get to charge you double for the experience of getting it done by yours truly?" Dominic quipped.

"You're not charging me at all," she laughed.

"Of course I'm not. That'll be about a quarter's worth of ink."

"Let's have some coffee, then we can drop the bags off in your room before we head over there," Kate smiled and grabbed the attention of the waitress.

"Are you ready for me to use that tattoo gun on you again?" Dominic said, as he put his arm around her lovingly.

"Babe, I'm ready for you to do anything to me," she winked at him.

CHAPTER TWENTY

The two couples walked the few blocks over to South Beach Tattoo, holding hands with their partners and chatting without a care in the world. Nicole had a year to get comfortable with the happiness, but it was still new to Kate. It still felt too good to be true at times.

At the shop door, Dominic fumbled with his keys. Nicole was talking, telling him about Kate and Gael's habitual Battle of the Wits contests. She was still mid-story when he found the right key and held the door open for his friends. Laughing at the image of Kate sparring with Gael and preoccupied with the door, he didn't realize that the other three had become silent and stone-faced as the door closed behind him. When he finally turned, he saw Tiffany standing with a man, who had a gun pointed straight at them. Kate was the only thing that went through his mind. He was not in arm's reach of her, and he didn't like that.

It felt like time stood still, but his brain knew that it was a blink of an eye before he moved. He jumped in front of Kate before there was a chance for the man to tell him not to move. He knew it was coming though.

Sure enough… "Don't move again!" the man yelled with a thick Hispanic accent. Tattoos crawled down his arms and up his neck, peaking up through the collar of his bright white t-shirt.

Dominic shoved Kate completely behind him and lifted his hands in the air slightly. He wasn't ready to completely surrender; he just needed to get a sense of the situation. He glanced over and made eye contact with Derek, who was standing in front of Nicole, shoulders squared. Nicole's face was a mixture of horror and a resigned here-we-go-again. Kate had told him about Nicole's encounter with Derek's ex-girlfriend when they were in Puerto Vallarta last year. Dominic was sure that Nicole couldn't believe this was happening to her again. Dominic also remembered that Derek used to be a MMA fighter. That could be helpful.

He felt Kate shaking behind him, but he could tell that she was trying to keep it under control. He hated that he couldn't stop and tell her that he would always protect her. That he would find a way to get them out of this mess. He turned his head just a bit and whispered to her, "Just breathe, baby." He heard her breathe in deep, trying to get control over her body.

He figured he'd start with his employee. "Tiffany, what are you doing?"

"Dominic, I'm sorry, but the money was too good to refuse." The smile on Tiffany's face didn't look one bit remorseful.

"What money?" he asked, slightly confused.

"This man was pretty determined to get inside this place. He offered far more than your stupid meddling mother did to sleep with you. I told you about that so you wouldn't ever suspect I was involved in anything. You know, a false sense of trust." Her eyes turned hateful above her cruel smile. "You don't think that Jax really wanted to steal from you, do you? This man can be rather persuasive, though." She nodded towards the gunman. "And missing money is only a small part of his grand plan."

"Shut up, bitch!" the man snapped at her.

Dominic scanned the area. He saw what looked like a few bricks of cocaine on the ledge behind the intruder. He could only assume he and Tiffany were going to plant it, but the four of them walked in and ruined their plans. Dominic wasn't stupid. "Santino Reyes, I presume? Nice to meet you," he said, shaking his head. This wasn't good. He was face-to-face with a man that people said didn't have a soul. To make matters worse, there are three innocent people now involved. One of whom he was madly in love with.

"Tie up the bitches. I'll take care of the men first," Santino ordered to Tiffany. She looked at him, slightly concerned. Dominic could sense that this wasn't part of the deal. She probably took a large bribe to get Reyes into the shop to plant the drugs. Maybe the plan was for her to tip off the cops? And then, to make it go away, Dominic would tell his family to play ball with Santino. It seemed like the most logical scenario. Dominic knew that there were cops on the payroll for some of the gangs and crime families. Luckily, it looked like Tiffany wasn't prepared to tie anyone up. Maybe Santino could get her to hold the gun while he tied them up, but that was still better odds for him and his friends.

Oh shit! Kate thought to herself, tightening her grip on Dominic's arms. Did "take care of" mean "kill"? She shot a look over to Nicole. How did she handle this last time? Suddenly, she had a new-found respect for what Nicole had experienced. Granted, Nicole's enemy had been a crazy little ex-girlfriend, and this man was most likely a drug-smuggling gang member with delusions of grandeur.

"That's not going to be happening!" Dominic shouted, his tone authoritative as he stood his ground. In that moment, Kate could not have been happier to have her bad boy as the one protecting her.

"I'm the one with the gun, *ese*." Santino nodded towards the weapon.

Dominic quickly looked to Derek and then threw a glance to the front counter, trying to communicate his plan quickly and discreetly. The counter stood between Reyes and the far wall. If they could at least get the girls behind that counter, Kate and Nicole would have some cover, while Derek and Dominic might have a chance to gain control of the situation without them getting hurt. Derek looked quickly at Kate, then to Nicole, and nodded. Dominic knew he understood his plan to get the girls to safety. They only had one shot at this.

"Let the others go," Dominic told Reyes. "They have nothing to do with this. You can deal with me and this grand plan of yours afterwards. Plus, I can only assume you need access into the port. And that will never happen if any of them get hurt."

With that, he looked at Derek and, almost simultaneously, threw Kate as far as he could behind the counter. He knew it would hurt her, but a few bruises were far better than the current alternative. Derek followed his lead and tossed his wife to safety as well. Then the two men stood next to each other, prepared for a fight.

Dominic shot a quick look over at the girls. They were curled up together with their backs to the wall. Seeing that look in Kate's eyes, Dominic knew he needed to do something before she cried. He could tell there was a small tear falling from the corner of her eye, but she was fighting it.

"This isn't going to end well for you, Santino," Dominic said. Maybe he could reason with the guy. Or at least stall until he thought of another way to get them out of this. "I'm not even in the Port business, so I have to be your last hope at getting my family to agree to your terms."

"They will agree. I'm going to run this whole city soon." Reyes threw his arms out wide.

Derek had been watching closely, waiting for his chance. This was it. This guy's ego gave him an opening. With Reyes' hands outstretched, bragging about his power to come, the former MMA fighter prepared for one of the moves from his championship days.

From behind the counter, Kate could barely see what was going on. She had been inching her body up just a bit to get a better view, wanting to be prepared for whatever was going to happen. She needed to know Dominic was safe. Everything seemed to be in slow motion, just like she had always heard people say. When Santino flung his arms out, she saw Derek move in. But so, too, did Santino, who regained control of his gun quickly enough to aim it right at her head.

Time slowed to a crawl. Her eyes found Dominic's. His were full of the terror that they both felt. He threw his body towards her. She didn't close her eyes. If this was the end for her, she wanted to see him for as long as possible, to make the sight of him her last memory.

The gun fired, a deafening sound that made her ears ring, but not loudly enough to cover her screams. Dominic landed on top of her. They were both covered in blood. He was lifeless, unmoving. Kate felt herself lose control, like she was drifting out of her own body. She watched herself scramble from underneath Dominic and get him into her lap. She tried to see how badly he was injured, but there was too much blood, and she didn't understand what she was looking at. Finally, she found the source, somewhere between his heart and his left shoulder. *Please, God*, she thought to herself, *don't take him from me*. She rocked him ever so slightly back and forth, trying to soothe him, telling him to stay with her, all the things she had seen play out in front of her on TV and in the movies. Just a moment ago, she had felt that things were too good to be real life. Now, everything felt unreal for an entirely different reason.

Meanwhile, Derek had swung his other leg up and around, knocking Santino out with one kick. He fell to the ground. Derek grabbed the gun, shoving it in the back of his waistband. Kate didn't notice any of that. All she saw was Dominic. He was all she cared about. Nicole had run over to Derek and was sobbing, staring at the seemingly lifeless body on Kate. "Dominic! He can't be dead, he can't be dead," she was yelling to Derek, not realizing Kate could hear.

"Shut up! Shut up! Shut up!" Kate was yelling at the top of her lungs. She felt present in her body again. She searched for a pulse on Dominic's neck and kissed his face when she found it. She looked around and saw that the blood wasn't black. She had no idea what it would mean if it was, she just remembered it would be bad. Was he knocked out from the pain? It didn't look like the bullet could have hit his heart, but what did she know? It could have opened a major artery.

Derek looked over and saw a blur of color run past and the door closing behind it- Tiffany, sneaking out past the chaos. They could deal with her later. It seemed like Tiffany was just in it for the money; she clearly wasn't one to cause any harm. *Hopefully, she hasn't been paid yet*, Derek thought to himself, as he fished his phone out of his pocket. As Kate was doing her best to be an amateur doctor, Derek called 911.

"Grab any towel you can find," he said to Nicole, giving her a job to keep her focused.

Nicole was trying to keep it together. "Okay, I'll rip up sheets and boil some water."

Derek almost laughed, but the situation was too dire. He squared her shoulders. "Love, he's not having a baby! We need some towels to stop the blood."

"Don't blonde out on me now!" Kate yelled.

"Got it." Nicole's brain took charge again, and she ran for something to stop the blood.

Crouching down, Derek leaned Kate back into his chest to help support the weight of Dominic's shoulders and head.

"I found a pulse," she whispered, as he took her hands in his and put them over the bleeding wound.

"Good job, Little One. You're doing great. We've gotta help stop the bleeding." Derek was trying to help, but he made sure to keep an eye on Santino, knocked out only a few feet from them. They didn't need any more problems right now. Dominic needed to be their focus.

"He can't die." Kate couldn't make her voice any louder than a whisper. She wasn't sure she had anything left in her.

"He won't. An ambulance is on their way. We'll keep him comfortable until they can do their work." He brushed her hair out of her face, so she had an unobstructed view of the man she loved. Derek remembered how he felt when Nicole was in danger. His feelings for her went into overdrive. Once you have a glimpse into what life might be like without someone, you find out how important they are.

He knew Kate wasn't as much of a romantic as Nicole. He knew there wasn't really a chance he'd be attending their wedding within the month, like what had happened with him and Nicole. But he also knew that Kate was now discovering exactly how strong her love for Dominic was. He already knew Dominic had those feelings for her, because they were exactly like those he had for Nicole. He wasn't at all surprised that Dominic was lying there, bleeding, so that Kate would remain unharmed. True love is to the death.

Nicole brought over a hand towel she had found in one of the tattooing stations. She may have been sobbing before, but once Derek gave her a job, he knew she'd focus on that and keep it together. He knew his wife, though. She'd lose it again later, when they were alone, and she could fall apart. He was proud of both girls. This sort of situation was new to him, too, and he wasn't really sure how to handle everything. Derek knew he needed to at least appear like everything was going to be okay, even if he was unsure that it would be. There are no guarantees in life, after all. He said a quick silent prayer for Dominic to whatever god was up there listening.

Nicole sat down beside Derek after helping put the towel under his and Kate's hands. She leaned into her husband's shoulder and rubbed her best friend's arm in comfort. That was all she could do for now. They waited, hearing only the sounds of Kate's sweet whispers to Dominic, until they finally heard the beautiful wails of sirens coming towards them. Never again would any of them be annoyed by their blaring shrills. When they sounded in the future, they would think about the people on the other side, waiting for help.

Kate watched helplessly as Derek pulled her away so that the paramedics could do their job. She didn't want to leave him, and she wasn't thinking clearly. Derek convinced them to let her ride in the ambulance with Dominic. He held her shoulders firmly and looked at her. "Kate, are you with me?"

Kate was in a haze; she wouldn't take her eyes off of Dominic being moved onto the stretcher. But she finally turned her eyes to Derek.

"You're going with him. Nicole and I will be right behind you. Are you going to be okay?" He was a little worried about her mental health at the moment.

She nodded her head and fell into him. "Thank you," she said quietly.

He hugged her for a moment and then walked her out to the ambulance and helped hoist her up when it was her turn. He turned to Nicole, grabbed her. What if it had been her? What if he couldn't have gotten to her in time? He hated having those thoughts. But they reminded him of how lucky he was to have her in his life.

"Thank you for helping with her," Nicole said, as she framed his face with her hands. "I love you."

"I love you. Let's get to the hospital so she's not there alone."

Kate watched as her friends had their moment. She figured they were each thankful that the other wasn't hurt. With that thought, she looked down at Dominic. Still no sign of life, other than the slow beeping coming from the machine to show his heart was still pumping. She wasn't upset with Nicole or Derek. This was just how the chips fell, and she was thankful, too, that no one else got hurt. For the entire ambulance ride, she sat there, helpless, holding Dominic's hand and watching as these strangers fought to keep him alive.

CHAPTER TWENTY-ONE

Kate hung up the phone with Stan Murphy, one of the partners at the Murphy and Simmons Law Firm. One reason she wanted to stay with them, and become a partner there herself, was that they put family first. Stan was extremely understanding and agreed that she needed to stay until Dominic's condition looked more promising. Kate knew that she was running the risk of losing the Preston case. The case would be huge for her, but Dominic was worth it. Stan said he'd hold out as best he could, but, based on when she would return, he may have to turn it over to someone else. Secretly, she hoped it wouldn't be Ethan. She didn't have any bad wishes for him, but this was her baby, and if she couldn't have it, she didn't really want to know that he had gotten it.

She walked back into the hospital room and watched Carolyn Price holding her son's hand. He may be her sexy bad boy and a forty-year-old man, but that was still Carolyn's baby boy. Dominic was out of the woods for the most part but still under strict observation. Most of the medical terms were gibberish to Kate. But she had gathered that, while the bullet had missed all vital organs, there was some damage to his arteries that needed to be watched closely. Dominic had lost a lot of blood and, from what she could understand, his body had shut down to protect itself, hence him passing out at the shop. That was the layman's explanation for it, at least. He had been in the hospital for several hours, but it felt like days. The doctors had performed emergency surgery, so now he was on some pretty strong meds to sleep it off.

Kate wasn't sure what to say to Carolyn, who didn't know the whole story yet. She was currently grieving under the idea that this was all Mr. Drug Smuggler's fault. That was technically true, but how did she explain that this woman's youngest son was lying in the hospital because he took a bullet for her? Their relationship was somewhat fragile; the two women had just become friends. How was his mother going to take it when she found out? Kate realized it was best she hear it from her rather than Dominic.

"How is he?" she asked, walking towards Carolyn.

"Handsome as ever," Carolyn responded with a forced smile. What would she have done if she lost him? He was her diamond in the rough, her black sheep in the family. She wouldn't change a thing about him.

"I feel like you need to know how this happened." Kate's heart was beating like crazy. She wished she had Nicole here, with a huge shot of tequila for some liquid courage. Once Carolyn and Sean arrived, Nicole and Derek had headed back to the hotel to give them some privacy with their son.

"What do you mean, dear?" Carolyn looked confused.

Kate was used to being in control of her emotions. Now, she was so far outside of her comfort zone that she was having a hard time keeping a check on anything. Tears formed in her eyes as she took a deep breath.

"It's okay, dear. What's wrong?" Carolyn sounded so mothering that it only made it worse.

"The man was aiming at me. Dominic jumped in front of me," Kate spoke quickly so that she could get the sentence out. "I'm so sorry!" She finally let the tears flow.

"Oh, darling, please come here." Carolyn took Kate's hand. "I was just thinking to myself that I wouldn't change a thing about my son. One of the many wonderful things about him is how much he's willing to protect the ones he loves." She paused for a moment and looked at him. "Did you know that when the kids were little, even though he was the youngest, he grew the fastest? There were times when Nicky was standing up to bullies for his brothers. He's always been a protector. I am not surprised one bit, and I am not upset he chose to protect you. He loves you." She smiled sweetly and pulled Kate toward her in the chair. Kate tried to take in deep breaths so that she could stop the tears.

Sean Price returned from getting some coffee for the three of them to find the women hugging. Assuming that they were consoling each other over the possibility of the worst, he told them, "He's a Price, he'll pull through just fine."

Carolyn knew her husband. He was acting tough so as not to show any weakness. She was the only one privy to all sides of her husband; he'd tell her later how scared he truly was. She appreciated him keeping it light in the moment. It helped her to not assume the worst.

Sean handed his wife and Kate each a coffee from the cafeteria travel tray. Kate liked Sean the instant she met him. He was very tall, with black hair like his sons. Kate knew that Dominic got his eyes from his mother, but she recognized the Price nose. He had broad shoulders, a booming voice, and a bigger frame than Dominic's. Kate felt small next to him. He put his free arm around her. "Glad to finally be able to meet you. Wish it was under better circumstances. Like maybe a bottle of red and a nice steak."

"Honey, she's a vegetarian, too, remember," Carolyn chimed in.

"Huh? That works out well for Dominic. Okay, the wine can stay, but you can bring some tofu or something. You eat that stuff, right?"

Kate would have laughed if she wasn't in Dominic hospital room, worried for his health. His dad was such a real, say-what-you-mean kind of guy. She felt that way about herself, to an extent. Sean pulled it off probably far better than she did. Nicole always said Kate was very matter-of-fact. This might be what she meant. "Yes, I eat that stuff," she replied.

"I hear you're from Chicago," he stated.

Kate wasn't sure where he was going with that. Hopefully, he was merely trying to fill the air with conversation. She didn't want to get into any questions about the seriousness of her relationship with Dominic. Today made her realize she couldn't live without him, but she also knew that there was no need to rush anything.

"Yes, I just got the approval from my law firm to stay a few more days. At least until we know more about his condition," Kate said as she looked down at the sleeping Dominic.

"Law firm? You're a lawyer? Corporate or criminal? Always want to know if I have any free legal advice coming for work. But we also need a good one to help prosecute that asshole."

She liked the way he thought. "Divorce, actually," she smiled and shrugged her shoulders.

"Well, the wife and I are good. So, it looks like you're off the hook," he smiled at both women.

"Oh, Sean." Carolyn rolled her eyes, but Kate caught the loving look she gave her husband.

"When are the other boys going to get here?" Sean looked around, annoyed at their absence.

"I've been in touch with everyone. The boys are finishing up a meeting with the office. No one is sure if this Santino Cruz or Reyes or whatever-his-name was working alone. They're coordinating extra security. Your friend Gael has been brought on as a security consultant for us as well." Carolyn looked towards Kate. "Carrie will be here soon, and Natalie doesn't want to scare the twins. She has the nanny coming to watch the boys, and then she'll be here, too."

It warmed Kate's heart to be enveloped in Price family support and love. She was glad that they didn't seem to have any intentions of asking her to respect their privacy. She wasn't about to leave Dominic's side. What if he woke up, and she wasn't there? Yes, he'd have his family, but he saved her life. What if she wasn't there to thank him? Though she had been prepared for that fight with the Prices, Kate was relieved that it was one less battle to overcome.

...

Kate genuinely liked both of Dominic's sisters-in-law. Carrie told her that they'd been waiting for Dominic to finally fall in love, and both she and Natalie worried if they'd like the woman. Kate could tell that Natalie and Carrie had become like sisters; they had high hopes that Dominic's future wife would make a third sister for them. She figured their telling that story meant that they liked her. She smiled at the thought.

After some time, she heard two loud voices, long before their owners walked through the door. She immediately recognized Adrian, and she knew the other man was Justin, the oldest of the three Price sons. Both were dressed in business attire, somewhat disheveled by the events of the day- shirts untucked, sleeves rolled up, hair mussed.

The brothers and father were handsome, but none could compare to Dominic. Then again, Kate may have been a bit biased in her opinion. The brothers' eyes softened as they saw their baby brother laying helpless in the hospital bed, with tubes coming out of him.

"Any changes since we spoke?" Justin asked, looking down at Dominic.

"No changes. We're waiting for him to wake from surgery," Carolyn said, her voice slightly unsteady from the day.

"How are you doing, Mom?" he walked over to hug her.

"I've been better, honey, I'm glad we're all here now." She leaned into her oldest son's chest and let him be the strong one for now. Sean patted Justin on the back and gave Adrian a solemn hug.

"That son of a bitch," Adrian said. "Was I really jumping the gun with the added security?" He looked at Justin.

"At least he's in custody. We'll make sure he goes down for this," Justin said authoritatively, as he patted his brother's arm, keeping the other around his mother.

Carolyn took in a deep breath, feeling slightly better. "Boys, come meet Kate, the woman your brother was protecting."

Great, you couldn't have be one of those families that keeps secrets. Through everything, at least Kate's internal voice was still able to find some sarcasm.

"We were introduced last night. How you holding up?" Adrian asked, as he gave her a quick hug.

She loved this family. His brother was shot, and he thought to ask how she was doing. "I've been better, thank you," she smiled at him.

"Nice to meet you, Kate. I've heard Dominic finally found someone that could compete with his love for art," Justin said and put his arm around her. *These guys could be triplets*, Kate thought to herself. Justin did look a bit older, but otherwise, the resemblance between the three was striking.

"Oh, I don't want to compete with that. I loved his work before I met him." Kate smiled as best she could. She couldn't help feeling weird, talking about Dominic without him being part of the conversation. She realized his brothers were just putting on a brave face, but it felt like they were doing something wrong. Like talking behind his back. Then again, he very well may be able to hear them.

...

Dominic had been put in the largest room possible; Carolyn had made sure to that. Yet, with all of the family, it was still rather crowded. When visiting hours were over, all but his parents needed to leave. Kate was pacing in the corner as his brothers and their wives were kindly asked to finish their visit. Kate couldn't leave him. Carolyn and Sean both noticed her, and Sean went to the nurses' station while Carolyn comforted her.

"Sean is rather persuasive. He'll find a way to let you stay," she said to Kate, trying to calm her worries.

"Thank you for understanding." Kate hugged her. "I know I have Nicole and Derek here, but I just can't leave him."

"And I love you for that, dear," Carolyn said, hugging her for the millionth time over the past several hours. If anything could bring people together, it was fearing for a loved one's life.

···

Kate texted some updates to Nicole. The nurses checked on Dominic regularly, and the doctor said he should wake slowly as the medicine wore off. He needed to stay medicated for the pain. Though the dose would be reduced a bit, the doctor warned them that he might still be rather incoherent. Kate needed to remember not to worry if that happened.

After the doctor left, Sean passed out on the couch with his head back, snoring slightly. Carolyn looked exhausted but couldn't sleep. Of course she couldn't. She was a mother.

Kate had taken Dominic's hand again. She had been talking to him on and off all afternoon, not caring what his family heard. She wanted to make sure he could hear her voice, if it could make any kind of difference. She talked about everything she could think of. She remembered times they had spent together. Even with the short time they've known each other, she was surprised at how many stories she could think back on.

Kate was still holding his hand and rambling on about nonsense when he stirred. She called to his parents and leaned forward to look for any sign of life. Without any warning, he opened his eyes and looked at Kate.

"Thank God," was all he said, before his eyes rolled back into his head, and he was out again. He had tried to save her life, and now he was completely sure he had. He could sleep again.

CHAPTER TWENTY-TWO

Those two seconds Dominic was awake were amazing. Looking into his eyes was all Kate needed to recharge her batteries. She had been exhausted for the past few hours, but that brought her back. Now, it was a waiting game again. She played a few card games on her phone and worked on the brain teaser app that she was addicted to solving. Slowly, time went by.

When she was just about to get tired again, Dominic began to stir. Kate called out to his parents and began to run her fingers gently through his hair.

"Hey there, Nicky," she said softly, hoping his eyes would open. She wanted to see into his soul and know that he was okay.

Dominic moved his head back and forth a bit, as if he was fighting through the drugs to wake up. She heard a slight moan escape. It wasn't his normal forceful moan that he made when they were alone. This felt weak and that worried her a bit. Slowly, his eyes opened and searched for hers. "You stayed," he stated, voice scratchy.

It was what she had said to him their first morning together. She repeated his reply from that day. "I wasn't going anywhere."

He cleared his throat and asked for some water. After a few sips, he continued, "I didn't know...if I was dreaming. I could hear you talking. Everything is jumbled...mixed up... I can't piece it together…remember he was going to shoot you," Dominic's heart began to pound. "I couldn't...couldn't bear to lose you. I only saw you and... everything else faded away." He smiled and reached for her hand. Then realization dawned on his face. "Where are Tiffany and Reyes? Are Nicole and Derek okay?"

"Yes, babe. They are safe," Kate smiled and leaned over to kiss him. "The police arrested Reyes or Cruz or whoever he is. But Tiffany snuck out during everything. Gael is working with the police to find her, and they will."

"He can help find Tiffany?" Dominic's brain wasn't thinking clearly yet, but he knew he hadn't heard of Gael being any kind of private detective.

"He's some sort of blood hound," Kate told him. "This involves your family, and they have asked him to be a security consultant through all of it."

His parents had been very nice, giving them a moment together, but Kate knew they were dying to be with Dominic, too. She looked over at them, knowing his eyes would follow her gaze.

"Mom! Dad!" he exclaimed, sounding almost surprised.

"Oh, Nicky, we've been worrying something horrible. Don't you ever do that to us again, you understand, mister?" Carolyn smiled and leaned over and kissed his forehead.

"I've been telling her, you looked right as rain to me," Sean said, but Kate saw the relief in his eyes. "Glad you're back with us, son." He patted his shoulder.

Suddenly, Kate decided to mess with him a little bit. "You've missed a lot over the past six months," she told him. She figured Sean would get a kick out of it; she wasn't so sure about Carolyn.

"SIX MONTHS?!" Dominic shouted.

Uh oh! Kate thought, worried about his blood pressure.

Just as she suspected, Sean joined in on the fun. "Yep, you must have been pretty tired. We toyed with pulling the plug a few times, too."

Carolyn hit her husband's arm, but she smirked and didn't deny any of it. Deep down, she must have a pretty good sense of humor.

"I quit my job to be by your side until you woke. I knew it would eventually happen." Kate was still concerned about his blood pressure, but couldn't resist continuing with the joke.

Dominic started looking around the room in confusion. Kate couldn't let it go on any longer. "Oh, Nicky, we're just kidding. I'm sorry. Too soon?" She leaned in and nuzzled her head into his neck. God, even lying in a hospital bed, he smelled amazing.

Dominic turned his head into hers, laughing, and kissed the side of her cheek that he could reach. He loved her wicked sense of humor. "That's actually pretty funny. You had me really worried there for a minute." They both closed their eyes and enjoyed the moment together.

Sean's booming laugh brought them both back to the present. "In all seriousness, you've only been here overnight," Kate told Dominic. "You still scared us all to death. There was no reason for you to throw yourself in front of me."

Dominic lovingly placed his hand on her cheek, and she instinctively leaned her head into it. "No reason, huh?" he asked her.

Knowing he shouldn't be moving too much, she reached her body forward to kiss his lips and whispered, "I love you, Nicky."

"I love you," was all he said, and his eyes closed again.

...

Two days after his release, Dominic was still trying to figure out how to get around with the use of one arm while the other was in a sling, keeping his shoulder stable. Kate was doing everything for him, so he hadn't had to fend for himself just yet.

"You need to get back to work, babe," Dominic insisted. "You are not missing this case because of me!"

He readjusted himself on his couch. It hurt, but he wasn't about to let Kate know that. She had told him about the Preston case that she had landed. This could mean good things for her with the firm. That's what mattered right now. He would be fine.

Kate wasn't sure what to do. Work and Dominic were currently the two most important things in her life. How did she balance the two in this situation?

"What did the partner tell you again? Stan, right?" He hoped she would be honest about how quickly she needed to get back.

"I need to be back by Monday," she stated. "I've already checked with Nicole. I can leave at the crack of dawn Monday morning and go straight to the office. I'll gain an hour with the time change, so I can be in the office by 10am. I've emailed Mr. Preston already and set up an 11am lunch meeting with him." As she spoke, Kate adjusted the pillow behind him.

Dominic wanted to help her keep her eye on the prize. He loved watching her talk about work. He was raised by a mother that stayed home and, though he loved having her there as a kid, he also liked seeing Kate's strong work ethic. If they had a daughter, he'd like her to see that side, too. *Wow, now I'm thinking about children?*

"Anything exciting about this case yet? Is one spouse to blame, or is it more about splitting assets equally?"

"Well…" She sat down like she had the juiciest gossip to spill. "From what Mr. Preston tells me, Mrs. Preston has not been the doting wife he thought she was." She looked up, trying to remember the facts. "She's all kinds of crazy. First, they were supposed to be trying to have a baby. Yet, he found birth control pills. Then, he went snooping, though he said he wasn't proud of himself. He found condoms, and they don't use condoms. That led him to contact a private detective. Turns out she was having visits to their house from a young man multiple times a week. And when I say young, it sounds like it's barely-legal young!"

"The plot thickens," Dominic made a dramatic face.

"Yes! She claims he's her personal trainer. I asked him to look for some form of money trail that would show she's paying him. Given the amount she could be spending, it may help distinguish if he's there to assist her in her workouts at the gym or somewhere else." She giggled at the innuendo.

"Any kind of prenup?" he asked.

Kate appreciated that he knew such a pertinent question to ask. "Yes, they have one. But it doesn't stipulate anything as to faithfulness. However, he was smart enough to include that any assets they had going into the marriage were to stay with each party, should the marriage end. His company was already extremely successful when they married. He won't have to worry about her getting a share of that."

"I love it when you talk *lawyer*. You are the complete package: sexy and smart." He leaned towards her to kiss her lips.

Kate moved her body to straddle his lap. She didn't want him moving too much. He seemed so strong and capable, but she still worried. She ran her hands through his hair, brushing the longer pieces out of his face. Kate was grateful for how she was so fortunate to have this man love her. How was she lucky enough that she could straddle the sexiest artist alive? She agreed, Dominic was the complete package, too. She loved the man beneath her, his body, his handsome face, everything about his appearance. She was incredibly attracted to him, but she also loved the brain inside that gorgeous head, the creativity and talent that his body held.

Kate lightly kissed his lips. She bit down on his lower lip ever so slightly and pulled his hair back to give her access to his neck. She trailed kisses from one ear, all along his chin, over to the other ear. He moaned as he leaned back into the couch. She loved the sound of that moan, so unlike the weak one in the hospital. He may still be recovering, but her strong bad boy was back. He held onto her hips as she pushed her body into his. She could feel his hardness against her, and it sent chills through her body. How had she gone six months without being with a man, before Dominic? Now, a few days had her going crazy. She wanted Dominic inside of her, to feel every part of him.

Kate brought her lips back to his and kissed him deeply as she moved her hips faster over him. When Dominic began to fumble a bit with her shirt, she leaned her body back, lifted it up over her head, and tossed it across the room. She removed her bra, knowing he wasn't very capable of this part with only one working arm. Next, she stood up and removed her jeans, and Dominic groaned, realizing there was nothing beneath them. Then, she slowly unbuttoned his shirt to expose his amazing chest, not bothering with trying to remove it over his shoulder. She helped him slide off his jeans, with another sexy leather belt attached. How many did he have? When he was completely healed, he may just need to spank her with one.

There he was, half-naked and all hers. Kate climbed back on top of him. Not wanting to hurt him, she kept it slow and sensual. She rode him intimately, showing him how much she had missed his touch. Dominic explored her body with his good hand and kept a firm grip on her hip with the other. They relished their time together on that lazy Saturday afternoon, home from the hospital and together, before she needed to leave for Chicago.

"So, how often do you go commando?" Dominic peered at her from under his lashes. They were still catching their breath, Kate curled up into his good shoulder.

"And lose the element of surprise? I don't think so," Kate smiled. "I like keeping you on your toes."

Dominic moaned, realizing that any point in the future, she could be commando under her clothes.

They lay together, still naked except for Dominic's shirt. Kate's face was leaned right up against a swirl of blue on his chest. She thought of how much they had been through together in such a short time. Her mother once told her that you should go through something difficult with someone in order to know how strong your relationship is. Kate smiled to herself, thinking about what a great job she and Dominic had done in navigating the past week. She had cared for him and done prep work for her case, always keeping an eye on her sexy patient. The experience had only brought them closer together.

Dominic had jumped in front of her to save her life. How many people said, "I'd take a bullet for you?" How many people got to prove it?

Thinking back on everything reminded Kate of why they were in the shop in the first place- her getting a tattoo with Nicole. She knew that Dominic had put his manager Jason in charge of cleaning up the shop. She wondered how that was going. "Any word from Jason? Is everything back to normal at the shop?"

"Yes, he said there wasn't much to do. Since I was nice enough to keep the bullet inside of me, it didn't damage anything," Dominic joked, though Kate didn't find the memory funny.

"I'm not sure I'm ready to go back there just yet," she snuggled further into his good shoulder.

"I get that," he said and kissed the top of her head.

"I still want you to do my tattoo with Nicole," she looked up at him and smiled. "I don't think I would ever want someone else to tattoo me. I know it sounds stupid, but it would feel like I was cheating on you. Even if you were there."

Dominic laughed and rubbed her arm lovingly. "Okay, we'll figure something out. I can always have my equipment sent here," he told her. "Check with Nicole. We could do it before you leave."

"So… you could tattoo with one arm tied behind your back?" she laughed at him. "You're that good?"

"I'm that good!" he responded, imitating her tone. "Seriously, though, that design is simple, and it's on your wrist. Luckily, I'm right handed, and, if you hold still, it shouldn't be an issue."

"'Hold still?' Easy for you to say. You're the one doing the stabbing with your mean little gun, not the one getting stabbed."

Dominic laughed at her in response. "Do you think these were drawn on with markers?" He pointed to the art all over his chest and shoulders.

"Point taken. How quickly can you get your stuff here?" She raised her eyebrows in excitement.

"I'll have an artist bring the stuff by now," he answered back, picking up his phone.

"Perfect!" Kate jumped up and grabbed hers. She sent Nicole a text, hoping she was on board with the idea.

...

Once again, Dominic held a tattoo gun up, ready to permanently mark her body. "Are you ready?" he said, with a twinkle in his eye.

"Do you enjoy hurting me?" she teased.

"Not one bit. I just love that there's a piece of me always with you." And with that, the gun came to life.

Nicole held Kate's hand while he began to form the friendship symbol. She looked up at her friend to try and ignore the pain. She realized quickly that her wrist was more sensitive than her shoulder, wincing as the gun dug into her skin. She looked into Nicole's eyes, remembering everything they'd been through together since college. Nicole smiled back, and Kate figured she was thinking about the same thing.

Derek walked up behind Nicole. "You're doing great," he told Kate.

"Thanks. This hurts!" She closed her eyes as Dominic redrew over an already sensitive area.

"It'll be worth it, though," Derek reminded her.

The entire thing only took about fifteen minutes. A long fifteen minutes. Soon, Nicole would be in the chair, and she was dying to get there. All it took was seeing a tattoo being done, and she wanted another one. She wasn't covered in them, hers all being small little accents, but she did still have quite a few.

When Kate was finished, she looked down at the gorgeous friendship symbol, now permanently part of her body. She loved it and loved it even more since Dominic was the one to put it there.

"What do you think?" Dominic asked both women.

"It's perfect," Kate said, watching him cover it for protection. She was definitely sure that tattoos were addictive now. Though she would be smart about it, given her profession. This symbol was small enough to add a cuff bracelet and go completely unnoticed.

"Gotta say, this is pretty cool, seeing a tattoo done at your place and not a tattoo shop," Derek commented, as he watched everything going on.

"Kind of like a tattoo party. The artist brings his supplies, and all of the people at the party get tattoos, one after another. Artists can clean up at a party," Dominic explained.

"I've never heard of that... Interesting," Derek replied.

Now, it was Nicole's turn. "You're an old pro. This should be a breeze for you," Kate said to her friend.

"I'm just so excited the world-famous Dominic Price will be tattooing me!" Nicole jumped up and down, joking with Dominic.

"Do you want the friendship symbol or a flying penis?" he threatened with a laugh. "Now sit."

Nicole and Kate kept their eyes on each other while a symbol of their relationship was again tattooed onto one of them. Kate was reminded, all over again, of everything that they had been through together. She couldn't believe that she may have found a way to love her more.

CHAPTER TWENTY-THREE

It was time to say goodbye again. Though Dominic still couldn't drive, he insisted on coming along in the car to see Kate off. It was 6:00am and still dark outside, though hints of orange and red had begun to fill the sky along the water's edge, like a huge paint brush had swiped watercolors across the horizon. Kate noticed Dominic watching it, too, and she wondered if he wanted to paint every beautiful thing that he saw. His work didn't look like anything from nature, but was he being inspired this very moment?

"I wish you could come with me," Kate said to him, as she nuzzled into his good shoulder. "I'm sorry again for how I left us last time."

"Babe, you've apologized a million times." Dominic tried to soothe her conscience. "I know that relationships, especially long-distance ones, are scary."

"I should have had the faith in us that you did," she reminded them both.

Dominic didn't respond. He kind of agreed with her, but he also knew that it was the over-thinking, intelligent brain of hers that was scared before, not her heart.

"How soon can you fly again?" Kate asked, hoping the length of time would change from the last time she had asked the question.

"The doctor needs to give me the once over on Friday. If I get the okay, I'll meet you at your place after work." Dominic said, kissing the top of her head. In actuality, the doctor had told him he could come in on Wednesday. As soon as he heard that, Dominic decided to surprise Kate. Knowing they both loved surprises, he wanted to create a new, happy one at her apartment. This was going to be a difficult secret to keep, but Dominic would try.

"We'll make this work!" Kate exclaimed to them both.

"We will," Dominic agreed.

Kate felt completely different boarding the plane this time. The sense of dread was gone. Her heart was full, instead of empty. Missing Dominic was still in the front of her mind, but this time, there wasn't a worry about the future. Neither of them could promise forever, she knew that. Her career would always offer that reminder. However, she knew they would figure this out together.

It was Monday morning and, God willing, he'd be in her apartment Friday evening. That meant there were three days in between when she wouldn't see him. She could do three days. The Preston case would keep her busy.

Kate leaned the plush seat back as far as it would allow and closed her eyes. Sleep hadn't come easy the past few days. She barely closed her eyes in the hospital and worried about Dominic when they were at his place. Any movement or sound from him had woken her. Hoping she could catch up on a few hours now, she tried to drift off.

…

Dominic was determined to get the okay to fly on Wednesday. Taking care of himself and his shoulder was the first priority. Carolyn happily agreed to come and dote on her youngest son in Kate's absence. With her waiting on Dominic, his shoulder would heal faster. Carolyn loved his idea of surprising Kate in Chicago and wanted to help make that happen.

When Dominic arrived back at his place, Carolyn was already there, with an enormous spread across his breakfast bar. Knowing his mother well, Dominic guessed that she ordered in from a restaurant. She wasn't a woman you'd usually find in the kitchen. Carolyn was very understanding about his eating choices. If it were Justin and Adrian coming over, they'd have a pile of bacon and sausage waiting for him. Not his mother. She always thought of everything and tended to go a bit overboard. Especially when she was feeling guilty and making up for her deplorable actions. There were eggs scrambled together with onions and peppers. Sliced tomatoes and avocado were lined along cubed pieces of cheese. A bowl of fruit sat next to a platter with pancakes and toast piled high.

"Nicky, dear," Carolyn sang, approaching him with open arms. Not wanting to hurt him, she leaned toward his good side and hugged him lightly.

"Thank you, Mom," he said, hugging her back. "I'm starving and glad you're here." They stayed like that for a few moments, mother and son, comforting each other. "I miss her."

"I know, darling," Carolyn rubbed the small of his back. He towered over her, strong and masculine, but forever her baby.

"I forgive you, Mom." He knew it was all that needed to be said.

Carolyn sighed. Of course he forgave her. He was so much like his father. "Let's get you better so that you can surprise her in a few days."

Carolyn walked Dominic over to the table. She prepared his plate with a bit of everything. He was going to need his strength, and that should start with a good breakfast. The less he moved his shoulder, the faster everything would heal. Planning to do as much as she could, Carolyn brought over the plate and filled his glass with orange juice from the pitcher on the table.

Dominic laughed as she tried to open his napkin for him. "I think I can do the napkin, Mom."

"Very well," she smiled and sat down next to him. "Your brothers have both called me. You remember your friend Gael has been working with them as a security consultant for the family. He would like to talk with you about that Reyes/Cruz man."

Dominic sighed. This was the man that shot him. The man that tried to shoot Kate. Talking about Reyes or Cruz or whoever-the-fuck-he-was wasn't tops on his list. "I'll give him a call after breakfast."

"He's going to come by," Carolyn said. "I suggested a breakfast meeting, hence so much food. I can make myself scarce."

Dominic appreciated her offer, but he didn't have anything to hide about what happened. "Mom, you can stay."

"He should be here any minute," she said and went to make herself a small plate.

...

Kate realized she had missed her office. She had missed the wall of ebony shelves, full of law books, and the solid desk and table, made from the same wood, where she spread out her books to stay organized while she researched. Two comfortable white chairs brightened the room and offered seating to clients. A small corner table held a large flower arrangement, her way of adding a touch of femininity to the room. The place was a physical representation of all her hard work had achieved.

All through law school, she had imagined been finished, graduated, with an elegant corner office. Her own mother had stayed home with three kids, her parents having started a family when they were young. Her mother was a member of a generation that still went to college for their MRS degrees. They landed the doctors and lawyers; it wasn't popular yet to become one themselves. Mom worked hard to teach her children that both parents' roles were equally important, and Kate grew up believing that her mother was completely happy with her choice. Then one day, in her senior year of high school, she overheard her mother talking with a friend, staring down the fact that she and Kate's father were about to become empty-nesters. She had sounded so lost and confused, unsure of what to do with herself now that her children were gone. Had she made all the right choices? What if she had worked outside the home?

Hearing her mother's words, a burning desire to succeed grew inside of Kate, ultimately manifesting in the dream of a partnership and a corner office. Looking around the room now, Kate reminded herself that it wasn't quite a corner office, not yet. But that didn't seem to matter so much anymore. There was a new prize in her life, taking a place right beside her career goals. It wasn't an office, wasn't an inanimate thing at all. Her bad boy on Ocean Drive, wounded when he saved her life. He was her prize now.

Kate sat at her desk and turned on her computer. With a few minutes to spare before her meeting, she reviewed her notes and got her head in the game.

...

Carolyn let Gael into Dominic's condo, and Dominic stood up from the table to greet him (recovering from surgery was not a reason to forget his manners).

"Please, sit," Gael said to him, as he shook Dominic's good hand. "You look good. How are you feeling?"

"Everything seems to be healing nicely, thanks," Dominic replied, reclaiming his chair.

"Go make yourself a plate. I'm going to read while the two of you talk," Carolyn said as she walked towards the balcony. Dominic still wasn't concerned about what she would hear, but appreciated her gesture.

"Have you got some news for me?" Dominic asked Gael.

"*Sí, amigo*," Gael responded. "I found the girl, Tiffany, at a relative's house. She wasn't hiding from the Price family. She was worried that Reyes would send someone for her, or come himself, if he was released from police custody.

"She *should* have been hiding from my family! That bitch smiled as a gun was pointed towards us!" Dominic knew they didn't have a close relationship, and she didn't owe him any personal allegiance. But she put them in danger. Over money. If Kate had been hurt, Tiffany would have needed protection from him!

"I understand," Gael told him. "I was finally able to convince her that I did not work for Reyes or his gang. An officer was waiting to take her into custody."

"Good," Dominic said, nodding his head as he piled more food onto his fork.

"She maintains that he forced her to help him. She will not admit to taking any money. The department has given me the professional courtesy of allowing me to speak with her. I'm not sure she will know if Reyes was working on this alone, but we'll find out what she knows," Gael stated matter-of-factly. "I found your employee, Jax, while I was looking for Tiffany. He would like to speak to you as well." Gael paused. "I think once you see him, you'll be inclined to forgive him."

"What does that mean?" Dominic asked.

"Reyes was not happy that Jax was caught. His arm was broken. I saw the pictures of what he looked like after the beating. The cuts and bruises healed. Some scars have remained though."

Oh fuck! Dominic thought to himself. He had been so angry with Jax, he wouldn't listen to a word he said. Thinking back on that scene in the office, which he often did, he realized that Jax wanted to tell him something. It seemed now like Jax may have wanted to warn him. Maybe he was too scared. "Damn it!" Dominic exclaimed, "Jax has nothing to do with the port. He was just a poor kid trying to get his chance at tattooing. Working the front counter was his in. He was learning from some of the guys."

Dominic's head hung a bit, and he pushed his plate away. Suddenly, the smell of eggs, mixed with the vegetables, made his stomach turn. Smuggling, and all that came with it, wasn't the reason he avoided the family business, just disinterest. It was a sad reality of an industry that he wasn't technically a part of. Apparently, being a Price was close enough; those around him may always be affected. He felt like he owed the poor kid an apology.

"Is it okay if he stops by here this morning as well?" Gael asked. "He said he'd like to apologize to you."

"That kid doesn't owe me any apology. I'm the one that's sorry he got into all this mess. Is this the price people pay for knowing my family?" He gave a bitter laugh. "No pun intended." Still shaking his head, his thoughts went straight to Kate. He wasn't going to let anything happen to her. He needed to call the real estate agent and make some plans to see a few places while he was in Chicago this week. Since he still wasn't sure whether to tell Kate about his condo idea or surprise her, he'd schedule a few showings while she was at work on Wednesday. Then maybe he'd show her his favorite, before signing on the dotted line.

"The fault lies with Santino Reyes," Gael replied simply.

Dominic knew he was right, but he still couldn't imagine what poor Jax went through because that maniac was looking for a way into his family's business. How did Justin and Adrian handle this shit? Were they always worried for their families? Dominic had never been a man to run from something. This wasn't exactly running, though. It was protecting someone he loved. Dominic wasn't willing to risk another gun being pointed at Kate's head. Or anything else that could happen to her.

…

Kate's case was progressing well. Jack Preston was a nice, older man. She hated to see his marriage fail this way. Before returning to South Beach, she had prepared all the initial paperwork and worked with Jack to file the petition for divorce. They had met briefly a few times, going over his financial information. He was a very wealthy man, and it turned out that his younger wife was going to fight for as much of it as possible. She contested almost every point in the petition.

As Kate worked to prove that Mrs. Preston was bringing men into the house, she realized that she hadn't thought about Dominic or their relationship throughout any of the sad stories of Mrs. Preston's cheating. She smiled to herself, proud that she could keep these things separate from her feelings about her personal life.

But even the most skilled lawyer needs the occasional break. And so Kate found herself walking into the office kitchen for a quick coffee. She never asked her assistant to bring it to her; Kate was perfectly capable of making it herself. And performing the mundane task helped her clear her head for a few minutes. Stirring in her cream and sugar, her thoughts on Dominic, she absent-mindedly turned around and almost walked right into Ethan. She really had to stop doing that!

"Sorry," she muttered, not wanting to look up from her coffee cup. They hadn't seen each other since their lunch, the day after Dominic's surprise visit. Though that ended relatively well, it didn't take away from the fact that Ethan thought she led him on. Lifting her eyes ever so slightly to sneak a peek at his face, Kate didn't see what she had been so crazy about for all those years. He was still classically handsome, but so were half of the men out there. Maybe truly being in love with someone takes those old desires away.

"I heard about what happened," Ethan said to her. He wasn't sure how to continue in a way that made his words sound at least a little sincere. "I bet that was scary."

Kate took a sip of her coffee, stalling for some time. "Extremely. I hope to never have a gun pointed at my head again, that's for sure."

How did I go all that time not seeing how wonderful she is? Ethan asked himself. Ever since he had heard the story, Ethan had tried to imagine if he would have been brave enough to jump in front of a bullet for her. For anyone, for that matter. He'd like to think so, but until the moment of truth, no one could say for sure. He was mad at Kate and at that Dominic guy, but mostly he was mad at himself. Looking at Kate, he was frustrated that he hadn't asked her out on day one, when she walked into that same kitchen for her cup of coffee, wearing a grey dress and black boots. She still wore it occasionally; it was his favorite outfit of hers. It is very true that you don't know what you have until it's gone. He could have had her as his girlfriend for years. Who knows, maybe his wife and mother of his children. Now what did he have? A front row seat to watching her every day. Maybe she'd move to Florida to be with this Dominic. That might be better for him in the long run.

"Well… I'm glad everything turned out okay." He didn't know what else to say.

"Thanks. I've got some emails to catch up on." She smiled at him and walked out of the kitchen. *That was brutal!* she thought to herself. Was it always going to be awkward around him? Hopefully not. They had been friends in the beginning, maybe they could get back to that. It still amazed her, how her idea of the perfect man had changed so drastically. Sitting back down at her desk, she smiled, thinking about Dominic. She had memorized everything about him. Like his particular smell- a mixture of his soap, cologne, and natural masculine scent. Closing her eyes, it felt like he was there. She leaned back into her chair, imagining it was his body she was snuggling against. Could she make it until Friday without him?

With that thought, Kate picked up the phone and dialed his number. She had made a point to commit it to memory, perhaps out of a bit of nostalgia for the days before cell phones, when there were no contact lists to do it for you.

Dominic answered almost immediately. "Hey, babe."

"Hi...." She sighed into the phone. "I don't have much time to talk, but I needed to hear your voice."

"I'm glad you called. My mother is taking great care of me in your absence," he joked.

"That makes me feel better. I'm glad she's there." Kate was more comfortable knowing he wasn't alone.

"Now go be super lawyer and put the bad guys away."

"The cheaters and liars? I'm on it." God, she missed him.

"That's my girl. Someone needs to stick up for us good guys."

Just the sound of his voice could make her melt. "Yes, you are one of the good guys. I love you," Kate told him, wishing he was there.

"I love you, too," he replied.

I can make it to Friday, Kate reminded herself.

CHAPTER TWENTY-FOUR

Jax arrived just after Dominic hung up with Kate. Hearing her voice was going to help him get to Wednesday. He needed to get out of this godforsaken city and back to her.

Staring across the table from Jax, Dominic wanted to hurt Santino Reyes Cruz. Thinking all three names to himself, he rolled his eyes, frustrated with everything. "Why the fuck are half the people calling him Reyes and half are calling him Cruz? Which is it?" he exclaimed.

Gael answered, "We take both our father's and mother's last names in Mexico. His father's last name is Reyes, his mother's is Cruz. His full name is Santino Reyes Cruz. Here in the States, most of you only take the father's family name. He is more commonly known here as Santino Reyes. Cruz is helpful at giving him aliases. You should see his rap sheet. He's listed under every combination of those three names."

"Wonderful," Dominic stated, pushing himself away from the table and heading for the couch. "Let's hope he's not able to get away with this."

The other men joined him in the living room. Gael spoke first, "He has a long list of priors on his record, and the prosecutor is pushing for attempted murder. That will get him plenty of prison time, for sure."

"Am I going to have to testify? Will Kate and the others?" Dominic asked. It hadn't occurred to him before. He wasn't keen on any of them reliving the experience, and he hoped that at least the other three wouldn't have to. He especially didn't want Kate to have to tell her story to a courtroom full of strangers.

"The prosecutor will most likely want you to testify," Gael replied, knowing Dominic wouldn't like the answer. "As for Derek and the girls, he will want to talk with them. If their experience can help the case, he may ask for them to testify as well."

"Fuck!" Dominic leaned back on the couch cushion and rubbed his head with his good hand. "I'm done with this shit. This Price name has gotten me nothing but trouble!"

"Remember, *cabrón*, this is no one's fault but Reyes."

"Dominic, I'm sorry I didn't warn you," Jax said, staring out the window at nothing in particular.

"I think you tried," Dominic said, trying to make eye contact with the poor guy.

"I shouldn't have been so vague. I should have told you or gone to the police."

"If he found out you went to the police, it could have been way worse," Gael added in.

With Gael's statement, Dominic looked closely at Jax's face. There was a scar that went the length of his right cheek, most likely from a knife. Another scar divided the eyebrow above his left eye. Dominic guessed it was the result of stitches repairing damage from repeated blows to his eye. Jax was lucky to be alive. "Way worse" probably meant death. And Jax's death most likely wouldn't have stopped what happened at the shop. Dominic would still be sitting here with Gael, but Jax would be in the ground.

"Before I had the pleasure of meeting Reyes, my brother told me it was like the man didn't have a soul." Dominic paused. "You must have been terrified to tell him you got fired. I'm sorry, man."

"I tried to tell him over the phone," Jax spoke quietly. "But they came to my place. It was crazy, Dom. I've been in regular fights. You know, the school yard, at the bars when guys get out of control. All normal stuff. This wasn't normal. They didn't even wake me up first. I woke up with a bat to my head. The guy didn't hit me hard enough to knock me out. They wanted me to feel the pain." Jax stopped and took in a deep breath before continuing. "I didn't think I was going to make it. I thought 'this is it', and you know what? I thought of my parents."

Jax paused and looked out the window. The others instinctively knew not to speak. Jax didn't seem done. So, they waited until he spoke again, "I moved out so young. My mother found weed in my room. Weed, of all things! She told my father, and he was so strict. He kicked me out. I was seventeen years old. I crashed at some friends' houses here and there. Even though I knew I'd never become a business man or anything, I wanted my diploma," Jax laughed. "I knew I was fucked without that. I wasn't going to end up on the streets. My parents kicked me out as a kid, and the first thing I thought of, when I thought I was going to die, was them!" He sniffed slightly, trying to cover the urge to cry.

"Have you talked to them since?" Dominic asked. Being so close to his family, he couldn't imagine that sort of situation.

"I've never thought about it, not once in five years, until now. But I just can't pull the trigger." Jax kept his eyes focused on the view outside. "Who kicks their kid out of the house over weed? Whenever I get close, that's what makes me stop dialing the phone. Though I've been worried about money, so I think about calling them from time to time."

"You know that you're welcome back at the shop, right?" Dominic interrupted him. "I'm going to catch you up on your bills, and we're going to get your training finished up so you can get your own station." He wished he had known all of this about Jax. The guy had never said a thing. Just came in as a kid from South Beach that wanted to learn the ropes. After everything he went through, Dominic was going to make this right.

"You sure?" Jax's voice practically cracked, shooting up a few octaves in surprise.

"Of course. We'll go in later today and tell everyone the good news. They've missed you around there," Dominic smiled. No one said anything directly to him, but he heard the whispers that Jax was missed. No one seemed to believe that he would have stolen anything.

"Thank you. It's hard out there right now. Shops aren't hiring. I appreciate it." Jax looked relieved. "I know I'm not as cute as my replacement, especially now," he added, gesturing to his scars.

"Well, look how well she turned out," Dominic smiled, trying to lighten the mood.

...

"I'm coming tomorrow night," Nicole told Kate. They needed this surprise to work. She knew that Dominic needed a reason to make sure Kate didn't have plans after work. Nicole figured she could keep Kate from scheduling a client dinner or drinks with girlfriends, so that Dominic wouldn't have to be waiting outside her door until she got home.

"You don't have to do that. Dominic will be here on Friday." Kate wanted to tell her best friend to get on the plane immediately, but knew she shouldn't.

"Well, tough. I'm coming. Derek's trying to be super-secret spy and help Gael with this investigation of Reyes. I'm getting bored."

Nicole tried to sound pitiful, but Kate wasn't buying it. It made her laugh into the phone. "I needed that, thank you. Okay, I'll be home by 5:30pm," Kate said, still laughing. "Thanks, Nic. Some girl time is just what I need. Actually, I need Dominic. But you'll do." Kate took a deep breath, feeling better with that laugh. "And Nic, I'm sorry for being so difficult with this Dominic thing. I hope I never insulted your relationship with Derek. You know that I'd never do that on purpose, right? I'm in awe of you two. I didn't think it could also happen for me."

"Oh, sweetheart!" On the other side of the phone, Nicole shook her head a little. "First, you could never scare me off that easily. And it would be impossible for you to offend me. We've both said it in the past. You are your own worst enemy when it comes to love."

"Do you think it's just the job?" Kate wondered out loud. "My parents are crazy happy together. My brothers' marriages seem perfect."

"I don't know," Nicole answered honestly. "Tom, back in college, did a number on you. You used to think you guys would get married."

"Oh my God, I haven't thought of Tom in years," Kate's jaw dropped in realization. "He did fuck with my head. I trusted all my boyfriends before him, and I bet they were all cheating on me."

"There you go," Nicole stopped her. "Why would they all cheat on you?"

"Okay, okay, point taken," Kate continued. "What I meant was that I never had trust issues before Tom. I blindly believed that 'happily ever after' just happened for people. I thought Tom was my happily ever after. I bet the combination of heartbreak, then going right into law school, screwed me up. I was in my post-breakup funk when I decided everyone was getting divorced, so I should just go into pre-law. I figured the industry would thrive." Kate couldn't believe how all the dots had just connected. Could Tom have been the reason she became a lawyer? She did love her work; she didn't regret her decision. But it was amazing to realize how things played out in people's lives. If Tom hadn't broken up with her, she may have stayed in the Art History field. She pondered again if she would have met Dominic through that avenue. Maybe they were destined to be together.

"That'll be two-hundred dollars for the therapy session," Nicole informed her.

"The check is in the mail," Kate laughed back.

"Luckily, I don't think this is permanent," Nicole continued. "Now you know why you're leery of everlasting love, but you've seen real-life examples of successful marriages. Plus, now you have a relationship with Dominic."

"Yes, my Nicky," Kate closed her eyes, smiling as she thought about that man.

Nicole laughed into the phone. "It really doesn't bother him when you call him that?"

"No, *Love*, it doesn't." Kate replied.

Nicole laughed again at her friend's wit. "Good one. It is cute, though, because he's so far from what you'd picture as a *Nicky*."

"Exactly. Plus, you got dibs on Nic."

223

"Yep, that name is mine."

After finishing their conversation, Kate curled up into her pillows and drifted off to sleep.

Her mind took her back to South Beach Tattoo, on that fateful day. But this time, it wasn't just Santino and Tiffany that surprised them. With Tiffany were all the women she had met through Dominic. Tiffany; Carolyn Price; Amanda; and Dominic's sisters-in-law, Natalie and Carrie, all stared at Kate and her friends with hate in their eyes. Santino wasn't alone either- his whole gang was there. Kate must have created a look for their gang based on movies she had seen in the past. They all wore the same baggie jeans, with white t-shirts and blue plaid shirts buttoned only at the top. Each one displayed a blue bandana. Most had them around their head, though a few hung them from their pockets, and a couple had them wrapped over their mouths and noses to hide their faces. Those guys scared her the most.

In her dream, Kate couldn't reach Dominic. She wasn't right behind him, holding onto his arms for comfort. Now she was alone, everyone out of arm's reach. It felt like Kate's heart stopped. Everything formed into a tunnel, and sounds became distant. Everything but the evil people in front of her. All the women were saying horrible things to her. They laughed and pointed, telling her that Dominic would never save her. Telling her that she deserved what was about to happen. The men eyed her up and down, with disgusting thoughts in their minds. She looked for Dominic, but he was a blur. She could barely hear him calling for her, trying to get to her, but somehow never able to. Derek and Nicole vanished. Now it was just Dominic and her against all these people.

Somewhere in her dreamlike state, Kate knew this wasn't real. She fought with her subconscious to wake up, yelling at herself not to believe what she saw, telling herself it was just a dream. Yet it seemed so real. The man next to Santino hit Dominic, hard. A few others grabbed his arms as he staggered back. Then Santino slowly walked up to Kate. Terrified, she backed away as far as possible, until she was stopped by the front door. "I'm going to take this out on you. Slowly… And I'm going to make your boyfriend watch."

Kate shot up in bed, wide awake and unable to catch her breath, no matter how hard she tried. Her body and sheets were soaked. Tears mingled with the sweat covering her face.

Why would this nightmare start now? Would this be the only one, or should she expect a visit from Santino every night? Grabbing a throw blanket from the end of her bed, Kate walked into her small living room and curled up on the couch. She was too scared and exhausted to change the sheets; the couch would work for rest of the night. She wasn't ready to fall back to sleep, anyway.

Kate's brain worked in funny ways, analyzing the situation to make it less scary. She would have expected nightmares to come right after that traumatic event. Why didn't she have any? She was at the hospital in the beginning, too focused on Dominic to allow for any dreams. Back at his condo, he still held her attention, and Kate never allowed herself to fully fall asleep. Then what about last night? Her first night back in her apartment and alone. That would have been the perfect time for a nightmare. Yet, she was sleep-deprived. Maybe too tired to dream? That all made sense. Now how was she going to stop them in the future? Kate needed her sleep, the same as the next person. This was going to be seriously inconvenient, if she couldn't get a good night's sleep every night.

It was only a dream! It wasn't real! That was her new mantra. Santino was still in some kind of county jail, and when it came down to it, Tiffany wasn't dangerous. She was a pipsqueak, no bigger than Kate herself. And Kate was in Chicago, far removed from all of that right now. Kate was a realist as well. If she was in South Beach for a visit and the nightmares returned, Dominic would be there as comfort. For now, she wasn't going to tell him about them. Not until they became a problem. He needed to focus on getting better so he could visit her.

It was only a dream, she told herself. It wasn't real… It was only a dream, it wasn't real…

CHAPTER TWENTY-FIVE

Dominic wanted to know more about Reyes' trial before he got to Chicago. He wanted to be able to give Kate some closure, if that was possible, and he knew that information would help her process everything. It would also help them know if the prosecutors would want to see Kate. Derek agreed to go with him as another witness.

Gael met them at the station. As he led them back to what Dominic guessed was an interrogation room, he wondered why Gael wasn't a cop. From what Kate had told him about his past with the Mexican authorities, Dominic would have thought the academy was a perfect fit for him. Maybe Gael had more autonomy as a consultant. Less rules to follow. Still, he fit the part perfectly. He walked them through what to expect. Neither Dominic nor Derek were in any kind of trouble, but Gael prepared them for how thorough Officer Zink would be. He told them that they would probably be repeating themselves multiple times, or asked for further detail. Dominic knew he needed to try to remember every detail he possibly could. Derek would have to take over once the gun was fired; Dominic's brain had produced no memories between that and waking in the hospital.

Dominic figured this had to be an open and close case. The police had Santino, the gun, and the drugs in their possession. His own testimony should only serve to corroborate the prosecution's evidence. They also had Tiffany. It was still unclear if she'd be prosecuted with Reyes or separately. Gael and Dominic agreed to leave Jax out of it for now. He wasn't at the scene and had gone through enough already.

Officer Zink was a large man with a wide smile, kind eyes, and salt-and-pepper hair cut short. Derek and Dominic began their story rather stone-faced. But Zink reminded them that, though they were in the station, they weren't being interrogated, just having a conversation to teach him all the details. That put them both at ease, especially when he told them to call him, "Big Z, just like the rest of my friends". Between the two of them, they hadn't missed a detail. Nothing particularly caught the attention of Big Z, until Dominic said he had seen four bricks of cocaine on the ledge. Or what he figured was cocaine.

Big Z stopped him. "You saw four bricks?" He took out a folder and flipping through a few pages, as though double-checking something in the notes.

"Yes, I saw four. There may have been more, but that's all I saw." Dominic looked up at the ceiling, trying to remember.

"Did you notice the bricks?" Big Z turned to Derek.

"There were two stacks with two bricks each on the ledge," Derek agreed. "I noticed because I've never seen that much blow in one place before."

Big Z rubbed his chin, which was covered with the white stubble of a few days' neglected shaving. "Hmmm. We need to have another chat with little Tiffany." Big Z looked over at Gael. "There are only three bricks in custody."

"In all that commotion, she thought to grab a brick of cocaine?" Derek was surprised.

"She could fetch twenty-five grand from that in South Beach. She was staring at a hundred grand in front of her. Probably figured no one would know how many were originally there." Big Z shook his head, realizing there was a brick of cocaine hidden somewhere in the city. A needle in a cocaine haystack, but it was there. "Let's get back to what you remember, and we'll follow up on that later," Big Z told them both. "I'm sure you'd rather not spend your whole day in this place."

"Whatever you need," Dominic replied, and Derek nodded in agreement.

...

The Price jet landed safely in Chicago. Dominic was surprised that, even in June, there was still a chill in the air. He hadn't expected that. A black town car was waiting at the Chicago Executive Airport. He knew that Kate always flew in and out of Midway airport so that she could take the train, but he wasn't about to trust himself with the mass transportation of Chicago. He'd get lost in five minutes.

The trip into the city was quick. His doctor's appointment had been first thing in the morning, giving him a chance to be in Chicago before lunch. Now he was meeting a realtor and checking out three condos, all within walking distance of Kate's building. Knowing that they shouldn't rush into things, it was best to be close, but not too close. Then, when it was time for them to take the next step, his place would be ideal, since she would still be close to her office and everything she loved about the city.

A water view was important, so he chose condos that were on the highest floors possible. The first two were nice, and he could have been happy with either choice, but the third was definitely it. Even the building reminded him of his building in South Beach, the same cubes of glass scattered across its face, with thick lines from the balconies providing contrast to the glass. He loved it.

The realtor listed off the building's amenities and had to pause in the middle to catch her breath. Along with the typical work out facilities and pools, the list included some surprises that he hadn't expected. There was a garden and indoor/outdoor community kitchen with a private dining area to entertain, if they needed more space than their condo could fit. He would love to hang out by the fire pit, and, if they had children, there was a huge playroom for when the weather didn't allow for the playground.

Once inside, he couldn't wait to show Kate. It was still modern, but the place had an elegant feel. The floor-to-ceiling windows were contemporary, but thick crown molding framed each pane. The color palette consisted of trendy shades of slates and grays. The dining area sat in a corner of windows, and he could immediately imagine their intimate dinners together. A comfortable-looking blue couch filled one living room wall, with a plush white chair next to it. The television was hidden in an ornate piece of furniture, keeping to the elegant aesthetic. The sleek black coffee table and lighting helped keep it modern as well. Though it wasn't as open as his current place, it felt like a home.

Dominic couldn't wait to cook in the kitchen, which looked like a French country kitchen dropped on the twenty-first floor of a Chicago condo. The focal point was the massive stove, wide enough to allow for six large burners and a double oven below. The lavish hood above it was brilliantly designed. Dominic thought it looked like a piece of art in and of itself.

This condo was a three-bedroom, which Dominic realized was perfect. He pictured future children in the play area downstairs, so having a nursery as well as an art studio made sense. The master bedroom had a lavish bed with a huge white headboard, covered with a thick fabric.

"It can come furnished," the realtor added when she saw his reaction to the bed.

"The whole place?" He looked over, extremely interested.

"For a price," she smiled.

"Everyone has their price," he joked.

"If you remove the bed, the second bedroom could be perfect for your painting. Lots of light. Let's check it out," she said, as she walked him towards the second room.

It was exactly what he needed. One entire wall was floor-to-ceiling windows. The master bedroom had a private balcony, which was fabulous, but this wall would give unobstructed light for his work.

The third bedroom had a smaller window, but the size of the room itself was good. "Future baby, maybe?" the realtor asked.

"You never know," Dominic smiled. "I would love to show this to Kate. I don't want to sign anything until she's given the okay," he told the realtor, as they finished touring the building's amenities.

"Absolutely. We can come back tonight, if she'd like. That would allow for you both to check out the view. We could also set up to have dinner delivered from the restaurant below. With a cash offer, I'm sure the owners would be willing to let the two of you try it out for the evening."

"Excellent. Let's pick up a menu on our way out. How about 8:00pm? I'll tell her I made dinner plans for us." Dominic was excited for this added surprise. They'd eat dinner, and he'd tell her the place could be theirs if she liked it. Well, his for now, but ultimately, theirs.

…

As Kate walked home, she looked around at the bars, with their summer outdoor seating, and thought of Dominic. Two more days. Then it would be them that sat outside, staring into each other's eyes, talking about anything and everything, as the rest of the world passed them by. She remembered seeing Nicole and Derek outside the Ocean Azul, only hours before her bad boy walked into her life. The way the Stones looked at each other, she had yearned for that. Still too cynical at the time to think it was possible, she had envied them. How had it been possible for her to find the same thing? She wasn't going to lose it this time. Kate would fight for a life with Dominic. Distance be damned, they'd make this work.

Opening the heavy door to her building, she waved hello to her door woman, Cynthia, and headed for her mailbox in the adjacent room.

"Hello, Kate." Cynthia sounded overly happy today. Maybe she was in love as well?

Holding the few pieces of junk mail and bills, Kate walked back to the desk. Cynthia was still smiling.

"Date tonight?" Kate asked her with a smirk on her face.

"Something like that." Cynthia stifled a laugh.

"Have a great time. I'll see you tomorrow. Thanks," Kate replied as she walked through the locked glass doors to the elevator. She smiled, happy that someone else was lucky in love as well.

The elevator door opened. She turned to walk down her short hallway.

And there he stood, with a single rose in his hand, looking devilishly handsome with his sharp jaw line. His head had been tilted down; he looked up through his lashes first, and she wanted him right then and there. The sexy scruff covering his face showed that he hadn't shaved in days. Kate didn't think it was possible, but it made him even more irresistible.

Kate dropped her workbag from her shoulder and the mail she had been carrying, and ran as fast as she could move her body to his. She jumped up and wrapped her legs around his waist. Dominic grunted as he leaned forward to kiss her. She pulled on his long strands of hair, unable to get enough of him.

"Oh my God, am I hurting you?" In the moment of surprise, she hadn't thought about his shoulder.

"No, babe! That greeting was worth it," he laughed and kissed her again.

Kate savored the taste of him, exploring every part of his mouth. It had been too long. Here he was, flesh and blood, and all hers. She was wearing a maroon colored pantsuit with a cream camisole, dressed the part of the attorney. He was in his relaxed jeans, sexy-as-hell thick belt, and a fitted gray t-shirt, looking like her perfect artist.

"How are you here?" she asked between kisses.

"I lied, but a good lie. My doctor's appointment was this morning," he answered and kissed again. "I promise to only lie for a surprise." More kissing.

"Take me inside," she panted, ready to strip their clothes right there in the hallway. "You are mine for tonight."

"I am always yours. I have dinner plans arranged for us, but we have time. I want you on your bed again."

Dominic set Kate on her feet, and they both went to gather her things. Luckily, no other residents had witnessed their reunion. Kate unlocked the door for them. "I should get you a key," she said, when they were inside.

"It would give me a more comfortable place to wait when I surprise you," he said, moving her dark hair from her neck and nibbling from her ear to her collarbone.

"Mmmmm, exactly," she stopped and relished the feel of him behind her.

Turning her body into him, Dominic removed her jacket and lifted her camisole over her head. She lifted his shirt over his to reveal the colorful tattoos that she'd missed too much. They fumbled their way to her bedroom. Not able to hold himself over her just yet, he turned his body and fell back onto the bed, pulling her with him.

Kate laughed and unbuckled his belt. She helped him out of his pants and took in a quick breath as she saw he was already hard and ready for her. Once he was free, she threw his pants aside and stripped hers off as well. She crawled on top of him, kissing every part of his body. She stopped and took his full length into her mouth. He pushed his head back into the mattress and moaned. Only wanting to give him a sample of their night together, she continued to kiss her way up to his mouth again. Pausing for a moment, she found his gaze and smiled, "Thank you."

He kissed her lightly. "For what?"

"For everything," she said, still smiling. "For surprising me, for loving me, for saving my life, for being you." She punctuated each answer with a soft kiss. "Should I continue?"

With that, he took her mouth into his, and the moment changed from sweet to sultry. Kate moved her hands down and wrapped her fingers around him, before sitting up and climbing on top. Closing her eyes and leaning her head back, they found the rhythm that would take her body over the edge. He had missed the feel of her warmth, the taste of her skin. Dominic held her hips, his left arm getting stronger every day. He guided her hips, and they increased speed. Kate held her last one until she knew that they would orgasm together. Exhausted, she fell onto his chest, and there they stayed while they caught their breath.

"I have missed you," Kate stated simply.

"There aren't the words to explain how much," Dominic added. Kate knew exactly what he meant. Once she allowed the walls to come down, the flood gates opened, and there were feelings never allowed before. Too scared to trust that much before, she never gave her full heart to anyone, not until him. Dominic was right; there were no words to explain it.

CHAPTER TWENTY-SIX

"Where's dinner?" Kate called out to the kitchen, as she zipped her dress up the back. It was a perfect choice- red and ever so slightly flared, to show off her waist. She chose a necklace with chunky white beads on a thick, gold chain to go with the dress' simple wide straps. She smoothed down her dark hair, styled straight with some product, and double checked her makeup. Slipping into a pair of nude heels, she grabbed her purse, and walked out to see Dominic standing with two martinis.

He looked drop-dead gorgeous, more dressed up than she'd ever seen. She wasn't quite sure which she preferred: Bad Boy Dominic or Refined Dominic. Luckily, she didn't have to choose. He was both. Now, he was wearing a light blue shirt under a charcoal vest and matching pants. The colors were dark enough that she could just see the pin-striped detail in the suit. There was a matching jacket flung over the back of her couch. His sleeves were rolled up high, and the shirt's few top buttons were opened to keep that little bit of bad boy showing through. His dark hair was still cut short in the back, but he had let the strands in the front grow a bit longer. A few sexy locks refused to stay styled back, and Kate loved it. His appearance was the embodiment of his personality.

"You'll see. I told you, it's a surprise," Dominic smiled as he handed her cocktail to her. "You look amazing."

"So do you," she kissed his cheek lightly, not wanting to mess up her makeup. "You clean up nicely."

"You approve?" he joked.

"Most definitely," she agreed, eyeing him up and down. "Do I need to call for a cab?"

"Nope, it's in walking distance."

"Hmmm, that narrows it down a little bit." She twisted her mouth in thought.

They sipped their martinis together, Dominic careful to time their arrival at the condo perfectly. He had walked back to her place earlier in the day, so that he knew how long it would take.

At the exact right moment, he grabbed his jacket and told her, "We should head out."

Hand in hand, they walked through the streets of Chicago. Kate remembered back to when they first talked about him visiting her city. Smirking, she realized they'd already visited her bedroom. But here they were, walking together like she had imagined. Leaning her head into his shoulder, she wondered where they could be going, and tried to mentally list all the restaurants within walking distance. But in under five minutes, Dominic walked towards the entrance to a condo building and held the door open for her.

"After you," he smiled.

"Why are we taking the residence entrance? The restaurant is down there just a bit," she asked, confused.

"Trust me, babe." Dominic winked at her, and she wanted him right then and there.

Kate took a deep breath, knowing she needed to trust him with more than just dinner. "Always," she smiled back.

The doorman had been informed of the surprise and, with nothing more than a quick "hello" and "enjoy your evening", he held the door open for the couple. Dominic let Kate into the elevator and loved how confused, yet excited, she looked.

When he pushed the button for the floor, she smiled more. "The twenty-first floor? Do you know someone that lives here?"

"Possibly." He was determined to keep quiet.

"Ahhhh!" Kate laughed and reached up to kiss him. Makeup be damned, she loved this man.

Dominic pinned her against the wall, all too willing to help her destroy her lipstick. Would there be this kind of passion every time they rode an elevator? He knew anything in life could become ordinary and routine, but it didn't seem possible to ever see a life with Kate as ordinary.

Hearing the ding, they pulled themselves away from each other as the doors opened.

"This way," he tilted his head to the left and took her hand again.

The door was left unlocked by the realtor, who had done a great job at planning the dinner, ensuring that the food was hot and on the table at 8:00pm exactly. For all he knew, she was hiding around the corner to make a safe escape. Once again, Dominic held the door open for his love.

Kate gave him an inquisitive look as she walked past him. *What is he up to?* "Wow, this place is amazing. Look at that view!" She stopped, wide-eyed, as she took in her surroundings. "And there's dinner!"

Dominic walked up and held out a chair for her. There was a bottle of white wine chilling on the table. As Kate sat, Dominic poured them each a glass and lifted the silver domes to reveal ginger-soy tuna over jasmine rice and vegetables.

"You are just full of surprises, Nicky," Kate said, smiling from her chair.

"I'll find a way to keep surprising you," Dominic replied, sitting down in the chair next to her. The round table, large enough for four people, was only set for two. Both chairs faced the view outside.

"This is unbelievable." Kate sipped on her wine as she looked out to watch the sky turn brilliant shades of pink and orange. The sun had fallen behind the buildings, leaving a breath-taking view of the city she loved.

"You have to try the dinner. It's from the restaurant downstairs," Dominic said, after sampling the fish.

Kate took a bite, and her eyes rolled back in her head. Laughing together and talking between bites, they continued until they finished their dinners. "I could get used to this," she joked.

"Would you like to?" Dominic asked. With his usual off-the-cuff style, he hadn't planned how he'd tell her about the condo. This seemed like the perfect opening.

"What do you mean?" Kate asked, wide-eyed again.

"A realtor showed me this place today. It's for sale. I didn't want to get it without you seeing it first. I'm going to keep my place in South Beach, but I thought a place walking distance from yours would be smart. I want to spend at least part of the year here, too. I haven't figured it all out..." He had begun to ramble. It wasn't as eloquent as he had hoped, but there it was.

"What?" Kate stood up and began walking around. Between the view and dinner, she hadn't noticed anything else.

Dominic stood to follow her. She didn't seem upset, more in shock. Taking her hand, he led her into the kitchen. "Let me show you around."

"You can just up and buy a place so you can be close to me? Of course you can, you're Dominic Price." Kate joked out loud, but it was meant more for herself. "This has to be over a million dollars. Nicky, this is crazy."

"Don't worry about the dollars. You're the one I'm crazy about."

Standing behind her, he slid his arms under hers and kissed the top of her head. Kate leaned her body back into him, trying to take everything in.

"Look at the kitchen! I even want to cook in it. This place is gorgeous."

"Come see the room that will be my studio. You'll love the bedroom as well."

Kate followed Dominic in a daze. Their quiet dinner together felt so normal. Tears began to form in her eyes as she realized she wanted more of those dinners. Her dreams of spending more time together had seemed rather far-fetched. Now, they were real.

With each room they saw, the sun sunk further in the darkening sky. By the time they made it to the master bedroom, it was black, the buildings around them lit beautifully by the lights inside them. The residents of the buildings lived their own existence, unaware that they helped create a wonderful view for Kate and Dominic.

"Check out this bed!" Kate said in awe. "Think they'll let you keep it?"

"I can have all of it." Dominic wanted to be sure not to say *we* just yet. "It can come furnished."

"Move-in ready, huh?" Kate smirked as she walked towards the wall of windows. "Not the view you're used to."

"During the day, you can see the water between the buildings. This view is just a different type. Inspiring in its own way."

Kate leaned her body into his again. He was perfect, and this was surreal.

"What do you think? Could you get used to hanging out here with me?" He lifted her chin, wanting to look into her eyes as she answered.

"Like I said, you're crazy," she smiled and kissed his lips. "Of course I could!"

"Well then, if this is going to be my bed, maybe we should try it out." He walked backwards, pulling her with him.

...

"Where is it?!" Big Z leaned over the table for effect. Tiffany just sat there, expressionless, while he pushed for information.

"We can do this all day. I'm not going to tire, little girl." Big Z was losing his patience with this little bitch.

"I've got nothing to say," she smirked.

"My client said she doesn't know anything," her court-appointed public defender stated.

"Let me have a try," Gael whispered to Big Z, as he circled the room in frustration.

"Please, try to talk some sense into her," Big Z said, glaring at the young woman cuffed to the table.

"Where would you meet Reyes when he contacted you?" Gael softened his voice, knowing that force wasn't working. He needed to go about this a different way.

Tiffany rolled her eyes and let out an annoyed sigh. "He'd meet me in the hookah lounge on Collins."

"Did you feel safe? People were around?" Gael was trying to get her to set the scene for him.

"Sure, I guess. That place is always packed."

"Why do you think he chose a busy place?" he asked.

"I don't really care." *She really is a little bitch*, Gael thought to himself.

"My guess is that he chose a place that you would feel safe, so you wouldn't reconsider your meeting." Gael kept his voice calm and cool. "Now, do you think someone would agree to meet you there if you were exchanging something? A brick of cocaine, say?"

Tiffany ran her tongue over her teeth, not sure she should answer. She hesitated, but Gael just raised an eyebrow, waiting for her to participate in the conversation. "No, I doubt it," she finally admitted.

"Exactly. If you were going to meet people willing to buy a kilo of cocaine, chances are… they'd take the drugs, keep the money, and each take turns raping you, over and over. Who knows when they'd decide to set you free, if ever?" He was harsh, but knew it was needed for effect.

Tiffany wouldn't answer, but her eyes told everything. The thought hadn't occurred to her.

"Now, tell me where the coke is. If anything, it may help with leniency in your case," Gael persisted.

Her attorney whispered into her ear. They went back and forth until they both seemed to agree on what would happen next.

"She will write a full statement, if we can keep jail time off the table," the attorney spoke for her.

Big Z slammed a piece of paper and pencil on the table. "We'll do our best, but no promises. Now write!"

…

"I was able to be present for Tiffany's interrogation," Gael told his friends, as he sat down at a table in front of the Ocean Azul Hotel.

"Did she have the brick?" Derek asked. Nicole leaned forward, interested in his answer.

"It took a bit of convincing, but I was able to get her to give it up," Gael explained. "Big Z sent officers to pick it up. He wanted it in custody immediately."

"What did you have to tell her?" Nicole asked.

"I explained how unsafe it would be to meet somewhere alone to drop off the brick. Most likely, the buyers would see she was just a small girl and use her body as they pleased," Gael said grimly.

Nicole's face scrunched at the mention of the last part. Why were some men such animals? She squeezed her husband's hand, thinking of how safe he made her feel. He had almost killed a man last year because he had tried to hurt her. Derek returned the squeeze, knowing full well what she was thinking about.

"That scared her enough," Gael continued. "Reyes had sought her out. He met her in somewhat of a public place. She was never asked to meet anywhere that made her fear for herself. If she was trying to sell a brick of cocaine, it would be an entirely different situation. She seemed to understand that fact. Most people can look past the money when the realization of what could happen finally sinks in."

...

"We had better get back. I don't own the place yet," Dominic said, rubbing Kate's arms absent-mindedly.

Kate was curled into Dominic's chest, her fingers running lightly over the bandage on his other shoulder, smaller than when she was last with him. At his words, she shot up. "Do they still live here? Ugh, do we need to figure out how to wash this comforter?"

Dominic laughed. "No, this is just staging. The owners have moved already."

Kate flung her body back down in relief. "Oh, thank God!" she said, laughing. "You were too tempting to care about the logistics of all of that before." Leaning over, she kissed him again.

"Hmmm. I wonder, if I call the realtor now, if they'll just let us stay the night?"

"Don't you have to get some kind of bank approval before they'd let you stay here?" She lifted her head to look at him.

"Just a wire transfer. Couldn't be official until the banks are open tomorrow," he answered and leaned his head up to hers, trying to take her lips again.

"Holy shit, Nicky," she almost yelled. "Are you kidding me? You see a place one day and can move in the next?" Kate was successful in business; she did very well for herself. But she had never even been able to imagine buying a condo like this, in downtown Chicago, in cash. That was unbelievable. "Let's go back to my place tonight. Is that okay?"

"Of course. I love your place. If I thought it would be smart, I'd ask to move in with you. But I think our own places in the same city is best to start with."

Kate knew he was right and knew that he probably said that for her benefit. She was madly in love, but didn't want to mess this up, either.

"Will you come over in the middle of the night if I ever have a nightmare?"

Why did she say that out loud? She hadn't planned on telling him about her nightmare. So far, there had only been the one. Maybe he wouldn't read into it.

He saw the worry in Kate's face. "Are you having nightmares?"

"You don't miss much, huh? Only one so far. I didn't mean to say that." A little embarrassed, she hid her face in his chest.

"Do you want to talk about it?" He lifted her chin again to see her scared face.

Kate tried to smile. "I'm not sure. I'm scared that if I talk about it, I'll have another one. I do my best to tell myself the dream wasn't real."

"I can understand that. Know that you can talk about it whenever you'd like." Dominic kissed her cheek. "Or a professional, if you need to talk to someone removed from the situation."

"Thank you. I really do appreciate it. I'm hoping it was a one-time thing," Kate answered, touched by his offer.

"Let's hope," he said again, kissed her lips lightly. "Back to your place?"

Kate stood up and slipped back into her dress (they never bothered to remove her shoes). Walking over to the glass door, she looked back at Dominic, "Can we go outside?"

"Let's check it out," he replied, as he rebuttoned his vest. *God, he's sexy*, she thought to herself.

As Kate stepped outside, twenty-one stories into the Chicago sky, a gust of summer wind blew around them. "This doesn't seem real," Kate said to the city below.

"It is." He wrapped his arms around her and leaned her body back into his.

"You're used to this extravagance. I'm not. It doesn't seem possible." Kate turned her head into his neck and breathed in his wonderful scent.

"It's convenient, I won't lie. But you and me, that's what counts. We'd make this work even if I couldn't waltz into Chicago and buy a place."

Kate laughed. He always made everything make sense. Always humble, he downplayed his family name and his success on his own.

...

"So what do you think?" Nicole looked at Derek, trying to read his expression. "Think they'll agree?"

"If it were up to me, I'd say write it! I think it would be a great book," Derek smiled as he answered. Nicole loved writing her romance novel, but her face lit up a bit brighter talking about her new plan.

It hit her the other day; the whole Reyes debacle could make a great plot for a book. Once the seed was planted, ideas kept popping in her head. She was already writing them down, as they came to life one after another.

"I could shelve the romance book. I do want to finish it, but this would be so much more exciting to write." Nicole's eyes widened with excitement. Now she just had to get Dominic on board. She didn't knowing the logistics of it all. Did she need to change the names to protect the innocent? That thought made her laugh to herself; she loved it when her brain told her jokes. She could base the book loosely on their story. She was pretty sure the Price family wouldn't want their names in a book, and she wasn't even sure she was allowed to use Santino Reyes Cruz as an actual character. She had some research to do.

"If you keep it vague, you may not need his permission. But it would be a courtesy," Derek explained.

"That's what I'm thinking. I'd rather get his approval," Nicole smiled. "I'm going to call and ask."

...

As they lounged in bed early the next morning, Kate looked around her room. It wasn't large, maybe half the size of what Dominic's new bedroom would be, but it fit all her things. With coffee brewing, they had about an hour before their day needed to start. Kate had an office meeting first thing, and Dominic was going to call his bank or visit a local branch if needed. They hadn't really discussed how often he'd come to Chicago or how long he'd stay. How often would she go down to South Beach for weekends?

Her heart began to race a little, and she took a deep breath to control her breathing. *We'll work this out*, she reminded herself. Snuggling up in the crook of his shoulder, she looked up to see his handsome face. *He would make the perfect hero of a book*, she thought. He was the hero of her story, after all. And Nicole was the perfect person to write it. She had promised to let Kate read the chapters as they were written, not to give any kind of opinion, but just because Kate was unable to wait until Nicole was completely finished. It would be strange to read herself as a character. Like looking inside someone's head and knowing exactly how they see you. Everyone must seem different in someone else's perspective.

"What are you thinking about?" Dominic asked, his eyes closed. He was dozing still, but could tell that she was fidgeting a little.

"Sorry, I didn't mean to wake you. I was thinking about Nicole's book idea," Kate told him.

"Thinking good things or bad things?" he asked and kissed the top of her head.

"Good things. I wonder if it'll be therapeutic for her to write? Not that she's having a hard time or anything...I'm not sure what I mean," Kate answered.

"I get it. She's the one in control while she's writing. None of us were really in control when it happened," he replied.

"Yes. You always know how to explain to me what I'm thinking," Kate joked.

"That's what I'm here for," Dominic teased back. "Now, let's have a cup of coffee before I become a part-time Chicago resident."

CHAPTER TWENTY-SEVEN

"You don't waste any time, do you?" Kate laughed, when she saw the second bedroom transformed into an art studio.

"I donated the bedroom furniture and ordered everything I need from that massive art store," Dominic explained. "I've been itching to paint. Walking around this city gives me all kinds of inspiration. The lines in the fire escapes and architecture of the buildings. Wanna take one of those river boat architecture tours with me?" He was rambling excitedly, and Kate thought it was adorable. In less than a week, he had made the place his own. "Next, I need to fill the closets," he was saying. "We should get some things for you to keep here, too. Want to do some Michigan Avenue shopping this weekend?"

"That was hot… say it again," Kate answered, with an eyebrow lifted.

He arched his own eyebrow in response. There was that wicked humor.

Kate wasn't sure her wallet could keep up with his type of spending. Like Derek, he dressed casually, but he did so in couture. Everything fit him like a glove as well. Did he get all his clothes tailored to his exact size? Kudos to the tailors, if he did; they did a fabulous job.

"After some shopping, what do you think about heading out to the 'burbs and meeting my family?" she asked.

"Sure. Your brothers, too, or just your parents?" Dominic asked. "They both still live in the area, right?"

"I'm sure John and Dave will both want to be there. They haven't been able to interrogate a boyfriend in years. They won't want to miss that," Kate laughed.

"I'll win them over once I explain how madly in love I am with you." Dominic walked up and lifted Kate off the ground, kissing her. His arm almost had its full strength back.

"Given your grand gesture," Kate motioned towards his shoulder, "the entire family will love you. Even before you saved me, my mother was dying to meet you. She loves art. I'm pretty sure I got that from her. And my father will be happy once he marries me off. He loves me, but I think he was always a bit scared, having a daughter. Passing along the worry to another man will help some of his go away." Kate smiled, thinking of her father. He also made her want to roll her eyes. Was it that he was old-fashioned? She wasn't exactly sure, but she liked to think that he just loved her too much.

…

"Are you happy with Natalie?" Carolyn asked her middle son, Adrian. It was blunt, but she wasn't going to sneak behind her sons' backs anymore. She learned her lesson with Dominic. She was going to find out if Adrian was committed to his marriage. If not, maybe Amanda would be right for him. Determined to let Adrian decide, upfront and direct was her new approach.

"What?" Adrian set his orange juice down. He should have known the "offer" to have brunch, one that was more than a request, was not because she missed spending time with him. If his mother wanted to have brunch, there was something else that she wanted.

"With Natalie? Are you happy? I've heard rumors of you and other women. Don't ask me why people think a mother wants to know that about her own son, but they do." Carolyn looked at Adrian and shook her head a little.

Adrian hung his head slightly and took a deep breath. "I've done things that I'm not proud of. Things that I shouldn't have. Natalie has threatened to leave me before but never did, because of the boys. But, Mom, I'm telling you. After Reyes, I realized what I could have lost." Closing his eyes, he shook off the vision that came into his head. "We visited Dominic in the hospital because, thank God, he survived saving Kate. I would have jumped in front of a bullet for Natalie without a second thought for myself. I don't want to lose that. I've apologized to her, and she's decided to cautiously forgive me. I'm going to prove to her that I won't take her for granted again."

Carolyn smiled. She had been looking at life all wrong for too long. Her boys' happiness with their spouses was far more important than growing the empire. The Price empire was big enough. Why hadn't she seen that before? Justin had always been in love with his wife, anyone could see that. Adrian drifted, and love had eluded Dominic for a time. Now, she was lucky enough to have three sons that were all happy in their love lives.

"That's wonderful. I'm happy for you, dear. You, Natalie, and your boys deserve to be a family." Reaching across the table, Carolyn patted her son's hand. Physical affection wasn't exactly comfortable for her, but she made an effort. "I believe that you mean it. Natalie will trust you do, too, just give her time."

"I'm not sure I'd trust me, if I were her. I've put her faith in me through the ringer," Adrian sighed. "We're going to start by taking a weekend trip to see Dominic's new place in Chicago. Nat really liked Kate."

"Oh, they'll love that. Dad and I are going soon, too. Ask Nicky about their friend's hotel. It's very close by and apparently luxurious," Carolyn informed him.

…

"How long will I have you here?" For some reason, Kate hadn't asked the question yet, and she wasn't sure why.

"I may have to take some quick trips back to visit the gallery, but Jason has the shop under control. I'll need to meet with him at least once as well, but ultimately, I'd love to be able to hand over the keys and be a silent partner. I figure I'll stay till winter really kicks in."

"Okay, Mary Poppins," Kate laughed. "You'll stay till the wind changes…"

Dominic hadn't seen that movie in decades, but he got the joke. "Funny, babe. I was born and raised on the beach. I've never experienced a winter before, especially a Chicago one. All I've heard is that they're brutal."

"Imagine bundling up and walking through Grant Park with hot chocolate. Or snuggling together in front of that huge fireplace in the lounge downstairs. Did you notice that, by the way?" Dominic laughed in response and she continued, "I bet you'd look sexy as hell in winter clothes. Thick sweaters and scarves with overcoats," she smirked at him.

"You make it sound wonderful," Dominic smiled but then sighed. He had never been in the cold; he wasn't sure how he'd like living it, day in and day out. That was something they'd have to deal with when the time came.

Both felt the mood change from playful to somber. Given how quickly Kate jumped on a plane home in the beginning, she didn't feel like she could complain about him going back to South Beach for the winter. It was just hard to hear it out loud. A week in, she was already used to him being here. How hard would it be in a few months?

"It does get extremely cold," she said, trying and failing to hide her emotions.

"Kate?" God, she loved it when he said her name. "Talk to me."

"I have no right to be upset. You bought a place here to be close to me. It's going to suck when you leave, though." Kate took a deep breath. Leaning her head back on his blue couch, she closed her eyes to try to contain the tears that were welling up. She had gotten used to his place. They were splitting the time evenly between the two buildings, but so far, they went to bed together every night. They didn't plan it that way, it's just how it turned out. How was she going to fall asleep without him there?

"We're going to figure this out together, right? I won't dictate anything. It's just winter. I'll need to go back for trips, but if I'm ever gone too long, you can tell me. The only portion I don't have much control over is the Reyes' trial." This was new ground for Dominic, and he didn't want to make his schedule alone. Kate's job wouldn't allow for her to be away often; it was his career that had the flexibility. He knew that. Once he'd testified, that piece of the puzzle could be removed as well.

Kate opened her eyes and looked at Dominic, sitting on the white chair next to her. "Thank you." She stood up and climbed into his lap. Curled up and snuggled into his neck, she tried not to think about when he was gone. It was hard to block out the thoughts. Maybe she needed a plan. Work...work always saved her.

"I can try to pick up extra cases when you're gone. Stay busy," she whispered into his neck, savoring his scent.

"There you go," he said, brushing her hair out of her face. "Let's go do something. Chicago winter is inevitable, but right now, it's a beautiful summer day."

...

"My mom wants to see us while we're there," Dominic added from the kitchen. Kate was in her bedroom, packing a small suitcase.

"Great." Excited for their weekend in South Beach, Kate chose some of her new dresses from their shopping trip last weekend. She went a little overboard, though, and they almost fought publicly every time they got to a register to pay. Dominic won most of the time, but she did sneak off and buy a few things with her own money when he thought she was still browsing.

Nicole and Derek would be back in Chicago in a few weeks, but Kate was still looking forward to seeing them. Nicole loved summertime in Chicago; she said that the city came to life in the summer. The Stones' current plan was to always be there for at least a month while the weather was nice. Kate had already reviewed the list of summer festivals to visit while Nicole was there. Throughout the entire summer, city streets were closed, and "street fests" would appear in different places for a week or two. People would gather to eat food from vendor tents, and browse for trinkets and everything from clothes to handmade jewelry, to artwork and elaborate candles. Everything was made locally, and both women loved supporting the "indy" companies. Kate was excited for Dominic to experience them, too. His success as an artist may have outgrown festivals, but if he was even a part-time resident, it would be fun to get a tent and sell some prints occasionally, as a bonus to his fellow Chicagoans. She would have to suggest that sometime.

Dominic might stay in South Beach a few days longer, depending on the Reyes' trial. Kate couldn't take any extra days off for this trip; she had too many meetings scheduled. Knowing she'd miss him, Kate remembered how busy she would be at work anyway. Dominic kept himself occupied during the day with his art, but she had quite a few business dinners the following week. He was meeting some people in the art world, which made her happy. She knew he needed friends there, too. Maybe he could open a gallery in Chicago one day.

Rolling her suitcase behind her, Kate walked back into the kitchen. "Are you nervous about testifying?"

"Honestly? A little. I really don't want to see that fucker. Adrian was right, he doesn't have a soul inside him. Anyone that would want to hurt you is not of this world." Dominic scooped her up and sat her on the counter in front of him. Instinctively, she wrapped her legs around his waist. "I'm glad *you* don't have to testify." He added.

"I would in a second, if it helped to put him behind bars." She leaned into his chest, feeling his heart beating.

"I know, babe." Dominic cupped her face in his hands. "The car should be downstairs. Let's get in the air."

As they left, Kate reflected that having access to one personal jet was strange enough, and now there were two…

…

255

"You're back!!" Nicole shouted as she grabbed both Kate and Dominic, one in each arm. Derek smiled and shook his head, laughing at his wife's reaction.

"We're back," Kate said after hugging Nicole and went to greet Derek, too.

"I'm so happy for you two," Derek whispered while they hugged.

"Thank you," she whispered back.

After saying hello to Dominic, Derek took his wife's hand. "I hear I'm to entertain you two ladies while Dominic talks with the prosecutor."

"Lucky us," Kate joked.

"It should only take a few hours," Dominic said. "They're just prepping me for questioning."

"I feel like we should be there with you. We were all there when it happened," Kate said, leaning into Dominic.

Not wanting her to feel bad, Dominic tried to downplay it, telling her, "There's no need for any of you to have to deal with this."

...

The four of them sat at a table outside of the Ocean Azul. As Nicole and Dominic talked about her book idea, Kate answered a few emails for work. Derek was reviewing paperwork about another property for sale. A server brought over a tray of nachos to share. They had all settled into life together quite nicely.

There was a delay in the trial and, while Dominic was prepped and ready to testify, he wouldn't be needed for a few weeks now. Kate was happy she could plan her work schedule to be there with him. Worried that she'd have nightmares again, Dominic wasn't thrilled about her reliving the day, even from the audience. He didn't like the idea of Kate being in the same room with that soulless bastard. Derek promised him that he and Nicole would be sitting on either side of her. While it had been scary for all three of them, Kate had almost lost Dominic that day.

"Once this trial is over, where are we going next?" Kate asked, looking back and forth between Nicole and Derek.

"How about we celebrate Reyes going to prison and go somewhere new?" Derek suggested.

"What do you have in mind?" Dominic asked, eyebrow raised in curiosity.

"I'd love to have dinner at the top of the Eiffel Tower with my wife." Derek looked around the table to gauge their reaction.

"Paris!" Kate and Nicole yelled in unison.

"I think you've got yourself a winner," Dominic laughed. "What do you think, babe? Could you get some time off for Paris?" He knew her schedule was hectic. Dominic loved how important work was to her, and he wanted to respect that. But he also wanted her to enjoy life as well.

"Even if it takes until I'm forty-one to become partner, Paris is worth it!" Kate said, laughing.

...

Dominic and Kate laid together in the exact same bed where they spent their first night. Dominic watched her sleep the way he had then. He knew, even then, that he loved her. Would he have trusted her love, if it had happened for her right away? Would he have worried that she wanted him for his money or fame? Dominic knew that Kate's brain was far too logical to believe in love at first sight. It made him trust in her love even more. She was there because she loved him and nothing else.

"I love you," he whispered and kissed her head.

Kate snuggled her body further into him and kissed his neck softly. "I love you, too," she said and immediately drifted back to sleep.

EPILOGUE

Looking around her apartment from the front door for the last time, Kate felt a bit sentimental. And this time, it probably wasn't the hormones. So many memories were gathered in those eight hundred square feet. Nicole was there the day she moved in, and Dominic was there the day she was moving out. Good start and good finish, with life happening in between.

Kate stretched her coat over the growing bump underneath it. She gave the bump a mothering rub without realizing her action. She couldn't believe how her life had changed over the past year. It turned out that, when dressed for it, Dominic liked the winter. They'd bundle up and still enjoy the city as it frosted over for a few months. They'd visit South Beach as often as possible, but Dominic did sell his condo. They stayed at the crash pad or Ocean Azul during their visits. When he had decided not to fly south for the Chicago winter, he hadn't needed a permanent place there anymore.

The monthly visits with Nicole and Derek continued as well, and their men had become thick as thieves. It warmed Kate's heart as she pictured her husband and Derek together. Kate looked down at the sparkling ring on her finger and smiled. Carolyn Price, her new mother-in-law, had been determined that they have an over-the-top, elaborate wedding, even if she only had a month to plan it. She outdid herself. During that weekend extravaganza, Kate had felt like royalty or some sort of celebrity.

Now she was Kate Price and soon to be "Mommy". By day, part-time, she would still be Kate Price, attorney-at-law. That dream wouldn't die just because she had a new dream. Wife and mother would always be her most important job now. But she still wanted to be partner. Closing the door for the last time, Kate thought about how much she loved her life. She was lucky and knew it. Dominic was an amazing husband, they were going to have a beautiful child, and their careers allowed for her to keep working while being present in her home life. Dominic's art had taken off in Chicago. Plans to open a new gallery were in the works. The new inspiration over the past year showed in his work.

Kate had asked for a few minutes by herself to say goodbye to her apartment. Dominic waited downstairs and, when she was ready, they would walk back to *their* home. She couldn't be happier. Fighting over names and picking out cribs filled her heart with a peace that she had never felt before. Neither of them had expected a baby right away. But life has strange ways of deciding what's best.

THE END

Thank you for reading *Love on Ocean Drive*! If you enjoyed it, please consider taking a moment to leave me a review at your favorite retailer. And don't forget to check out a sneak peek of my next novel, *Love on the Rockies*, at the end of this book!

Thanks!

Acknowledgments:

Thank you to my mom. You always find the way of being the perfect combination of supportive mother and critical eye. You've made time to be there with me every step of the way.

Thank you to Kate Seiwert. The amazing woman you are needed to be sensationalized and written. You brought Kate to life, and there was no stopping her.

Thank you to Kelly from For the Love of Books and Alcohol. You have always been one of my biggest cheerleaders. Thank you for beta reading and for the hours of laughing as we review your notes.

Thank you to Christina McGrath. Thank you for always being there when I needed support. You helped *Love on Ocean Drive* become what it is today with your beta reading. The countless miles and time zones between us disappear when we chat. You are a true gem.

Thank you to Lindsay Marie Miller. Thank you for all of your support and beta reading. You believed in me from *Love on the Malecon*, and I'm thankful every day for the friendship I found in you.

Thank you to Alexander Von Ness at Nessgraphica for my amazing cover. You find a way to bring the Love on… series to life visually.

Thank you to Allison for editing and formatting the book. My mind may be a little dirty at times but so is my grammar.

Thank you to my husband for working so hard. You have allowed me to follow this dream.

Aubrey Parr

Biography

Aubrey Parr waited until her she was forty to publish her first novel. Although she received her Master's in Accounting, Aubrey always knew that she wanted to write. She was inspired by her great-uncle, author Evan S. Connell. With a few years of life experience under her belt, she decided it was time. She lives with her husband and daughter outside of Chicago, Illinois. When she's not chasing after her daughter, she sneaks off to create steamy stories of wonderful love affairs.

Connect with Me:

Follow me on Twitter: http://twitter.com/aubreyparrbooks
Friend me on Facebook:
http://facebook.com/aubreyparrbooks
Follow me on Instagram:
http://instagram.com/aubreyparrbooks
Follow me on Pinterest:
http://pinterest.com/aubreyparrbooks
Follow me on Goodreads:
http://goodreads.com/aubreyparrbooks
Favorite me at Smashwords:
http://www.smashwords.com/profile/view/aubreyparrbooks

Love on the Malecon

Make sure to check out Book One in the Love on... series, *Love on the Malecon*, and read about Nicole and Derek's love story!

In the heart of downtown Puerto Vallarta, there is a magical oceanfront promenade known as the Malecon.

As a tribute to her father's life, Nicole James travels to his favorite place on Earth. On the cobblestone streets of charming Puerto Vallarta, she meets Derek, an ex-MMA fighter who invested his winnings into land for luxury hotels. Derek is fabulously wealthy, aging like fine wine, and lives on resorts like an endless vacation. Could her father have orchestrated this chance meeting with Mr. Right from beyond the grave?

Derek Stone never thought a woman would fit into the world he created, until Nicole came along. She's beautiful, smart, and sexy. More importantly, she has no idea of his money. Derek has taken care of himself for his entire life. He's not used to trusting anyone. Can he tear down his walls and let Nicole inside?

And here is a sneak peek of Book Three in the Love on... series, *Love on the Rockies*:

Love on the Rockies: Sneak Peek

CHAPTER ONE

Her name was Nora Johnson, and it wouldn't occur to most people to call her pretty. Then again, it never occurred to Nora to try to be pretty. She had classic features but was too busy with her causes to take the time to accentuate them. Never enough hours in the day, Nora chose to spend her time fighting for the rights of everything, from animals to trees to grub worms. Her current cause was the green white firs that lined the canyon walls of Ouray, Colorado.

Her twelve o'clock meeting was running late. Nora reviewed her paperwork again. The name must have been misspelled. It read Gael Flores, probably supposed to be Gale. Unsure as to why this woman wanted to meet with her, Nora looked out the window of her small office at the back of the family inn, admiring the magnificent view of the mountains. The land was for sale, and this woman must represent an interested party that wanted to purchase it. Nora's family didn't own it anymore. Other than the fact that their small inn was built just across the property line, she couldn't imagine a reason for Gale to meet with her.

The snow hung further down the mountain peaks in the winter, and it gave a completely different feel to the view. Summer in Ouray was gorgeous, but winter was breathtaking. Taking a deep breath herself, Nora closed her eyes and leaned her head back. It gave her strength somehow- the mountains and trees, the earth and the sky, all of it. What if this Gale was going to help destroy the view that gave her such strength?

With that thought, there was a knock at the door. Nora hated that she expected the worst. Protecting the land around Ouray was turning into a full-time job. Keeping the city quaint was important to its residents. Large ski resorts were great but not for their home. Nora was ready for a fight.

"Please, come in." Nora tried sounding pleasant.

The words left her mouth before she turned away from the window, wanting to soak up every drop of strength for whatever came next. Expecting to meet a woman named Gale, Nora found herself face-to-face with the embodiment of sexuality. He was a walking cliché. His skin was the color of delicious caramel; she wanted to taste every ounce of him. His thick, lustrous hair was a bit wild from the wind outside. It was black as night with curls that couldn't be tamed into submission. For some reason, Nora was already imagining how striking he'd look dressed in a tuxedo.

Her mouth dried immediately, and the English language seemed to escape her. Then he spoke. His voice was smooth, with a Latin American accent that almost brought her to her knees.

"Nora Johnson?" he asked as he walked towards her.

"Yes." Nora forced the word out of her mouth.

"I am Gael Flores. I apologize for keeping you waiting." He took her hand and kissed it lightly.

Could this man be for real? For starters, his voice, his accent. The way he said her name…and his. If it had been spelled the way it sounded, Guy-el, she may have realized a sex pot was walking in to meet her. Nora never found time for men, but she may be able to rearrange her schedule for this one.

Immediately, her brain reminded the rest of her body that this man may be there to destroy her view and her beloved green white firs. This could be the beginning of the end for quaint Ouray. She needed to regroup...and fast. This was war, and she was staring into the sexy face of the enemy.

Clearing her throat gave her the few seconds she needed to get her head in the game. She was going to fight a huge ski resort, even if it was against this Gael Flores.

Gael hadn't expected Nora to be his age. For some reason, he pictured a plump, older woman with grey hair tangled up in a bun. Nora was far from that. Though he guessed she was in her early forties, her face did have deep lines. He hoped they were from years of laughter, rather than work. It was too early to tell. Her kind eyes were a beautiful color of green, without a drop of makeup to accentuate them. Her clothes were chosen for comfort over style- an oversized maroon sweater that tied at the waist and jeans of a soft material, two sizes too big. Long black locks fell over both shoulders, with nothing to keep them out of her face. Gael was used to being with women that spent hours preparing themselves for an outing, making sure everything was perfected. Nora Johnson was nothing like those women, and he was intrigued.

Determined to stay focused, Nora spoke, "It's quite alright. What can I do for you?"

"My research has shown that your family is one of the oldest in the area. I was hoping to get some information on this city of yours," Gael explained, as he claimed the empty chair across from the cluttered desk.

267

"Yes, that's true. I'm not sure how I can help." *Keep your enemies close, huh?* Nora added to herself. "Does this involve the land for sale?" She motioned out the window as she spoke. It made sense to get right to the point.

"Yes, my company is interested in acquiring the land," he said in that velvet voice.

That was it. Nora's blood boiled, and her heart raced. She clenched her jaw momentarily, deciding what to say next. "Well, from what I understand, the owners will not sell it off in pieces. What are your company's intentions for over a thousand acres?" Sarcasm escaped along with the words, and she didn't care.

Gael liked that she had grit. The residents of Ouray were pleasant people, kind and welcoming, but leery of outsiders as well. At least those that were land developers. Apparently, Nora was the same way.

"I can be very persuasive. You never know what the owners will agree to. May I take you to lunch to discuss it?"

Lunch? Really? Nora couldn't even think of food. The knots that had grown in her stomach wouldn't allow her to take a bite of anything. If this man thought he could smooth talk his way with the owners of the land, that was fine with her. If he had any plans to use that same velvet voice on her, he had another thing coming. She wasn't about to fall for something so ridiculous.

"No, you may not. I'm not exactly sure how I can help you, Mr. Flores." She hated being so dismissive, but with this man, it was the only way she'd survive. "If that's all, I have some things that require my attention."

Nora stood and walked to the door. She held it open as a silent request for him to leave.

"Until we meet again," Gael crooned as he walked past. *This is only the beginning, mi amor*, he thought to himself.

"Indeed." Nora closed the door just as the scent of his cologne found its way to her. She leaned against the door for the support she suddenly needed. Every cell in her body came to life over his smell. What was she going to do if they met again? How on Earth was she going to stay strong?

She had to. Ouray was counting on her.

www.ingramcontent.com/pod-product-compliance
Lightning Source LLC
Chambersburg PA
CBHW051421170626
46809CB00006B/2262